LEGEND

OF

AURORA

Cover by Ken Farmer

THE AUTHORS

AUTHOR

Ken Farmer didn't write his first full novel until he was sixty-nine years of age. He often wonders what the hell took him so long. At age seventy-seven…he's currently working on novel number twenty-five.

Ken spent thirty years raising cattle and quarter horses in Texas and forty-five years as a professional actor (after a stint in the Marine Corps). Those years gave him a background for storytelling…or as he has been known to say, "I've always been a bit of a bull---t artist, so writing novels kind of came naturally once it occurred to me I could put my stories down on paper."

Ken's writing style has been likened to a combination of Louis L'Amour and Terry C. Johnston with an occasional Hitchcockian twist…now that's a combination.

In addition to his love for writing fiction, he likes to teach acting, voice-over and writing workshops. His favorite expression is: "Just tell the damn story."

Writing has become Ken's second life: he has been a Marine, played collegiate football, been a Texas wildcatter, cattle and horse rancher, professional film and TV actor and now…a novelist. Who knew?

Ken Farmer's dialogue flows like a beautiful western river…it's the gold standard…Carole Beers

Web page: www.KenFarmer-Author.net

 **BUCK STIENKE** is a native Texan originally from Houston. He spent many of his formative years in the Texas hill country, and lived on the LBJ ranch when Lyndon Johnson was president. His love of almost all things Texan extends to movies, books as well as music. He's an accomplished guitarist and singer / songwriter. In fact, a country song he wrote inspired this novel. Buck has an extensive knowledge of guns, modern gunsmithing and ballistics.

Buck and his writing partner, Ken Farmer, have published ten novels to date. Six have been from a series of best-selling BLACK EAGLE FORCE Military/Techno novels : *Eye of the Storm, Sacred Mountain, Return of the Starfighter, Blood Ivory, Blood Brothers*. They also wrote a pair of historical fiction westerns: *The Nations* and *Haunted Falls* (Laramie Award winner - 2013). *Devil's Canyon* was Buck's first solo effort.

ISBN-13: - 9780990438908
ISBN-10: - 0990438902

Timber Creek Press
Imprint of Timber Creek Productions, LLC
312 N. Commerce St.
Gainesville, Texas

ACKNOWLEDGMENT

The authors gratefully acknowledges Loree Lough, Katherine Boyer, T.C. Miller, Alex Cord, and Doran Ingrham for their invaluable help in proofing and editing this novel.

Contact Us:
Published by: Timber Creek Press
timbercreekpresss@yahoo.com
www.timbercreekpress.net
Twitter: @pagact
Facebook Book Page:
www.facebook.com/TimberCreekPress
214-533-4964

DEDICATION

LEGEND of AURORA is dedicated to all writers of Science Fiction and their tireless efforts to keep the wonderful genera alive. Special kudos go out to Gene Rodenberry, Jules Verne, Issac Asimov, Edgar Rice Burroughs, E. E. "Doc" Smith and the father of SciFy, H. G. Wells. Much of what we see as science fiction, when it was written, soon becomes science fact.

First printing - 06/01/2014
Second printing - 02/10/2019

HISTORICAL FICTION WESTERN
THE NATIONS by Ken Farmer and Buck Stienke
HAUNTED FALLS by Ken Farmer and Buck Stienke
HELL HOLE by Ken Farmer
ACROSS the RED by Ken Farmer and Buck Stienke
BASS and the LADY by Ken Farmer and Buck Stienke
DEVIL'S CANYON by Buck Stienke
LADY LAW by Ken Farmer
BLUE WATER WOMAN by Ken Farmer
FLYNN by Ken Farmer
AURALI RED by Ken Farmer
COLDIRON by Ken Farmer
STEELDUST by Ken Farmer
BONE by Ken Farmer
BONE'S LAW by Ken Farmer
BONE & LORAINE by Ken Farmer

SY/FY
LEGEND of AURORA by Ken Farmer & Buck Stienke
AURORA: INVASION (Book #6 in the BEF) by Ken Farmer & Buck Stienke
HISTORICAL FICTION ROMANCE
THE TEMPLAR TRILOGY
MYSTERIOUS TEMPLAR by Adriana Girolami
THE CRIMSON AMULET by Adriana Girolami
TEMPLAR'S REDEMPTION by Adriana Girolami

Coming Soon

HISTORICAL FICTION WESTERN
NO TIME to DIE by Buck Stienke (sequel to Devil's
Canyon by Buck Stienke
BONE'S GOLD by Ken Farmer
ZARKOV PARADOX by Buck Stienke

HISTORICAL FICTION ROMANCE
DAUGHTER of HADES by Adriana Girolami
ZAMINDAR and the LADY by Adriana Girolami
MILITARY ACTION/TECHNO
BLACKSTAR RANCH by T.C. Miller

SY/FY
ANTAREAN DILEMMA by T.C. Miller

Thanks for reading *BONE & LORAINE*. If you enjoyed it, I would really appreciate a review on Amazon. My Author Page is:

www.amazon.com/Ken-Farmer/e/B0057OT3YI

Email - pagact@yahoo.com

Personally autographed books available at my web site:

Web page: www.KenFarmer-Author.net

TIMBER CREEK PRESS

PROLOGUE

APRIL 17, 1897
SOL SYSTEM
INSIDE MARS ORBIT

A fleet of twelve giant globular shaped, iridescent green space craft moved silently through the black void toward their destination, the third planet from the sun—a brilliant blue and white marble designated as Tellus, but known by the inhabitants as...Earth. As they passed the fourth planet—a red orb called Mars—an area of space far in front of them shimmered and a fleet of ten huge triangle shaped silver craft—five heavily armed Mauler Cruisers and five gargantuan Superdreadnaught Carriers—emerged one at a time from the vortex. Each of the five larger carriers was over a mile wide and slightly over four miles long and carried two hundred fighters.

Ahead of the marauding green fleet, Earth and its moon were looming larger. The triangle craft quickly formed into an immense cornucopia-like cone formation that covered thousands of miles with the Maulers at the open end—like a giant maw—directly in front of the globular craft. The military grouping was able to encompass virtually the entire formation of globular craft.

Hundreds of smaller triangle shaped craft—tiny two-crew versions of their giant mother ships—began to spew from the Superdreadnaught carriers like angry wasps from a nest. They took positions inside the cone, between the Maulers and their carriers that completely encircled the globular craft formation.

The ball-shaped space vehicles—each over two miles in diameter—began firing with pulse lasers of unimaginable power on the smaller craft. The multi-layered force fields of the small fighters flared with titanic intensity as they darted, looped, gyrated, dodged and spun to keep away from the ravening beams. Several of the smaller craft took direct hits, flared through the visual spectrum from violet to white hot incandescence and then vaporized into the cold inky vacuum of space, leaving only wispy particles of metal like coruscant vapors where the craft formerly were.

The five huge Maulers were designed to lock on and hold an enemy with powerful tractor beams to prevent their escape or even the slightest of movement. The great space battleships, Superdreadnaughts and the smaller fighters simultaneously began a centrally coordinated pounding with massive annihilating purple beams of pure energy from their projectors and launched wave after wave of Thorium torpedoes at the green enemy. The cone of annihilation formation enabled the triangle ships to direct their concentrated force beams into the formation of the globes from multiple directions, overloading the layered shields surrounding the greenish craft of the aggressors. Nothing made of ordinary matter could survive in the center of this unbelievable display of pure power and energy. The entire sector of the solar system glowed with the intensity of a small sun for the duration of the battle.

The trapped globular craft fought back with savage ferocity and poured pulse upon pulse of powerful multiphased vibrating greenish laser beams hundreds of yards in diameter in return. Protecting fields of force flared vividly on both sides with blinding regularity.

The smaller triangle craft flitted closer, encircling the giant ball ships like swarms of angry bees, constantly firing their force beams to add to the destructive power of their huge carriers and accompanying space cruisers. The overwhelming masses of silver fighters exceeded the number of defensive weapons the larger green craft could bring to bare.

Inside one of the tiny fighters, small gray hands flashed over a touch screen, directing the craft toward one of the giant globes seen through the panoramic cockpit window. In the second seat, another set of tiny gray hands worked over a weapons console targeting a pair of small, but ultra-deadly Thorium torpedoes toward the nearest globe—the fighter abruptly spun and darted away at maximum free velocity after releasing its missiles.

In the fire control area of the globe, sharp claws at the end of five finger-like scaly greenish-blue appendages tapped on a similar type screen. The globe fired a pulse laser at the quickly retreating fighter and scored a grazing hit exactly where its force field was the weakest—along the aft quarterdeck. Due to the fact that the ship was in the free inertialess mode—essentially massless—at the instant it was hit, the monster laser pulse knocked the craft out of the battle area like a major league batter smashing a fast ball. The tiny fighter seemingly vanished as it streaked away—initially at near the speed of light or the same speed as the pulse.

The globe's monstrous force field flared with sheets of whiteish-blue hot plasma as the first Thorium torpedo struck and partially collapsed it, creating a quarter of a mile circular area devoid of defense. The second torpedo followed in, hot on the tail of the first, penetrated the hull and detonated with a force well over a thousand kilotons.

The two-mile diameter sphere shook with the power of the fusion explosion deep within its bowels. Large chunks of debris flew out into the stygian darkness lit only by the repeated flashes of nearby spacecraft force fields successfully repelling attacks or failing spectacularly.

Three other fighters from the same squadron darted in and targeted the weakened globe with force beams that sliced through its exposed Aranak skin like a hot knife through butter. The globe's force field flared like a mini-sun to violet, through the entire spectrum of colors—then the globe vaporized into a billion points of instantaneous brilliance and faded quickly into the absolute zero cold and vacuum of interstellar space.

The triangle ships and their fighters systematically began targeting the other globular craft and one by one, the force fields of the giant spherical ships flared into even more frenzied displays of pyrotechnic incandescence with rainbows of color and then failed as the ships were vaporized. Only clouds—merely silver mist—of tiny atom-sized metal droplets drifting through their own momentum in the ether were left in the center of the cone.

Many of the small fighters had taken near hits from the enemy vessels, but were able to return to their mother ship's docking bays—except for one. The damaged craft spun out of control in the direction of the blue and white planet some 33.9 million miles in the distance.

The two gray figures inside worked frantically to stabilize their fighter—to no avail. The tiny ship's inertialess drive was severely damaged at the moment of contact from the pulse laser, causing it to return to its original mass and therefore Newton's First Law of Motion took effect: *Every object in a state of uniform motion tends to remain in that state of motion unless an external force is applied to it.*

The battle zone was positioned such that Tellus was at aphelion—its most distant point from the Sun—and Mars was at its perihelion—the closest point to the Sun. In other words, the two planets were orbitally on opposite sides of the sun. The gravitational force of the massive star began to slow the passing vehicle as it approached Earth.

The triangle mother ships continued the destruction of the remaining globular craft with a tremendous flare of expended energy until the last craft ceased to exist in this plane. The surviving viable fighters formed up and headed toward their giant space carriers and were taken back on board.

The fleet of triangle space Maulers and Superdreadnaughts reformed into a line with carriers in the lead as a distortion in the very fabric of space-time appeared in front of the fleet. One at a time, the ships entered the wormhole with a bright flash and disappeared to reemerge from hyperspace thirty parsecs away in another part of the Orion Spur just minutes later.

APRIL 17, 1897
AURORA, TEXAS

The damaged fighter finally began to regain some degree of control as it entered the outer thermosphere portion of the Earth's atmosphere at a speed approaching Mach 5. The crew tried repeatedly to reactivate the inertialess drive, but it was too badly damaged and only functioned intermittently. As a result, the ship started to glow from the heat of the friction.

If the drive had been fully functioning, an elliptical bubble field in the shape of the craft would have been generated around the ship, not only making it invisible to any light spectrum, but also giving it full antigravity capability as well—known as being *free* and therefore making it massless. The neutralization of inertia removed the limitation of any *free* craft to instantaneously reach the velocity which the force of her cosmic engines could generate—depending on size—in any direction. The larger the craft, the more ultimate velocity could be achieved—allowing the jump to hyper-space—per Newton's Second Law of Motion: *The relationship between an object's mass (m), its acceleration (a), and the applied force (F) is F=ma. Acceleration and force are vectors; in this law the direction of the force vector is the same as the direction of the acceleration vector.* The tiny fighters were not of sufficient size to permit hyper-jumps, but performed very well in dense atmospheres like Earth in their *free* inertialess state—but the little stricken vessel was unfortunately subject to the normal atmospheric friction and gravitational forces exerted by the planet.

"Can we reach the Ley Magnetic line near the thirty-third parallel?" asked one of the gray beings.

"Trying. If we can, we should be able to recharge our accumulators."

A full moon was setting on the western horizon and dawn was just starting to lighten the horizon to the east as the small silver craft—still glowing from the heat of its passage through the Earth's atmosphere—moved erratically north across the sky, losing altitude.

Tiny gray hands again flashed over a touch screen. Through the panoramic cockpit window, the occupants could see a metal tower with a circular array of numerous blades at the top in the distance, rapidly coming closer. The craft yawed sharply, shuddered, dipped, and then regained altitude and stability for a brief moment.

The three lights on the bottom of the flat triangle craft flickered on and off. Then like a shot quail, it plummeted toward the surface, striking the tower and its adjacent water tank before impacting the ground, tumbling and exploding in a fireball, scattering wreckage for more than a hundred yards.

Some fifty yards away, in a large white frame house with a wraparound porch on three sides, a woman was startled awake by the resulting explosion and sat up in bed. Hazel Proctor nudged her husband, Judge Henry Proctor.

"Oh, my God!...Henry!...Henry, wake up! What was that?"

A small gray figure, silhouetted against the fire, stood shakily from a portion of the wreckage. It looked around, then knelt down for a moment in the wreckage next to another gray figure. The being stood erect again, picked up a metallic looking case and disappeared into the darkness outside the flickering glow of the numerous small fires.

Judge Henry Proctor, a portly man in his fifties with full mutton-chop gray whiskers, stirred from a sound sleep and rolled over to face his wife. "What?…What are you babbling about, woman?"

"An explosion!…Over to the windmill!…Get up, Henry!" She looked out the open window. "There's a fire!"

He snapped awake. "A fire!…Where?"

"I told you…Over to the windmill!"

He jumped out of bed, threw a flannel robe over his long white night shirt, shoved his feet into his slippers and charged out of the door, followed by his wife, Hazel. She had grabbed a faded pink chenille robe and slipped it over her skinny frame.

Jagged bits of wreckage and flames were scattered everywhere. The windmill and water tank were destroyed as well as Judge Proctor's garden. Nearby neighbors, most still in nightclothes, were rushing toward the wreckage. The top edge of the springtime sun had just started peeking above the horizon.

"What the Sam Hill is it?" one of the neighbors asked.

"I seen it pass over downtown when I was gittin' up, a few minutes ago...It's some kind of flyin' machine," another answered.

"What on earth can fly?...'Cept a balloon."

"'Twern't no balloon...it was shaped like a triangle with three flickerin' lights on the bottom. I can tell you that..."

One of the ladies gathered at the wreckage gasped, "Look!...There in the wreckage...is that a body?"

The gathering crowd looked and pointed toward a large piece of the craft a short distance from the fire. Lying near the twisted silver metal—with strange hieroglyphics on it—was a small gray body.

"Everybody get back...get back," said Proctor as he and his wife Hazel arrived from their house.

She moved forward. "Oh, my goodness, Henry...It's a child!"

The judge moved forward himself for a closer inspection and knelt down by the body. "Maybe yes...maybe no, dear ...but, whatever it is..." He looked up at the crowd. "...it's not of *this* world."

A small silhouetted figure watched from the darkness under a large bois d'arc tree at the edge of the cemetery, and then it shimmered very slightly and disappeared—metal case and all.

AURORA CEMETERY

Aurora, Texas, a small farming community located in Wise County, just northwest of Fort Worth boasted a population in 1897 of over three thousand residents. A somber group of the town's people gathered around a small grave that had been dug under a gnarled oak tree with a large L shaped crooked limb sticking out overhead.

A preacher opened a bible and began reading, "'The Spirit himself bears witness with our spirit that we are children of God, and if children, then heirs—heirs of God and fellow heirs with Christ, provided we suffer with him in order that we may also be glorified with him.'...Lord receive this creature to thy bosom that it may have everlasting life...In Christ's Name we pray. Amen."

There was a scattering of 'Amens' as four townsmen lowered a small child-size wooden casket into the ground with ropes. At one end of the grave a stone marker of native rock had been placed. Carved into the sandstone was a *V,* lying on its side with three circles etched inside and beneath was an inscription that read:

NOT OF THIS WORLD
April 17, 1897

A small figure watched the funeral in the shadow of a tree in the distance. It touched its left wrist and again shimmered and vanished...

***

CHAPTER ONE

CROSS TIMBERS COUNTY, TEXAS
September 6, 2013

Detective Darrell Ulysses Bone and Captain David St. John of the Cross Police Department moved quietly through a remote field of mostly blue stem and grama native grasses quail hunting on a warm Indian summer day.

"Better sharpen your eye, Cap'n, you're behind two to three," said the giant of a man—weighing near 280 pounds—fifteen feet away from a smaller, black man. Bone was just wearing a yellow T shirt with a black ballistic nylon cartridge belt around his waist. Two small pouches, one for extra ammo and another for game birds he had bagged were attached over each of his hips.

"You just lucked into a larger covey, Bone…Don't seem to be as many quail this year," the stocky middle-aged man with a shaved pate in a tan canvas hunting vest with a pouch in the back commented.

"Yeah, noticed that right off."

Just then a small covey of Bob White whirred from a clump of sage about thirty feet in front of St. John.

"There you go! Take 'em!"

St. John snapped off two quick shots from his Remington 870 12 gauge pump shotgun. One of the birds fluttered to the ground on the other side of a five strand barb wire fence. "Now we're even."

A smile came to his somewhat craggy face. Years of playing defensive end had left him with a slight bend in his nose and a couple of small scars on his chin. "Yeah, and if this were baseball you'd be batting .500…But, it ain't…Maybe you oughta be shooting a skeet choke instead of a modified."

"Kiss my ass, Bone."

The two men walked up to the fence. St. John went through first, handing over his shotgun before he eased through the third and fourth stands. Bone passed both weapons over to St. John on the other side, and then pushed the slightly slack top wire down and stepped over. The captain returned Bone's Benelli semiautomatic shotgun back to him.

"Being 6' 8" has its advantages over 5'9", I suppose."

"Yeah, unless you want a Ferrari," quipped Bone.

"You don't have to worry about that...no way in hell you could afford one anyway."

They both turned to look for the bird and see a very small—less than five feet tall—woman, appearing to be in her fifties, standing about fifteen feet away. Her light brown hair was bobbed short in what might be called a pixie cut. She was wearing a pair of child's green bib overalls with a matching light green shirtjac. A muscular yellow and white pit bull, sat on his haunches beside her, his mouth open in what looked like a giant grin. Both men were startled.

"Wow, didn't see you come up, ma'am," Bone said as he doffed his Black Eagle Force gimme cap, revealing a unruly shock of short dark hair.

"I'm kind of hard to see, sometimes." She walked up to them. "You gentlemen aren't from Global Energy, are you?"

"No, ma'am, we're just quail huntin' on the Diamond S Ranch...I shot a bird and it fell on this side of the fence. We're just trying to retrieve it," St. John replied.

"Well, the fence you just crossed is the property line…You're on my land…I own this 640 acre section that adjoins Buck Stienke's Diamond S on the east." She pointed back behind her.

"We apologize, ma'am. We had no intention of trespassing." The big man extended his hand to the diminutive woman. The dog immediately became more alert, the hair along his back began to rise and a deep rumble started in his throat.

"It's all right, Tyrin," she said and the dog instantly relaxed.

Immediately as he touched her hand, Bone had a montage of quick flashing images—the woman tending her garden—a slightly younger version setting a small device on a hilltop—a triangle shaped silver spacecraft—a lavender sky with two suns—a space battle with large triangle ships, small triangle fighters and giant green globes—a small gray people in hooded suits with large almond-shaped black eyes, in a type of cockpit—an old fashioned windmill coming fast in the cockpit window—a flash of light. He quivered a little bit and released her hand.

"Are you all right?"

"Uh...yes, ma'am...Uh, I'm Detective Bone and this is Captain St. John...We're with the Cross Police Department."

"I'm Lucille Wilson...and this is my friend Tyrin. His name used to be Sparky...he's a rescue dog I adopted from Noah's Ark animal shelter in Cross...I needed one to keep the coyotes and other varmints away from my chickens. Just thought I'd give him a complete new start with a new name too."

"That's very kind...He looks like a good one for that and most anythin' else...It's a pleasure to meet you, Miz Wilson...and you too, Tyrin."

The blond and white painted dog woofed, grinned, wagged his tail and extended a paw. Bone took it like a hand and shook it.

"Hey, Miz Wilson, he smiled at me."

"Goodness, just call me Lucy, please and yes, the Staffordshire Terrier can do that."

"Yes, ma'am...uh, Lucy.

"Aren't they also called *pit bulls*?...Fighting dogs?" asked St. John.

"Yes, but they're known as *Nanny* dogs too, because they're so protective of their owners and especially of children."

"I read somewhere that the most decorated war dog of World War I, Sergeant Stubby, was believed to have been a pit bull," offered Bone.

"I had...ah, read that also."

"Lucy, I don't suppose you've got some fresh water? We neglected to bring any along." He shot a glance at Bone who just looked skyward and shrugged his shoulders.

"Why, yes. Where are my manners?...If you don't mind well water."

"Well water would be great."

"We better find the Captain's bird first," Bone interjected.

"Right," agreed St. John.

They started looking around in the calf-high grass, pushing the clumps aside with their feet. Tyrin was off a little way—he barked and wagged his tail. Lucille walked over to where he was standing and picked the quail up. She cupped it with both hands, held it for just a moment—with her back to Bone and St. John. Unseen by them, there was a very quick soft glow of pale blue light from inside her hands.

"Here's your bird."

She turned toward St. John and extended her hands and opening them at the same time—the quail flew up and away. "Oh, my…it must have only been stunned."

"Damn…Oh, pardon my language, ma'am…But, I could have sworn I thought I saw feathers fly when I shot."

"Cap'n, you know what happens when you think…Oh, by the way, believe that puts me back ahead."

St. John gave him a look that would melt steel.

They walked through the gate in the white picket fence and stepped into her yard. It looked like something from the early 1900s—large white frame pier and beam, dog run style house with a walk-around porch on three sides, two chimneys and a standing seam galvanized metal roof. Well kept flower beds adorned the area in front of the porch with a half-acre garden and chicken coop out back. The corn and most of the vegetables were past maturity and had turned brown—the fall planted onions, tomatoes, turnips and potatoes remained green. There was a combination fruit/storm cellar between the house and the garden.

"As I mentioned, I use well water." She pointed to the dug well with native stone casing and a wooden cover between the side of the house and a smoke house.

They walked toward it, Bone lifted the center dust cover and lowered the bucket twenty-five feet to the water. It filled half full and then righted itself. He cranked the bucket back to the top and pulled it over to set it atop the casing. Lucy handed St. John the white porcelain dipper that had been hung on a hook on one of the support posts.

"Oh, no, ma'am, you go first."

"Nonsense, you're my guests."

St. John nodded, took the dipper and dipped into the bucket. He took a long drink. "My, my, but that's wonderful…I'd forgotten just how good well water tastes." He handed the dipper to Bone who filled it and drank heartily.

Lucy continued, "I think there's something to be said for pure fresh well water unspoiled by man with his chemicals."

"I'll second that," Bone said as he filled the dipper again. He drank part of it, and then poured the rest in Tyrin's bowl next to the well.

"I see you like dogs, Mister Bone."

"Yes, ma'am, uh, Lucy...Dogs understand unconditional love."

"I've discovered that to be true, also."

"Lucy, earlier you asked if we were with Global Energy...Might I inquire why?...If that's not being too presumptuous."

"No, not at all...Global Energy has been trying to buy this place for the last two years...It's, ah, been Wilson property since...well, since before the turn of the last century, my, uh, grand parents moved here from Aurora in Wise county in 1897...I'm not inclined to sell or lease...and as of late, they've been trespassing and harassing me."

"In what way, Lucy?" asked St. John.

"With innuendoes and now...outright threats."

"As in?"

"Their representatives have stated that it would be a shame if my house caught on fire...being so far from town and all."

"Do you have a cell phone, Lucy?" asked Bone.

"Goodness no. Never had a need for one."

"Tell you what..." He handed her his Galaxy S4 cell phone. "Take mine...I'll get another...Do you know how to use one of these?"

"Oh, I think I can figure it out…Just because I live out here in the country without rural electricity or telephone service, doesn't mean I'm not informed."

"No, ma'am…Sorry, didn't mean to imply…"

"Don't judge everyone by yourself, Bone," St. John quipped.

He held up his hands. "Kings X, I surrender…Lucy, you have any problems with those yahoos, you call my office…The speed dial code is zero one…I'm open nearly every day."

Why thank you Mister Bone…that's very kind of you."

"It's just 'Bone', Lucy."

She smiled and nodded.

"Oh, by the way, don't mean to be nosey, but how do you get supplies? I didn't see a car anywhere."

"I don't need much. I grow most of what Tyrin and I require…But I do have an automobile, a 1930 Cord. I keep it in the barn."

"You have a *Cord*?" asked an amazed St. John.

"Yes, I…uh, bought it from a neighbor's estate some years ago. It only has 3,800 miles or so on it…Like I said, I only use it on occasion when I have to have something from town or go in to pay my property taxes."

"My, my, my…a Cord." The Captain grinned and shook his head.

"I would love to see it, Lucy, if you don't mind," said Bone.

"Certainly…This way," Lucy said as she turned and headed to the red barn some eighty feet from the house on the west side, with Tyrin close to her heels.

Bone and St. John glanced at each other and tagged along.

"Here, we'll get that for you," Bone said as he and the Captain each grabbed one of the ten foot tall strap-hinged doors and swung them open admitting the afternoon sun to illuminate the interior.

Lucy walked over to a painter's plastic drop cloth draped over the vehicle and pulled the thin sheet off.

Bone's jaw dropped. "I have died and gone to Heaven. That's a L-29 Coupe," he exclaimed as he gazed on a sky blue 1930 Cord convertible coupe with twin spare tires mounted on the twelve inch wide running boards.

"That is an absolutely beautiful machine, Lucy," said St. John.

"I think so, too. I much prefer this vintage as compared to what are produced today…They were made much better and with more personality, I might add."

"Cap'n, you know that the L-29 was manufactured by Auburn Automobile Company and was the first American front-wheel drive car to be offered to the public?"

"You're joking."

"Joke you not...And It's powered by Auburn's 4,934 cc, 125 horse power L-head Lycoming inline 8...It was the most innovative vehicle of its time."

"How do you know all this, Bone?"

"Well, you see, it's this way...The L-29 Cord was first choice for my restoration project...'til I found out how much it would cost to restore one...So, I went with the '73 Thing."

"Kind of a come down."

"Ya think?"

"Maybe you'll be able to get one some day, Bone," offered Lucy.

"That'll never happen, Lucy...never happen."

"Never say never," she admonished and smiled.

He nodded halfheartedly and smiled at the phrase he often used himself. "If you ever need anyone to change the oil or wash and wax her, you let me know."

"Why, I appreciate that very much, Bone. I may take you up on that."

"Cap'n grab the sheet and let's re-cover this masterpiece for Lucy."

"Thank you. It's so much easier removing the cover than putting it back on...It's one reason I don't drive it much," Lucy said as they covered the Cord back up and closed the barn doors.

"Well, one more dipper of water and we better head back, Bone."

"Thinkin' the same thing, Cap'n," he said as they neared the well.

From a hill four hundred yards away to the east, two men watched Lucy, Bone and St. John with binoculars—both were dressed in field khakis. One man, Jeffers, a tall burly individual with the beginning of a beer belly, put down his glasses, took a flask from his pocket and had a swig.

"You better lay off that stuff. Williams will can your sorry ass," the other man, Hollister, a fit engineer type with neatly trimmed dark hair, said.

"What he don't know won't hurt him."

Hollister put his eyes back to the binoculars and focused on Lucy's house again. "Wonder who the hell those guys are?"

Jeffers looked through his again. "Beats the shit out of me...They got shotguns, probably just bird hunters." He took another swig from the stainless steel flask.

Hollister glared at him.

St. John noticed a flash of reflected light from the nearby hill out of the corner of his eye. "Got company, Bone."

"I know...Saw a glint off their binoculars when we walked up."

"How do you do that?"

"My Padrino, taught me to look at nothing, but see everything," Bone said as he replaced the dipper on its hook.

"Padrino?" Lucy asked.

"Godfather...I guess you could say he's a shaman...Spirit teacher...We're descended from the Nasca in Peru...Me, on my mother's side."

Oh, yes, I'm familiar with the Nasca. I've had, ah...occasion to study their culture. I'd like to meet your Padrino sometime."

"I'm sure he would like that."

"Well, you and your good Captain St. John are welcome here anytime…I don't often have company."

Bone leaned over and gave her a hug—again the same flashes of scenes as before. St. John also hugged her. Bone rubbed Tyrin's head and got a lick in return.

"That's unusual…He doesn't like many people."

"He just doesn't know him yet," St. John said with a grin.

"He knows what he knows."

They bid their good byes and started walking back toward the Diamond S Ranch.

Bone and St. John were still calf-deep in native grasses as they neared the fence line.

"Cap'n, what say we slip around the other side of that hill and have a little conversation with those two jackasses?"

"Thought you'd never bring it up."

They veered to the left to head toward a ranch road on the other side of the hill. Bone and St. John approached a dark green Jeep, with a Global Energy logo on the driver's door, pulled off the road near the hill.

"Well, looks like they've been down some caliche roads." Bone wet his finger and touched a fender, and then put the tip of his finger to his tongue. "Yeah, caliche and bentonite, with a touch of barite."

"Come again?"

"It's a non-nutronic type of weathered volcanic ash used as *drilling mud*, especially on high pressure drilling operations like gas exploration."

St. John eyes sort of glazed over.

"It's a gift." Bone took off toward the side of the hill nearest the road. "Bet a donut, that we can just walk up behind 'em."

"No bet, you remember we spent twelve years together in the Recon Marines playin' in the sand pile...I've watched you too many times."

Bone and St. John eased up the back side of the hill. They separated until they were about twenty yards apart in a flanking maneuver.

The two men were still lying on top of the hill watching Lucille's house. Bone moved up, toe-heeled Indian style, until he stood right behind the two men. He carried his Benelli twelve gauge in the crook of his arm—St. John flanked off to the side.

"You boys peeping toms or are you just lost?"

Jeffers and Hollister both jumped up, obviously startled.

"Jesus!…Who the hell…" Jeffers blurted.

"Damn, man, what are you, Indian or somethin'?" Hollister added.

"Something," was Bone's simple reply.

St. John walked in tighter. "Just what *are* you boys doing here?"

"What the hell business is it of yours?" replied Jeffers.

"Well, one, I'm a Cross police officer, two, you're trespassing and three I'm holding the damn gun."

Hollister responded, "You're kinda out of your jurisdiction, ain't you?"

"Girls, he might be bound by his jurisdictional restraints, but, me…I don't just give a damn…I suggest you answer the question," said Bone softly, but with unmissed intensity.

Girls?…Why don't you put down that gun and I'll show you girls."

"Jeffers," Hollister cautioned.

St. John just muttered, "Mistake."

Bone placed his shotgun on the ground. "You know, I quit taking punks like you out behind the gym when I got out of high school…but, in your case…I think I'll make an exception."

Jeffers tried a haymaker to Bone's head, but was slightly inebriated and off balance. Bone grabbed his arm and easily flipped him over in a somersault—Jeffers landed on his back.

"Wouldn't get up, if I were you," St. John warned.

Hollister started to move toward Bone, but the 190 pound St. John side kicked him in the sternum, sending him down on his butt in a wheezing heap.

Jeffers jumped up and charged. Bone calmly stood his ground and did an overhead hammer fist to the top of the man's head—Jeffers knees buckled. He fell face forward, eating a mouthful of Cross Timbers County and lay still.

"Told you," commented St. John nonplused.

Bone walked over to Hollister, knelt down and looked him right in the eye. "Now, peckerwood, you want to tell us what you were doing up here? Or would you like a little more encouragement from my Captain?"

"No, no…I get the point…We work for Global Energy… and we were just told to keep an eye on that little woman."

"She's already told ya'll no sale…Now, why don't you look somewhere else," St. John interjected.

"I don't call the shots…Just do what I'm told."

"Well, that's good, sunshine, cause I'm gonna tell you something else…You girls come back here again and we're not likely to be so nice…Comprende?"

Jeffers struggled to his knees, spitting out grass and dirt, rubbing the back of his neck. "Damn, what'd you hit me with, big man?…I think I'm about two inches shorter."

"A sample."

FIRING RANGE
CROSS TIMBERS COUNTY
Next Day

Bone, Detective Cal Mitchell, in his late forties and Investigator Loraine Rodriguez, a beautiful Hispanic woman in her thirties with an ample bosom, lined up on the left of Captain St. John. To his right, officer Stella Johnson, a gorgeous twenty something blonde, another uniform officer, Dale 'Moomer' Alexander and the Range Master, Jim Bryan, took their postitions on the firing line at the range for their practice rounds.

They were uniformly dressed in gray Cross PD "T" shirts, black BDU trousers and black combat type boots. All range participants wore safety shooting glasses and ear protectors. Several other officers and Sheriff deputies watched—they had already taken their turns.

"From the holster, ten rounds, five and five, fifteen seconds. Go to the tactical position when finished…The line is ready, stand by…" Jim instructed.

The officers were facing their targets with weapons holstered, the man-shaped targets rotated to face the line. They all drew their weapons and commenced firing.

Each shooter reloaded at five rounds. At fifteen seconds, after the roar of sixty total rounds being fired, the range master pressed the button on the controller in his hand and the targets turned back away from the shooters. The officers all assumed the tactical position.

"All right, people, good groups…pick up your magazines and police the brass…Everybody off duty? Just nod…"

"Huh?" Bone asked.

St. John pointed to his ear protectors.

"Oh, right," Bone said as he removed the yellow rubber plugs from his ears.

The captain continued, "I'm calling a meeting of the Bridge and Road Club." He turned to Stella next to him on his left in the firing line. "You can come too, rookie."

"Thanks, Cap'n, thought you'd never ask."

St. John turned to detective Mitchell on his right. "Bring the B and R kit, Cal?"

"Always."

"Let's head to the lower firing range, then."

The group turned and headed down hill some thirty yards to the long gun and sniper practice location, euphemistically just called the lower range. At the edge of the first firing line Cal's blue Dodge Ram pickup was parked under the shade of a massive oak tree. A large red and white cooler sat on the lowered tail gate with BRIDGE & ROAD painted on the side.

Cal stepped up to the cooler, lifted the lid and started passing out cans of ice cold Shiner Bock beer.

"Ladies first…Here you go, Fresh Meat." He handed one to Stella.

"When do I get to lose the moniker, Fresh Meat?"

"When the next rookie comes on board…'til then, you got it."

"Joy."

There were several personal cars and pickups parked around under the shade of the numerous large trees that surrounded the range. Tail gates were lowered on all the trucks.

"Here, Loraine, you're next…You hard dicks help yourselves…didn't take you to raise."

The 5' 4", well-endowed Hispanic detective and Bone's partner, took the beer from Cal's hand. "You have such class, Cal."

"Just gotta call 'em as I see 'em, Loraine."

Bone stepped up and fished out two from the cooler, moved over and sat on Loraine's Red Chevy Apache tail gate.

"Two, Bone?" Loraine asked.

"Got two hands, don't I?…'Sides, saves a trip."

"I may have to have that sex operation I read about just to fit in with this group."

"What's that, Pard?" asked Bone just before he took a deep draught from one of the cans.

"An addadictome," Loraine said dryly and took a sip of her beer.

Bone blew beer out his nose while the rest of the cops, deputies and Stella moaned—several chunked already empty cans at her.

"Hey, Moom, crank a round from that new Barrett at Achmed," said St. John.

"I can do that," the big redheaded officer said as he opened the trunk of his vehicle and removed a Barrett semiautomatic .50 cal sniper rifle and inserted a five round clip.

Two hundred yards downrange a plastic store mannequin was propped against a fifteen foot high dirt berm. He was dressed in traditional Arab dress and a red and white keffiyeh and known affectionately as Achmed the Raghead.

Moomer pulled out the two supporting bi-pod legs from the rifle, got down in the prone position and sighted in on center mass. All the other cops put their ear protectors back on just before he squeezed off a round.

Instantly Achmed disappeared in a huge cloud of smoke as the six ounces of Tannerite inside where his heart would have been exploded with a tremendous roar on impact of the Vienna sausage sized projectile.

Moomer rolled up on an elbow, a grin on his face from ear to ear. "Went moooom!"

"Ya think?" commented Bone as he pulled his ear protectors out.

An hour and numerous beers later, Bone and Loraine were leaning against the driver's side of Cal's pick-up—Mitchell was on the opposite side. Most of the other cops were sitting on hoods or pickup tail gates, even a few had brought folding lawn chairs—all with a beer in their hands. A fire had been started in a big metal tractor tire ring for the proscribed cooking of hot dogs and hamburgers. The meeting of the B & R club was standard fare for off-duty cops after an afternoon of range practice.

Cal finished off another beer and set the can on top of his head. "Hey, Loraine, see if you can hit this can."

"Piece of cake, Cal."

She pulled her Kimber 1911A .45 and fired—the can went spinning away.

Mitchell looked up as if he were trying to see the can, then he felt the top of his head and grinned.

"Good shot, pard," commented Bone as she holstered her weapon.

Cal stepped over to the tailgate of his truck and grabbed another can out of the cooler—a full one. Moving back, he placed the fresh beer on top of his head and faced Bone. "Hey, Bone...let's see the hand cannon."

Bone, Loraine and the others were unaware that it was a full, unopened can Cal had placed on top of his head.

"Hold my beers and watch this." He handed Loraine both his beers, pulled his S&W 500 .50 cal magnum revolver and fired in one smooth motion.

The can exploded in a monstrous cloud of beer and foam, Cal instantly disappeared out of sight behind his truck.

After five seconds of stunned silence, Loraine slapped Bone across his chest with the back of her hand. "Damn you, Bone, you killed him!"

"No way I could miss at this range."

The other cops and deputies were too stunned to even go check on Mitchell.

Then, Cal staggered to his feet from the other side of his truck, beer foam covering his shaved head and face and soaking his CPD shirt. "Son-of-a-bitch!...What a rush." He held up his hands. "Ball of fire this big!...Hot damn, you should'ov been there!"

Everyone looked at each other dumbfounded, then they all broke out laughing.

Mitchell grinned and held up the remains of the can, just a couple of flattened pieces of shredded aluminum.

CONFERENCE ROOM
GLOBAL ENERGY
DALLAS, TEXAS

Two executives of Global Energy, Field Operations Director, C.W. Williams and Lease Acquisitions Manager, Barry Farlow, were sitting around a very large, very expensive burled walnut conference table. The conference room occupied a corner of the high-rise office building in downtown Dallas. The two solid glass walls offered a complete view of the city from Woodall Rodgers Freeway north and east to the Arts District.

CEO Jeff Davis, a tall well-built executive type with a touch of silver at his temples, blew a cloud of blue smoke from a Cuban cigar above his head, turned from one of the windows and faced the men at the table. He had several boxes of his favorite cigars smuggled in each month from Cuba through Haiti.

"What the hell is the hold up on that Wilson property?" he demanded.

"Lucille Wilson just doesn't want to sell or lease...That right, Farlow?" Williams looked at Farlow.

"To put it mildly. To be such a little snip of a thing, she's tougher'n boot leather...Additionally, yesterday, two Cross PD officers out hunting, had a run in with Jeffers and Hollister on her place. They told them they were trespassing and not to come back."

"Cross Police Department? You're shittin' me...Who were they?" asked Davis.

"Didn't give their names, but one was a big son-of-a-bitch, musta weighed close to 300 or so...apparently a detective and the other was a Captain," replied Williams.

"They have no jurisdiction out there and I don't give a good rat's ass in hell if she's Chesty Puller reincarnated, we need that section...It's up-dip from the best Barnett Shale gas play to date...We're talking over a half a billion dollars here."

"Do we have permission to go to plan B?"

"You have permission to do whatever it takes...Rig 12 will be setting pipe in seven days, we have to be able to move to a new location. I want that property and I want it by then!…Understood?"

Williams and Farlow looked at each other and both nodded to the CEO.

***

CHAPTER TWO

CROSS, TEXAS
SOUTH GRAND AVENUE

Cross was a somewhat smallish rural type community of less than twenty thousand citizens in the cross timbers area of north-central Texas, just five miles south of the Red River. Founded in 1848 and flourishing as a cattle and cotton center in its early years, Cross now boasted a wide spectrum of business from agriculture to manufacturing, but like many other rural cities and towns in the south, was unable to escape the occasional escapade of the local inebriated red-necks.

Stella Johnson and Juan Sanchez of the Cross PD on night patrol were following a couple drunks in a pickup truck.

Buddy Lemmons and Chad Bryson, two mid-twenty year old ne'er-do-wells, both with contusions on their faces, were talking about their bad luck that evening at a local honky-tonk as they drove back into town. Buddy was at the wheel of his battered lime green '94 Ford F-150.

"Daaamn, them two gals was hot…" said Buddy.

"Yeah, too bad about that fight. We'd be sitting pretty right about now…What started the whole thang anyways?"

Damn'fIknow. It looked like some fun so I just waded on in. Some skinny guy with long hair did some Karate stuff on me…Think I lost a tooth."

Buddy felt inside his mouth, looked at his teeth in the rear view mirror and ran over the curb. He almost hit a parked car, but reacted just in time to miss it and jerked back into the driving lane.

"Did you see that?" Stella glanced at Juan. "That truck almost ran into a parked car…Bet a dollar they're wasted."

"No bet…Light 'em up," said Juan.

She hit the flashing lights and bumped the siren for half a count.

Buddy and Chad heard the siren and saw the lights as they reflected inside the cab of the truck.

"Shit! I ain't got insurance on this truck 'ny more. If they catch me with this here pistol, they'll revoke my parole," Buddy said as he pulled small .380 semi-auto Kel-Tec from his pants and gave it to Chad.

Chad took it and looked at the gun like it was a bomb. "What the hell am I supposed to do with it? I ain't got a CHL!"

"Think of something," Buddy said as he pulled to the side of the curb.

Stella and Juan pulled in behind, lights still flashing. She typed in the pickup's plate information and got immediate license and registered owner information. "Let's go see what Mister Lemmons has to say."

"Got your back."

They exited the black and white patrol unit and walked up to each side of the truck. She approached the driver's side just aft of the window with Juan on the other, her hand on the butt of her weapon.

Buddy rolled down his window.

"Evening, sir. May I see your license and proof of insurance, please?"

Yes, sir…uh…ma'am…I weren't speedin'." He handed her some papers and his license.

"Sir, the reason I stopped you was because you were driving erratically…Have you been drinking?" she asked as she perused his paper work.

"Just a couple over at Cowboys." He belched.

Stella waved the foul smelling burp from her face. "Step out of the vehicle please, sir." She stepped back away and toward the rear of the pickup.

Buddy glanced over at a nervous Chad and gave him a *calm down* hand signal as he opened the door and got out.

She escorted the skinny driver back between the vehicles. He was wearing a black Lone Star Shooting Supply 'T' shirt with a pack of cigarettes rolled up in one sleeve, jeans and a multicolored short-billed welder's cap. Stella held up a roll of blue masking tape.

"We are going to perform a little field sobriety test here, Mister Lemmons. I will be asking you to walk a straight line…Sir, please hold the end of this tape."

Buddy took the end of the tape from her hand. Stella backed away from him and pulled the roll between her fingers until she had about twelve feet rolled out and tore it off. "Now, sir, please stick the tape to the asphalt directly in front of you."

She bent down and stuck her end of the tape to the street. Buddy leaned forward several times, loosing his balance each time. He regained it, bent down a third time and slowly fell face forward to the pavement as if in slow motion. He landed flat on his face, breaking his nose—he fell to one side as it started to gush blood.

"Now look at what you went and made me do!"

Stella covered her mouth as she started to laugh and motioned to Juan. "Better give me a hand over here, Juan."

Chad nervously watched Juan go toward the back of the truck and decided to make a break for it. He opened the door, pulled the pistol from under his thigh and tried to put in the front of his jeans as he ran—the gun went off inside his pants. He grabbed his crotch and fell down on the sidewalk.

"Oh, Jesus. Oh, Jesus!"

Stella and Juan reacted to the shot. They released Buddy, who fell on his face again. Both drew their weapons and moved in tactical positions to the side of the truck and covered Chad. Juan pulled out his D cel Mag lite.

The chubby counterpart to Buddy in a faded button shirt with the sleeves cut out—like Larry the Cable Guy—was lying on his side in a semi-fetal position with both hands on his crotch. Blood seeped through his fingers and stained his jeans. His beat-up straw cowboy hat lay several feet away.

"Get your hands where I can see them…What the hell just happened?" ordered Juan.

Chad rolled on his back and placed both bloody hands up in a surrender pose. "Oh, God…I think…I think I just shot Mister Happy."

Stella and Juan looked at each other and burst into laughter.

"That's gonna leave a mark," Stella said grinning. "Better call an EMT."

Juan just shook his head.

SMALL FRAME HOUSE

Dymonelle Satterwhite and Rhynelle Satterwhite, two scroungy looking young black men in their twenties stood in the kitchen of their ramshackle shack of a house cooking meth. Each wore bandannas across their faces to help block the smell.

"I cain't stand it no more! This meth cookin' is foul, bro'. The smell be killin' me," complained Rhynelle.

"I got me an idea. We can get us one of them new trailer houses from FEMA. I seen 'em on the news...they got thousands of 'em," his brother suggested.

"Fa'sho! Uh...How we go about getting us one?"

"You're too stupid to be my brother...know what I'm taking about? We tell 'em we 'lost everythang in Ike' and they give us one."

"But we never even been to Galveston."

"They don't care...They gots to give away the money or lose it...Give me the phone, fool. I'll show you how to finesse *the man*...What be the number for FEMA?"

"How the hell should I know? I look like a phone book? Call the directory assistance."

Rhynelle tossed the portable phone to Dymonelle. He pulled off his bandanna, glared at his brother and punched 911.

CROSS PD

The light on the dispatcher console marked 911 illuminated. Dispatcher Lauren punched the lighted button. "911 Police Emergency, what is the nature of your emergency?"

SMALL FRAME HOUSE

Dymonelle silently mouthed the word "Shit" and slammed the phone down. "That was the po-lice! Now look what you made me do!"

"Who the dummy now?" said Rhynelle.

CROSS PD

"911 Police Emergency. Hello? Policia Emergencia, Hola?" She turned to her computer and cross referenced the 940-555-3292 number. It generated an address: 1313 East Garnett St. "Alpha 122, Dispatch."

"Alpha 122, go ahead," replied officer Joel Newman.

"Alpha 122, 911 hang-up, 1313 Garnett."

"Alpha 122, copy, I'll check it out...Probably kids playin' around."

Over the radio came a report from the night supervisor, Sergeant Hung, "Delta 19, 10-8 departing Motor Pool."

"Roger, Delta 19...ya'll be careful out there."

SMALL FRAME HOUSE

Newman pulled up in front of the house, turned off his unit, got out and walked up to the front door and knocked.

Dymonelle looked through the curtains and sees Newman on the porch.

"Who at the do'?" Rhynelle asked.

His brother mouthed 'Po-lice', held up a finger vertically over his mouth and turned off the light switch in the living room.

Newman banged on the door harder. "Police! Open up...I know you're in there."

After no answer, he walked around the side yard with a flashlight in hand. The kitchen lights were still on in the back of the house. As he neared the back of the house the unmistakable stench of meth cooking hits him. He waved his hands in front of his face, turned around and headed back to his unit for his radio. "Alpha 122. Dispatch."

"Alpha 122, dispatch."

"Alpha 122, meth lab in progress, 1313 East Garnett. Request all available backup."

"Copy Alpha 122, meth lab in progress, 1313 East Garnett, standby for backup…Delta 19, dispatch."

"Delta 19, Copy Alpha 122's request. ETA four minutes," responded Sgt. Hung.

Wanda Stanton was filling out a booking sheet on a drunk and heard the backup request on her radio. She turned to the jailer. "Finish up this miscreant for me, will you, Kyle. Newman needs backup."

Kyle nodded and gave her a thumbs-up.

"Whaz a miscriaint," the drunk slurred.

"You may never find out," said Kyle.

"Huh?"

Wanda talked to dispatch over her radio on the way down the hallway, "Yankee 143, Dispatch. 10-8 Out of booking, enroute to cover on Garnett street."

"Roger, Yankee 143…Alpha 128, dispatch."

SOUTH GRAND AVENUE

Stella and Juan stood by their unit and watched as the EMT wagon started up and drove away with Chad. Buddy was in the back seat with tape across his nose and cotton plugs in his nostrils. A tow truck backed up and hooked on to Buddy's truck.

Stella keyed her mike. "Alpha 128, go ahead, Dispatch."

"Alpha 128, what is your status?"

"Lauri, we're 10-8 on the DUI and shooting. One to transport."

"Roger, call when 10-8 after booking."

Stella looked behind her and could see that Buddy had fallen asleep against the door. "Alpha 128, roger..." She released the button on her mike and turned to Juan. "Beer breath is asleep. Newman never calls for all available assistance...He's got trouble."

"10-4 on that. How 'bout we take the long way to book this guy?"

"Like via Garnett street?"

"Close enough."

They smiled and bumped fists.

SMALL FRAME HOUSE

Several police cars are pulled over on the street with lights flashing. Newman had donned a gas mask and carried a tactical shotgun. Stella and Wanda also held shotguns. Juan had a M-16.

Sergeant Hung barked out orders, "Sanchez and I'll take the back door. Stanton east side windows, Johnson west side. Newman, give us one minute to cut off the utilities and burn out any gas in the lines. We will wait for your signal on Tac 3.

The five officers took their positions.

Dymonelle and Rhynelle whispered as they crawl on their hands and knees into the kitchen.

"If we stay quite, they'll go away," said Dymonelle.

"I think I'm startin' to get scared."

The flame under the meth cooker flickered, then went out and then the kitchen lights followed.

"Yep, I'm scared all right," said Rhynelle.

Newman took his position at the front door and put a pair of breaching charges in his shotgun equipped with a standoff device on the muzzle. He glanced at his watch, pulled the weapon to his shoulder and rapidly blew off the doors bottom hinge followed by the top one. Kicking the door wide open, the young cop made a dynamic entry into the living room.

He quickly swung the shotgun around with the tactical light mounted on the top. "Police! Don't move. You're under arrest."

Dymonelle and Rhynelle scrambled toward the back door in the kitchen.

Newman talked into his microphone located inside his gas mask, "Two suspects exiting back door!"

Sergeant Hung had stationed himself close to the back door. Juan Sanchez stood several feet behind him with his M-16. As the suspects burst out the door, Hung held up one hand in a *Stop* signal.

"Halt! Poli…"

The two brothers stampeded over him like herd of cattle, they tangle and fall into a rolling pile of arms and legs. Rhynelle tried to get up, but Juan was right there with his M-16 muzzle six inches from his face.

"Live or die, your choice Einstein…I'm on full auto."

Rhynelle's eyes rolled back in his head as he passed out. Wanda and Stella came around to the back from their respective sides of the house. Juan extended a hand to the dazed Hung lying all the way out in the yard on the grass and pulled him to his feet.

"Nice stop, Sergeant…Gutsiest move I ever saw."

Wanda and Stella, who witnessed the whole thing, turned away and cracked up. They moved in to cuff the two brothers.

Dymonelle and Rhynelle were seated together in the back of Hung's patrol car.

"I think I peed my pants," Rhynelle said.

Dymonelle made a face. "That ain't all you done in them pants…Mister Policeman, can I get me another patrol car. I think I'm gonna to be sick! "

"That mean we're not gonna get one of those free trailers from the FEMA?"

Dymonelle started trying to hit his brother in the head with his own head. "Shut up, dummy!"

"You the dummy!"

Stella and Juan make their exit back toward their unit.

"Nice work back there," Stella said.

"Why thank you, officer."

"I particularly liked the smoke up Hung's butt."

Juan cracked up. "He'll probably put himself in for a medal of valor or at least a commendation."

"Let's get Mister Lemmons to the slammer before that beer Novocain wears off and he wakes up."

"Sounds like a plan, I could use some coffee. Got a feelin' it's gonna be a long night."

CROSS POLICE STATION

A white disheveled woman, Roxy Jones, stood at the dispatch window and knocked. Lauren walked over to the window from her dispatch desk.

"Yes ma'am, may I help you?"

"Yeah. I think I've been ripped off. Can you test some coke to see if it's real?"

"Excuse me?"

"I just scored this stuff, but I think they're trying to rip me off. Can you test it to see if it's the good stuff?"

"Oh, I think we can take care of you. Let me buzz you in and you can have a seat and one of our specialists will be right with you." Lauren grinned as she walked back to the dispatch desk and keyed the intercom back to booking. "Officer Johnson or Sanchez, please report to dispatch."

Stella and Juan were booking Buddy Lemmons. She shook her head at the request from dispatch.

"I wonder what Lauren wants…Take over," she said to Juan and headed down the hall.

"Can do."

Stella walked into the reception area. "You rang?"

"You are *not* gonna believe this. That woman sitting over there…asked us to verify the quality of some cocaine she just bought," Lauren whispered to Stella.

"Get out!"

Lauren snickered. "She's afraid she's getting ripped off."

"Is everybody in Cross taking stupid pills tonight…I'll get my field kit and we'll check her buy…Service with a smile."

Stella, Juan and Roxy are seated around a gray metal table in one of the department's ten by ten plain vanilla interrogation rooms. Stella set out the testing kit.

"So, Roxy how much of this stuff did you buy?"

"Almost half a week's worth of food stamps...an' my Obama phone...I kin git another one of those, though...Just tell 'em I lost it."

"Let's have a look at your buy and see if it's real, okay? Sure don't want you to get cheated."

"That's why I'm here. Just cain't trust people these days...know what I mean?"

"Uh, huh," commented Juan.

Roxy got out a small pill bottle with a white powder in it and placed it on the table. Stella slipped on a set of blue surgical gloves, took the bottle from the table, opened it, grabbed a small stainless steel spatula and removed a sample. She placed it in the test tube, added a little reagent and shook it—the sample turned blue.

"It's coke, all right but I think they stepped on it real hard."

"Thieving bastards! Can you arrest them and get me my food stamps an' Obama phone back?"

Stella and Juan smiled at each other.

"No problemo, ma'am. You tell us who ripped you off and we'll go pick those dirty thieves up right now."

"Ya'll are just the nicest po-lice peoples."

CROSS PD PARKING LOT

Captain St. John, after putting in a very long day, was the last of the day shift to leave the station. He had worked past supper to try to catch up with the mountain of paperwork generated by the previous night shifts' full moon escapades. He unfastened his tie, pulled it from his neck and unbuttoned his collar button as he drove his white Explorer out of the parking lot and turned left off Main Street onto Commerce at the courthouse.

St. John braked his vehicle to a stop. In the middle of the street an Indian in full war paint, holding a long lance, mounted on a gray and black Appaloosa with just a multicolored saddle blanket draped across his withers stood facing his SUV. He blinked several times and rubbed his eyes—the mounted Indian was still there.

He pulled into a parking space at the courthouse reserved for county officials, turned off the engine and got out. The Captain approached the horse cautiously and looked up at the war bonnet bedecked Indian.

"Howdy, chief…kinda late for a little ride, isn't it?

"No chief. Running Bear strongest Chickasaw brave in Oklahoma."

"Right…You know you're in Texas, don't you?"

"Texas?"

"You crossed over the Red River five miles to the north."

"Raging river deep and wide, but no stop Running Bear… looking for White Dove."

"Uh, huh…Say, why don't we get out of the street before some drunk runs into us."

Running Bear slid off the Appy. St. John led him and the horse over to the courthouse steps and tied the reins to a welded pipe hand rail.

"You Buffalo Soldier?"

"What?…Buffalo Soldier?"

"You ride with Long Knives?"

"Huh?…Oh yeah…I mean no. I didn't ride in the cavalry. I'm a cop."

"You Lighthorse?"

"Ah…Yeah, *Lighthorse? Oh, right…That's what they call the Chickasaw police in the Nations.* I'm a…Lighthorse, but not in the Nations…Here in Cross."

"You arrest John Running Bear?"

"Did you do anything wrong?"

"No, but that no stop white man's law."

"What?"

"White man no live by treaty. Speak with fork tongue. Treat all red men bad."

"Yeah…some parts of our history, I'm not proud of."

"You white eyes all same."

St. John cracked up. "Who you calling *white eyes*, Dude? Look at the color of *my* skin!"

The captain held out his arm. Running Bear took it and turned it over and then back.

"Nice arm."

"Do I look white to you?"

"You go maybe…tanning salon."

St. John rolled over laughing. He started to say something, but stopped and then stood. "Hey, listen, I picked up some beer to take home, but I think I'll have one…How about you?"

"Running Bear drink tizwin with Lighthorse…No light beer."

St. John grinned and shook his head as he headed to the back of his Explorer. He opened the rear hatch, took out two beers from a cooler, walked back to the courthouse steps and handed the cold Shiner Bock to

Running Bear. They clinked their bottles in a toast to each other.

St. John and John Running Bear had moved over to the grass under a big red oak tree on the courthouse lawn and sat, laughing and drinking beer. There were several empty beer bottles scattered around them.

"...so, John, how long have you worked at WinStar Casino for the Chickasaw Nation?"

"Since they opened, eleven years ago."

"Accountant? Huh?"

"Well, actually CFO, Chief Financial Officer..."

"I thought you said you weren't a Chief."

They both laughed.

"I'm the chief bean counter...It's about to drive me crazy...I just had to twist off."

They toasted bottles again.

"Join the club. Been there, done that once or twice myself," said St. John.

Officer Wanda Stanton cruised by and saw the two men drinking on the courthouse lawn and a hobbled horse grazing nearby. She shined her spotlight on the two, bumped the siren into a short growl, got out of her patrol car and walked up to the two men with her

Mag lite. "Hey, no drinking in public in this county! Pick up your trash and move on."

St. John turned around.

"Officer Stanton, I believe I have everything under control."

Wanda immediately turned off her light. "Captain?"

"Yeah…Last time I looked."

"Did you know it almost 5am…sir."

"I do have a watch, thank you very much…officer. That will be all."

"Uh…Right…Yes, sir…Well, have a nice night, Captain."

Wanda shook her head, got back in her unit and rolled on. "Well, that's one for the books…on second thought, I'd better not put that in there."

* * *

CHAPTER THREE

PIONEER CEMETERY
CROSS, TEXAS

Officer Stanton started making her morning sweep of the old Pioneer Cemetery to chase out a handful of homeless derelicts. She cranked her spotlight across the sea of headstones, bumped her horn a few times and leaned out of the window of her patrol car as it slowly rolled down the narrow asphalt roadway near the central mausoleum. "Okay, folks. Head 'em up and move 'em out!"

One shabby derelict did not hear the horn nor Wanda. He was too engrossed in the throes of a rare and furtive sexual experience with a young woman in the shadows between two hundred year old tombstones.

"Okay, lovebirds, let's go! It's almost sunup."

The man paid no heed to the officer.

Damn, I hate this part. She got out of her unit, walked right up to the man and tapped him on the shoulder with her long Mag lite, before the man even knew she was there.

"Hey! You hear me?"

She noticed that the woman was too young, attractive and well-groomed; then that she might be drunk or even unconscious; then that there was blood spreading from underneath her head. "Oh, Jesus Christ! JESUS H. CHRIST!"

Stanton grabbed the derelict by the collar and yanked him off the girl, throwing him to the side. The derelict, still being drunk, took a wild swing at her. She ducked and with her off arm, used his momentum to push him around away from her. Then, by placing her right foot in front of him and her left hand between his shoulder blades, she took him to the ground, put her knee in the middle of his back, pulled a set of cuffs from her Sam Brown belt and snapped them on. He rolled back to the right to look up at her with wide bloodshot eyes.

"Face down, asshole! Now...do it now!" She kicked the perpetrator in the side and he rolled back onto his stomach. "Slimy bastard!"

After she frisked him, she stepped over to check the victim—knelt down and felt her carotid artery with the tips of her fingers. "Damn." Wanda moved back to the perpetrator, pulled him to his feet, walked him to her unit, yanked open the back door and placed him in the seat.

She fumbled for the radio mike clipped to her epaulet and called dispatch. "Alpha One-seventeen, Lauri, I need cover, 901H and 11-44."

"Alpha One-seventeen, 10-75?"

"Affirmative, Lauri."

"What is your 20, seventeen?"

"Pioneer Cemetery...Suspect is in custody."

CONVENIENCE STORE

Bone walked out of an all night convenience store with a styrofoam cup filled with hot coffee in his right hand as he pushed the door open. He heard the dispatcher calling him on his police radio installed in his '73 Volkswagen Thing.

"Kilo Twelve-thirty-six, did you receive?"

The top was down on the primer gray vintage vehicle and he reached over the door with his left hand for the mike hooked to its holder on the dash, spilling the hot coffee in the process. "Crap!" He keyed the mike. "Kilo Twelve-thirty-six. Negative. Repeat."

"Officer needs cover, Pioneer Cemetery. Suspect in custody."

"Ten-four, Lauridarlin', 10-51."

He went back into the convenience store and came back out with a large cellophane-wrapped hoagie.

PIONEER CEMETERY

Bone pulled through the arched gateway into the one hundred and fifty year old cemetery. Three patrol cars, with lights still flashing, were already at the scene along with an EMT ambulance. He pulled up behind one of the units with two uniformed officers standing beside it.

Stanton was leaning into the open driver's door talking on the police radio. In the back seat, the handcuffed suspect squirmed in protest and was shouting a flurry of invectives at all within earshot.

Bone approached one of the officers, Joel Newman, who extended his hand. "Bone."

"It wasn't me, I wasn't there and I didn't do it...You cuff 'em and stuff 'em?"

"Nope, Stanton sacked him. I'm back-up."

Bone walked closer to the unit and bent down to get a better look at the suspect in the back seat. "Lover's tiff?"

"I doubt it. She's much too good looking for this slime-ball!"

"You don't say."

"Yeah, real fox. White female...looks to be in her mid-twenties...She nailed the bastard, *flagrante delicto*!"

"She saw it happen?"

"Nope. When she walked up on them, this scum bucket was screwing the vic."

Bone felt someone touch his shoulder from behind. "What?" He turned and sees the oriental deep-night sergeant, Richard Hung.

He was puffing on a reeking briar pipe which he assumed gave him an *air of authority* and maturity. "Detective Bone, I have the crime scene well in hand."

"Well, Dick...I'll be workin' this, if it's okay with you."

"Oh, sorry, I thought you might just be a...uh, John Q. Citizen. You know, we have to protect the crime scene from contamination."

Bone glanced at the scene, and then back at him. "Would that be the same crime scene that your people are tramping through as we speak?"

Hung looked toward the officers who were randomly searching the tape barricaded area in the beams of their flashlights. "All right, people listen up..." His voice trailed off as he moved over to *take charge*.

Stanton had finished her radio business and joined Bone and Newman. "Hey, Bone...I'm the arresting officer. I assume Newman told you what happened."

"Pretty much, Wanda. Had his rights read?"

"First thing."

"Who is he?"

"His ID shows him to be one Vernon Edward Wyland."

Newman nodded. "Yeah, that's his name. I've arrested him several times. Mostly for being drunk, disturbances, petty theft, routine stuff. Looks like he made the big time on this one."

"When you searched him, did you find anything that belonged to the vic?"

"Nothing," answered Joel

"When you get him to…"

He was interrupted by the return of Hung. "Well, as you can see, I've made certain that the area is secure."

"Thank you…Dick…Now, why don't you just have your people run everyone off that doesn't have a good reason to be here." Bone noticed that a few news media types that had begun to arrive on the scene. "Starting with those inbreeds." He pointed to Channel 10 reporter, Lisanne Adamson, and her camera crew setting up for a live coverage.

"Yes, sir, I'll handle it."

The rookie sergeant scurried off to meet the press.

"That should keep the little turd occupied for a while…Kid is almost sharp as a basketball."

Newman and Stanton tried to suppress grins.

"While I'm talking to the suspect, get a unit to cruise the area and see if the vic might have left a car parked close by…Uncuff 'im first."

"You got it," said Joel.

Newman opened the back door and removed the cuffs from the suspect, while Bone took the hoagie out of his sport coat pocket. The scruffy suspect was still heaping verbal abuse on the uniformed officers outside of the car.

Bone held out the hoagie. "Hey, Vernon…Hungry?"

Vernon eyed the sandwich, snatched it out of Bone's hand and tore the wrapper off. He was somewhere in his forties—with thinning reddish-brown hair—and badly in need of a shave.

He began to calm a little at the sound of his name and took a monstrous bite. "Ain't got nothin' to say. Take me to detox," he mumbled.

Lisanne Adamson started interviewing Sergeant Hung live after her camera man counted down with his upheld fingers when they were on-air.

"Can you tell us what happened here, Sergeant Hung?"

Bone got in the open front door of the squad car and turned around to address Vernon. Stanton and

Newman stood next to the open back door, watching the suspect.

"How's the hoagie, Vernon?"

Answered with his mouth full. "Good, good."

"Vernon, do you know why you're being placed under arrest?"

"I didn't do nothin' wrong." He took another big bite. "She let me."

"What do you mean...she let you?"

"What'd ya think I mean?...She just laid there and let me do her."

"Do you think she might have had a good reason to let you?"

He grinned broadly, wads of partially chewed bread showing stuck to his yellow teeth. "Guess she wanted it...Huh, huh." He chuckled.

"Well, Vern, I can see how a classy looking woman like that might go for a suave and sophisticated gentleman like yourself...But, we do have a small problem."

He took another bite. "Yeah?...What kinda problem?"

"Well, an old cop once told me...never get caught with a live boy or a dead woman."

"She weren't no boy, I can tell you that."

"No, it was a woman you were romancing…but she just happens to be dead."

Vernon paused and stared at Bone. "No, she ain't! No, no, no! She ain't dead, by God! You take me to detox. That's where I'm 'sposed to go. Take me to detox!"

"I'm afraid a trip to detox won't cut it, Vernon. Now, I suggest you tell me all you know."

"Said all I'm goin' to say."

Bone exited the patrol car, the filthy man continued to rant about going to detox between bites. On his way to inspect the body, he stopped to have a word with Stanton while he pulled on a set of latex gloves. "Cuff 'im again when he finishes the hoagie and then haul him."

"You want us to take him to your office?"

"Hell, no! Have you smelled the bastard? Take him to county. I'll give him a day or two to dry out and think it over."

"Charge him with murder?"

"Yeah, for now…We may have to reduce it to a 4-5-0 later."

"What's a 4-5-0?" asked Newman.

"Sex with a corpse," Bone said as he walked away.

Newman and Stanton exchanged looks as Bone proceeded over to the murder scene. Several officers stood inside the tape, gaping down in silence. Someone had covered the victim's body with a sheet of white plastic.

Bone slipped on a pair of latex booties and gloves. "Okay, people, give me a little room here…"

One by one the officers turned and headed off toward the growing crowd of onlookers.

Bone knelt between the grave markers, peeled back the plastic sheet and stared down into the face of a beautiful young woman with natural strawberry blonde hair that was flared out like a halo. Her dead eyes met his with a vacant look that he had seen all too many times in his career. "Mother of God," he whispered.

He pulled the sheet free, exposing the victim's entire body. Her green plaid skirt was shoved up to her waist, with her white silk blouse ripped open and her bra pushed up above her breasts—she was devoid of undergarments.

Again he stared into her pale green eyes which were fixed and dilated. A puzzled look of recognition came over his face. Suddenly, there was a white hot flash that bathed the scene in a sea of blinding light.

"Man, that's what I call a beaver shot."

Bone turned to see the outline of Cal Mitchell, pointing a camera at him and the dead woman.

The flash went off again and again Bone was temporarily blinded. "Dammit, Cal!" He did not have to see the face to know who it was. They had been classmates at the Police Academy in Dallas when they broke in together with the Dallas Police Department, ten years earlier. Both were fresh out of the service in the sandbox—Bone the Marine Corps and Cal, Army Green Berets.

"What a looker."

"Just take the pictures, Cal."

"Say what?…The damned ringing hasn't stopped yet."

"I said just take the damned pictures!…And you need to research 'hydraulic force'."

"Want to see the bruise on top of my head"

"No!" Still half-blinded by the flash, Bone rose from his position beside the dead woman. He noticed a man in thick glasses a few feet away. It was the ME, Doc Fisk. The frumpy man always seemed to wear the same outfit consisting of a Hawaiian flowered shirt under his jacket and with black pants.

"Hey, Doc! We got a real cutie for you this time. Take a gander at this lil' darlin'."

Fisk stepped in for a closer look. "Well, I haven't had one like that in a while."

"Hey, Bone, you know Doc Fisk, don't you?"

"We've met."

"Huh?"

"Never mind!" Bone yelled.

The Medical Examiner was too busy admiring the corpse and eating a breakfast burrito, to acknowledge the big detective.

Bone continued to yell to communicate with Cal. "Look, I have to go have a word with dispatch before they transport." He glanced at Fisk. "And don't jack with anything 'til I have a chance to look it over."

"You got it…And you don't have to shout."

Bone just shook his head, pulled off his latex gloves, walked back to his Thing and picked up the mike. "Kilo Twelve-thirty-six, Lauridarlin'."

"Go ahead, Bone," the dispatcher came back.

"Darlin', try to raise the beat element checking the area around the cemetery for the vic's vehicle…"

"Bravo One-five-five. We've checked the area within a five block radius, Bone. Nothing."

"Thanks, five-five, expand to ten…Lauridarlin', no vehicles are to be hauled before I have a chance to inspect them at the scene."

"Ten-four…anything for you, Bone."

"Bone out."

He rejoined Mitchell, who was taking the last of the crime scene photos. Fisk stood by and waited for the two cops to finish their business.

"Bone, we've done about all we can until you do your thing."

He nodded, put on a new set of latex gloves and knelt down to examine the body in detail. "Yeah…Let's turn her over, Cal. Bag her hands first."

"What?…Oh, right."

Mitchell placed paper bags on her hands, securing them with rubber bands at the wrists and they gently rolled the victim over. Bone examined a puncture wound at the base of her skull.

"Looks like a small caliber round. .22 or .25 maybe. Five'll get you ten, we've got our boy in custody."

"Cal, how many winos you seen carrying around something they can hock or sell…particularly a gun?"

"Mitchell took some close-up photos of the wound at the base of the victim's head.

"Judging from the powder burn stippling around the entrance, I'd say it's a contact wound."

"Uh huh."

"Huh?"

"I just said, uh huh." He keyed his recorder on the new Galaxy S4 he had gotten to replace the one he gave Lucy. "Small entry GSW, base of the skull, appears to be .22 or .25 caliber…contact wound…execution style…She knew her assailant." Bone rose and walked off a couple of steps.

"Oh, well…still say we have our boy."

He turned back to face Mitchell. "Have you noticed something is missing?"

"Like what?"

"Like a purse, jewelry, not to mention her shoes. That tells me that some of these fine homeless citizens got to the body before lover boy happened onto her."

"He could have stashed it under some of this trash."

"Not likely, but just in case, I'd like every piece of trash and debris in a twenty yard radius of the body photographed, but don't touch it and leave a uniform here to keep it secure…I'll be back out later to do an on-site."

"And who's going to do this?"

"You got the camera. The job comes under the category of preservation and collection of evidence."

"It'd be just a big waste of time."

"I'm sure Sergeant Hung will be more than willing to head up the operation.

"Damn you, Bone, you're just screwin' with me."

"Tell you what, Cal, just look on it as doing our part to keep the city of Cross beautiful."

"Is there anything else I can do to make your life a little easier?"

Bone glanced over Mitchell's shoulder at Doc Fisk who was preoccupied with the corpse. "Come to think of it, there is something you can do."

"Of course there is…What?"

"You and good ol' Doc Fisk there seem to be asshole buddies. See if you can get him to schedule the autopsy for later this afternoon."

"How's about I show up this weekend and clean your damn house?"

He started walking away. "Thanks…Already have a house keeper."

"What?" Mitchell said to Bone's back.

CROSS POLICE DEPARTMENT

Bone walked in the CPD office shortly after eight am. As he moved down the hallway, Dispatcher Lauren Smith, a sexy twenty-two year old natural blonde in a dark blue police uniform with a tight fitted skirt, was headed the opposite direction.

"Lauridarlin'."

"Well, mornin', big guy."

Bone turned his head and watched her continue toward the dispatch desk. He grinned and shook his head. "Oughta be a law."

Loraine, wearing her work clothes, a blue pinstriped pant suit with her silver Inspector's badge clipped to the belt, had just poured herself a cup of coffee. She saw Bone, poured a second cup and had it waiting for him.

He took the cup from her. "Damn, Loraine, it's not my birthday…What's the special occasion?"

"Don't get used to it. I just figured you wouldn't have time to get your own before the captain calls you in his office."

"What th' hell did I do now?"

"He's been on the phone with the media types ever since he walked in…My guess is he wants to know what you have on that killing this morning."

Before Bone could take the first sip, he was summoned by a whistle from St. John. Bone stepped into the office, leaving Loraine at the coffee pot.

He was still on the phone. "That's all I'm at liberty to say right now. The investigation is ongoing and as soon as we have further information, our office will make it available. Thanks for calling."

St. John hung up without waiting for a response from the other end and yelled to the receptionist in the lobby. "Lacy!"

The heavyset black receptionist came to the door. "Yes, sir?"

"Lacy, direct all my calls to Sergeant Franklin until further notice."

"Uh…Sergeant Franklin is out sick, sir."

"Damn…Okay, then you take 'em."

"What do I say, sir?"

"Aren't you studying acting?"

"Yes, sir."

"Then act like you know what to say." He waved her back to her desk.

"Christ, Bone, what the hell kind of crap did you step in this morning?"

"Just a typical Jane Doe homicide."

St. John loosened his tie and unbuttoned his collar. "Typical my ass...The phones haven't stopped ringing since I walked in...What the hell did you tell them?"

"Actually, I didn't tell them anything...You know I don't talk to those bastards."

"Then what in God's name put them in such a feeding frenzy?"

"You might want to watch the six o'clock news."

"Why? I ask...as if I really want to know."

"Our police spokesperson on the scene was a kid passing himself off as the deep night supervisor."

"Please tell me it wasn't a little turd-merchant by name of Hung...He's like a bear cub playing with his pud."

"You've met."

St. John leaned back and stared at the ceiling. "Just what was there for him to tell?"

"Oh, not much...Except the suspect was screwing the corpse when he was arrested."

Captain St. John wilted forward, face down, on his cluttered desk and let out a long slow sigh. "Jesus, Mary and Joseph," he softly said.

"Actually, boss, in the suspect's defense...the vic *was* a real   looker...and still a tad bit warm, I would add."

The captain raised his head enough to look at him with one eye. "You are one sick puppy, Bone...and not a damned bit funny.

"Sometimes a little sick humor is what keeps us sane in this line of work."

"Yeah...So, I take it we have a good case on the suspect?"

"Personally, I don't think he did it."

"But you said he was apprehended in the act."

"No, I said he was caught dipping his wick in a freshly murdered female victim. But, after talking with him...I don't even think the knuckle-head even realized she was dead."

"Bone, please tell me you're not going to turn this into a media circle jerk."

"Boss, already told you, I don't talk to those bastards...Besides, I have a surefire way of not being misquoted."

"Okay, probably be sorry I asked, but I'll bite."

"Well, when some tight-assed little reporter sticks her microphone in my face, I just say 'Hell, I don't have a little dick. It just looks little on me!'...I don't even make news at ten.

Captain St. John just glared at Bone for a moment.

"Okay, so maybe it wouldn't work for you."

"All right, smart guy, so clue me in. What makes you think we have the wrong man?"

"Well, for starters, the vic's jewelry, shoes and purse were missing, and our suspect didn't have them when he was apprehended...Meaning someone else got to the body first."

St. John leaned back in his chair. "I want you and your partner to get out on the street and make a case on this killing. If this butt nugget didn't do it...find who did...Got it?"

"That's my job."

"Now, get the hell out of this office before the big cheese comes in with a bunch of questions we don't have answers to."

"Oh, anything on that Global Energy bunch?"

"Not yet, got some contacts out. Let you know...Now get out of my office."

Bone glanced at Loraine on her cell phone, standing by Lacy's desk. She finally saw him, he nodded toward the front door. She terminated her conversation and was waiting when he left the captain's office.

Lacy buzzed the front door. When it opened, there was Police Chief Art Froman, the big cheese himself—a large man, tending to portliness, balding with a mustache.

"Good morning, Chief."

"Morning, Lacy.

The two homicide investigators swept past him just as he stepped through the door.

"Morning, Chief," said Bone.

Loraine followed with, "Chief."

Froman turned toward them just as the door closed…

CPD PARKING LOT

Bone and Loraine approached his car—manufactured for sale in the United States from 1973 to 1974. It resembled a Jeep on steroids and was also known in Germany as Type 181.

"What in God's name is this?"

"It's my Thing."

"Excuse me?"

"Don't like squad cars…This is a 1973 Volkswagen Thing…I'm in the process of restoring it."

"When are you going to start?"

"Just get in…bitch."

They got in, Bone cranked the rear-engine car up.

"Hey, where are the lights and siren?"

"Captain won't let me have 'em."

They entered Santa Fe Street from the parking lot and headed south.

"You want to fill me in on what happened this morning?"

"Grab your ass, pard, you are not going to believe this…"

"…and, so anyway, ol' Vern is convinced it's true love."

"You're a warped bastard, you know that?"

"Just thought I might bring you up to speed on the investigation."

"You're all heart, Bone…Except the part that's taken up by your butt." Loraine suddenly remembered something she had to do. She checked her watch. "Damn, I need to make a call, I have a lunch date."

"We need to go dig through some trash at the murder scene…Tell him you'll take him to dinner."

Loraine gave her partner a good-natured go-to-hell look and she pulled her phone out of her jacket pocket.

"And tell him you'll make it someplace dark and romantic…and expensive."

She held up three fingers which Bone knew meant, read between the lines.

PIONEER CEMETERY

Bone and Loraine walked up to the crime scene barricade tape where Officer Stella Johnson was standing guard.

"Okay, Stella darlin', you can take off, we'll take it from here…Rookie duty's a bitch, huh?"

"It's okay, gotta pay my dues…It's been pretty quiet, a little spooky, but quiet…See you later…How's it goin', Loraine?"

"It is what it is, Stella."

"Heard that," she said over her shoulder as she walked to her squad car.

Bone looked around at all the trash the homeless folk had left. "Damn, there's enough crap here."

"This where they found the DB?"

"Yeah. I didn't want anything disturbed except the body transported to the ME's. Mitchell took pics of everything."

Loraine started putting on her blue latex gloves. "Do I get a clue what we're looking for?"

Bone sat down on the top edge of a tombstone. "Somethin' that doesn't belong."

"Aren't you going to help?"

"Well, I gotta sit and cogitate about this a spell, see if I can get a feel for the crime…It's my style."

"Style, my ass. That's so much horse crap. You just want to see me on my knees digging through this stuff."

"On your knees is good."

"Jerk off." She finished pulling on her latex gloves and started digging through the trash.

Bone smiled, looked around at the crime scene and then got his thousand-yard stare. He started visualizing his version of the crime. *The victim is being led by her arm by a man in shadows holding a small semiautomatic pistol in his other hand. He turns her around facing away from him. She looks directly at Bone. The perpetrator puts the pistol near the back of her head and pulls the trigger. There is a 'pop'. The victim's eyes go wide in surprise for a brief second.*

He sees the bullet burrow its way inside her skull, the hollow-point round separating as it tears through the brain matter. The victim drops like a felled ox. The perpetrator turns and walks away into the darkness.

A female nondescript homeless type comes onto the body and begins removing jewelry, shoes, panty hose, etc. Then a very drunk Vernon staggers into the scene, pulls down her panties, fumbles with the buttons on her blouse then just tears it open and gets on top of her... Bone shook his head and put his hands to his temples for a moment and lightly massaged.

He got to his feet, slipped on his blue latex gloves and started sorting through the trash on the opposite side from Loraine. He rose up and stretched the kink out of his back.

"I'm getting a little parched. Think I'll see if there's a drink machine at that station down the street. Want one?" Loraine asked.

Bone pitched her the car keys. "Dr. Pepper, and don't hurt my Thing."

"I'll be gentle."

Bone continued the search while she made the run. In just a few minutes, she walked back up. He was looking at a tombstone with a small mirror and an acrylic dome magnifier. "What are you doing?"

"Checkin' for blood spatter...A mirror reflecting sunlight beats the hell out of a flashlight."

"Anything?"

"Nada." He pointed to a tombstone. "Grab a seat, I'm just finishing up."

Loraine opened the two soft drink cans and handed Bone his DP.

He took the can and drained half of it in one swallow. "So, tell me about Mister Wonderful."

"What do you want to know?"

"Just tell me he's not a lawyer."

"He's a former investigative reporter turned crime writer, if you must know."

"Kiss a fat baby!"

"Aw, knock it off, Bone, we met at that in-service school I attended two weeks ago on Departmental Media Relations just before I was assigned to work with you...He was a guest speaker."

"Has he sold anything?...Being a big-time writer and all."

"Yeah, smart ass, as a matter of fact, his first true crime book."

"How many copies has it sold?...I know you bought one and so did his mom...uh...that makes two." He finished off the Dr Pepper and crushed the can with one hand.

"You just like to see me pissed off, don't you?"

"Better to be pissed off than pissed on, I always heard… So…was it love at first sight of your boobs or did it blossom gradually after he found out you were a homicide investigator?"

"You know, Bone, you've been digging through that garbage so long it's seeped into your brain."

"Look, pard, I'm just yanking your chain…" He smiled. "Still love me?"

"Love you? I don't even like you…Ass wipe."

Bone was at the spot where the body was when he picked up something that at first seemed unimportant. He tossed it aside into a pile of trash he has already been through and then stopped, pulled out a measuring tape and measured the small blood stain on the ground. He paused and then he went back over to the trash pile and began to meticulously dig for the object which he had just discarded.

"What is it?"

"Don't know…tell you in a second."

He retrieved what he had been looking for and held it up. "What does that look like to you?"

"Looks like three cocktail straws together."

Uh, huh…and it doesn't belong here…but, notice anything else? Look at the small stain on this one." He pointed at the center link.

"Lipstick, maybe?"

"Maybe…Then again, maybe blood…Get the Hemastix Strips out of my kit, let's see."

Loraine opened his kit, removed a box of blood reagent strips and soaked the tip of one with sterile water from a dropper bottle. Bone shaded it with his jacket while she touched the stain with the tip of the strip—it turned a shade of green.

"Blood."

Bone placed it in a small paper envelope and marked it for identification. "We'll have Peach in forensics verify, send it off for the DNA and then see if she can pull some partials."

"That will be a stretch…What about this other stuff?"

Bone looks at the pile of clutter. "We'll have a uniform sack it up." He checked his watch. "It's a little after one o'clock…Let's go."

"Where?"

"We're goin' to go watch *peel and crack 'em*."

***

CHAPTER FOUR

BONE'S THING

En route to the Medical Center, Bone pulled out his new S6 and hit a speed dial number. In a couple of rings it was answered on the other end.

"This must be Bone."

"Just checkin' on you, Lucy."

"Everything is fine. Haven't seen a soul."

"I actually would have preferred that you did…Don't like it when things are too quiet."

"Oh…I see your point."

"It dawned on me I need to bring out one of those solar chargers for your phone…since you're not on the grid."

"I can manage, Bone, but you're welcome to come out anytime…and your Captain also."

"Try to get out there in a day or so. Up to my neck in an odd case right at the moment."

"Odd as in unusual?"

"Could say that. Body of a young lady found murdered in the old Pioneer Cemetery…A homeless guy didn't know she was dead and proceeded to…"

"That's all right…I think I get the gist…Come when you can…I should be here."

Bone heard a woof in the background. "That Tyrin?"

"Yes, he says hello."

"Well, tell him I'll bring him a knuckle bone from Scivally's when I come…and I'll have my Padrino along too. He'll be anxious to meet you."

"And I him."

"Laterbye."

"Bye."

"Who was that?" Loraine asked.

"A little lady…and I do mean little…the captain and I met when we were out bird huntin' Saturday.

Very interestin' woman. Lives way out in the boonies on the west side of the county…just her and her dog. Has some oil company folks harassin' her for a lease…Just keepin' an eye on her."

AUTOPSY LAB

Doc Fisk was dressed in a bright Warner Brothers cartoon surgical gown and stood by the body on an *L* shaped autopsy table making notes on a chart. Bone and Loraine entered the double stainless steel doors and walked over to the table. The lab was all white tile and stainless steel.

Fisk turned and held out his hand to Bone, who hesitated and looked at it before shaking it.

"Doc, this is my new partner, Inspector Rodriguez."

He took her hand. "How do you do? Is this your first…"

Bone interrupted, "Oh, no, Loraine is an old hand at this. Right, partner?"

Loraine just nodded.

"Well, we might as well get started."

A bright track light hung suspended above the autopsy table next to a microphone.

"Hey, Doc, where are your deeners?" Bone asked.

"I decided to give this case my personal attention." Fisk pulled the sheet off.

Loraine touched Bone's arm and whispered, "What's a deener?"

Bone replied sotto, "Like the doctor's assistant...his flunky. The deener prepares the corpse for autopsy."

"Kinda like Igor."

"Damn, Loraine, that could almost pass for a sense of humor."

She poked him in the ribs. "I'll humor you."

Fisk grabbed a butcher's type apron from a hook on the wall and put it on, wrapping the tie strings around and tying a bow knot in the front. The apron was also imprinted with the *Yosemite Sam* cartoon character holding scalpels in each hand with the inscription across the top that read: *I'M A REAL CUT UP*.

He reached over to a nearby table and grabbed his partially eaten hamburger. Bone stepped in for a closer look, but Loraine hung back trying not to let her apprehension show.

The victim looked much the same as she did when Bone last saw her, staring up glassy eyed, from between the tombstones.

As Fisk worked, he recorded the procedure while he continued to eat. "External examination…Photographs and fingerprints have been taken for identification…The victim's clothing has been photographed, analyzed for trace and removed…I place TOD between midnight and 1am…Body is now in full rigor…"

Loraine's breathing was becoming shallow and rapid as the doctor continued his examination.

"…There is an indentation around the victim's waist indicating she had been wearing pantyhose post mortem." Occasionally, he glanced toward Loraine to see how she was holding up.

"You okay?" Bone asked her quietly.

Loraine nodded sickly as Fisk placed what was left of his burger down and removed the white paper bags from the victim's hands.

"The body is devoid of jewelry. There are indentations and pigmentary variations on both the right and left ring fingers indicating rings…I am now taking fingernail scrapings for later microscopic analysis..."

Bone watched as the doctor poked and prodded the corpse, taking fluid and hair samples as he went. Loraine had averted her gaze toward a digital clock on the far wall—but was beginning to get a little pale.

"The external genitalia are those of an adult female with light red pubic hair. Abdomen and pectoral regions are unremarkable...Uh-oh, what have we here?"

Bone stepped closer, but Loraine hung back. "Whatcha got, Doc?"

"Three inch scars under each breast...Augmentation mammoplasty." He grinned. "Our little gal has had a boob-job...Help me roll her over."

Bone took hold of the dead girl's ankles and Fisk lifted from the shoulders as they turned her over on her stomach. The back of the body had turned bluish-black.

"Post-mortem lividity is developed on the back and is of normal color. Back and buttocks are unremarkable...There is a puncture wound at the base of the skull approximately one inch to the right of the external occipital crest. The wound appears to follow a slightly upward trajectory, most likely COD...Won't know for sure 'til I complete the autopsy...Okay, let's flip her back over and see what's inside."

Loraine got a little more green around the gills as the doctor selected a large scalpel to make the first incision. He picked up his hamburger again, took a large bite and placed it back to the counter.

"This one isn't bad. You should see the floaters...The ones who've been in the water a couple of days...or when they've been cooped up in warm house for some time before they're found...and, of course the jumpers are always interesting."

Fisk began the thoracic incision, opening the body from the breast to the lower abdomen. "Bone, hand me that set of loppers over there."

Bone grabbed a three foot set of tree pruners laying on the counter and handed them to him. The ME made the first cut in the sternum, making a *crunching* sound.

Loraine began to sway, backed up and sat down heavily in a chair. Bone noticed and moved over to her.

"You okay?"

She nodded, careful not to look at the carnage on the table as Fisk continued cutting the sternum apart.

"If you're okay to walk, I think we've seen enough."

"I'll be fine."

"Tell you what, Doc. If we need anything else, we'll get it off the autopsy report."

"Forty-eight hours, Bone. Take that long to get the tox screen…This isn't TV, you know."

Loraine rose unsteadily to her feet and she and Bone pushed their way back through the double doors that led to the hallway.

"You sure you're okay?"

Loraine took a deep breath and nodded. "Does he always dress like that?"

"Naw, sometimes he gets kinda wild."

She glanced at Bone—*Why did I transfer here again?* They headed for the door leading to the hospital parking lot—Loraine stopped abruptly.

"What's the matter?"

"I need to make a phone call." She dug in her purse and came out with her cell phone.

"Another one? This must be true love."

"Bite me."

"Thought you'd never ask, darlin'…I'm going to check in with the office.

Bone grabbed his cell while Loraine stepped outside where she could talk in private.

She exited the door, scrolled to the number and waited for an answer.

After a couple of rings, Bob Ashworth looked at his caller ID and answered, "Hey, sweetie. How's the prettiest gal I know?"

"Fine…Just finished watching an autopsy."

"Sounds gruesome."

"Nah, you see enough of 'em, you get used to it."

"Homicide?"

"Yeah, the vic was found just before sunup in Pioneer cemetery."

Ashworth was seated on his couch staring down at several newspaper articles on his coffee table, covering the woman's homicide. He had, what some termed, an arrogant Ivy League patrician look. "Funny you should bring it up. I was just reading about that…Your case?

"Mine and my partner's."

"Come up with anything?"

"Not yet. We're trying to ID the vic…She's still a Jane Doe."

"That's unusual, isn't it? I mean somebody should have missed her by now."

"Depends. She was murdered around one this morning. Why the interest?"

"It's the old investigative reporter in me...Remember, I used to cover the police beat."

"Right."

"I'd sure like to see you. I have a great idea for my next project."

"How about after I get off work?"

"Oh, sugar pants, tonight is not good for me...My agent is expecting the final draft of my new book. I don't think I could keep my mind on business with you here...You know how you distract me."

Loraine saw Bone coming out of the hospital and cut her conversation short. "Okay, I'm going to let you off the hook...just this once. But you owe me big time."

"Deal...Say how about tomorrow evening? For cocktails and dinner?...I'll tell you about my idea."

"Works for me...Gotta go. My partner's coming."

"Say, why don't you bring him along? I'd like to meet him...get his views."

"Well...I don't know. He's not much of a socializer with people he doesn't know."

"Nonsense. Ask him...The worse he can do is say no."

Bone heard the last part of the conversation as he approached.

"Okay, I'll ask...Give me a call later, okay?"

"You got it, sweetie. Bye."

Loraine disconnected and put the phone back in her purse as they headed for Bone's Thing.

Bone pulled out onto Hwy 82. "Ask me what?"

"Excuse me?"

"Back there you told your honey, *you would ask.* I assume you were going to ask me something."

"I already know the answer."

"Ask anyway...might surprise you."

"Bob asked me to invite you to join us for drinks and dinner tomorrow...I told him you'd probably be tied up."

"Well, tell...what's his name...I'd be delighted."

"Bob...You mean you will?"

"Why not?"

"Wait a minute...You're going to pull some of your crap, aren't you?"

"No, honest...I'd just like to meet the guy...Besides, I've never met anyone that could spell before."

"Bone, you are so full of shit."

He pulled into the CPD parking lot. Loraine grabbed the door handle when she remembered something.

"Oh, hey...What did the Captain have to say when you called in?...Anything on the vic yet?

"Nothing, no one has come forward to claim the body and there are no missing persons matching her ID."

"What about our other cases?"

"Captain's ordered us to put 'em on hold."

"What makes this case so special?"

"Well, that's simple...A vic who is raped and murdered isn't as newsworthy as one who is murdered then raped."

"God, some people are really sick, aren't they?"

"You can thank our good Sergeant Hung for helping point that out."

Loraine got out and paused with the door open. "Where are you headed? Hot date with some tittie dancer?"

"Not tonight…got a bunch of reloads to do and then I'm gonna watch a Ben Johnson western I recorded I don't know all the words to yet…Think he and I will drink some tequila and stack some furniture…Oh…there's something I failed to mention…"

"And?…"

"For some reason, have the feeling I've seen the vic before…"

"It's been a long day…and don't tell me it hasn't affected you…Mister Hardass."

"Maybe you're right…guess I need to back off a little."

She closed the door. It didn't catch, so she opened it again, slammed it closed. "If you need me…I'll call you," she said over her shoulder as she walked toward her car.

"Bitch." He grinned and watched her flash the single finger salute over her shoulder before she got in her car. He put the Thing in gear, pulled away from the curb and looked back to watch Loraine drive away. In his rearview mirror, he saw the victim sitting in his back seat. Bone slammed on the brakes and turned around to look—there was nothing there…

CROSS POLICE DEPARTMENT
FORENSICS LAB

Peach Presley, the tall, attractive brunette forensics technician from Georgia, was working on the stir straw chain trying to pull a partial print. Cal entered the lab with two cups of coffee.

"Hey, Peach, brought you some coffee. How's it coming?"

She took the cup from his hand. "Bless your heart, that's so sweet. I needed this...and you don't really want to know."

"Whoa, who peed in your chili?"

"I've worked on this straw chain for three hours...there just isn't enough surface area to pull more than two points and we need a minimum of eight to make an legit ID. IAFIS has kicked it back twice...Makes my butt want to work button holes...And on top of that, the DNA lab in Atlanta is backlogged. We're number 617...gonna take five weeks. All I can get here is the blood type, A positive...same as the vic.

Cal stifled a grin. "How about the bullet from the vic?"

"That's worse."

"How so?"

"Doc Fisk sent over six fragments from the autopsy. Based on the entrance wound in the occipital crest, the diameter is consistent with a .22 caliber round…In my opinion, it was a .22 mag hollow point pre-segmented, copper-jacketed projectile designed to separate and fragment upon impact…Considering all the pieces, it's impossible to get a ballistic match…Good gracious, who in the world uses a round like that?"

"Someone who wants to be sure."

"Yeah."

"Well, check you later," he said as he closed the door.

Her cell phone rang. "Peach."

"Hey, how's the prettiest gal I know?"

"Oh, hi, Bob."

"Say, sweetie, I'm in dire need of someone to help me test a bottle of Caymus Cabernet 2002 vintage tonight…Do you know anyone?"

"Bless your heart…I might…She's about five foot ten…from Georgia…and a brunette…Will that do?"

"I think she'll do just fine. How about my place…about 7:30?" Ashworth asked.

"Works for me."

BONE'S GAME ROOM/RELOADING SHOP

Bone pulled the lever on the last reload, walked over to the counter and poured himself a tequila neat and reclined in his lounge chair. He picked up the remote and started the TIVO, absently stirring his drink with a red plastic stir straw.

Halfway through the second the movie on the TV had become a blur, its sound a din of indistinguishable gibberish. He nodded off.

"Bone?"

He stirred—at first, he wasn't sure if he actually heard anything—someone was calling his name from the darkness of the door into the hallway.

"Bone?"

Again he heard his name. Bone looked up to see the murder victim framed in the single bulb light from the doorway behind her. She was wearing a white gossamer lounging peignoir.

"Did you forget about me, baby?"

She floated across the room in a very fluid motion to his chair, holding out a red stir straw folded into a triangle in her hand. "Bone, help me...I'm frightened."

He looked into her face and saw that life had returned to her green eyes. "Who...?"

The beautiful wraith pressed a finger to his lips to silence him. "Shhh...Just hold me...You must look at nothing, but see everything."

He couldn't take his eyes off her as she sat down on the arm of the chair—her gown opening. Bone pulled her to him, caressing the smooth texture of her strawberry blonde hair. He was drawn to her eyes as they began to grow pale and dim until they were fixed and dilated as they were when he first saw her body in the cemetery.

His gaze drifted down toward the open gown and the sight of the stitched autopsy *Y* incision running from between her perfect breasts down the entire length of her torso suddenly filled him with unimaginable terror.

Bone sat bolt upright in his chair and let out a muffled scream. Like a madman, he flailed wildly at the air around him where the specter had been sitting—he was alone.

He fumbled for his drink and drained the glass. The commercial break signaled that it was time to freshen it. Bone walked over to the counter next to the refrigerator and mixed a fresh one, three fingers this time and went back to his chair…

BOB ASHWORTH'S LIVING ROOM

Ashworth got up from the couch and got the bottle of wine from the bar, walked back and refilled Peach's glass, put the empty bottle on the coffee table and sat back down next to her.

"Well, how's it going at the lab? Working on anything interesting?"

"Bless your heart, Bob, you just wouldn't believe."

"Oh?" He glanced at her over the top of his glass as he took a sip…

BONE'S GAME ROOM/RELOADING SHOP

A commercial for a local car dealership was playing across the screen of the TV. Bone picked up the remote and began to fast forward to the movie when something caught his eye. He backed up to the beginning of the commercial and replayed it. It was an ad for *King's Row Car Dealership*. As the camera panned across the rows of new cars, he saw something that made his blood turn to ice.

She was pointing to a car. "This is our top of the line model and today you can get $5,000 off list and zero percent financing. Come by and see us at King's Row." She winked at the camera and smiled. "You'll be glad you did."

The attractive strawberry blond was the same woman who just invaded his dream. Bone reached for the phone on the table next to his chair and called Loraine. He glanced at the clock radio. It was a few minutes after 12am.

A sleepy Loraine answered. "Hello?"

"Partner, you alone?"

"No, I've got the Mormon Tabernacle Choir in here…" She sat up in bed and checked the time on her clock radio. "Bone, you okay?"

"I'm fine."

"You don't sound fine."

"I know who the vic is."

"What?"

"Don't know her name, but I just saw her in a TV commercial."

"Have you been drinking?"

"I'm not workin', am I?…Just saw her on that western movie of Uncle Ben's I recorded. She's doing a car commercial for the King's Row dealership."

"Come again?…What are you talking about?"

"Look, I'll explain in the morning en route to the dealership. Pick you up around eight-thirty." Bone reached for his drink and saw something that made him believe he was still dreaming.

"I'll be out front…meanwhile, you get some sleep."

"Yeah…yeah…night."

He hung up the phone and reached for the thing that made him doubt his reason. On the table next to his glass was a red stir straw neatly folded into a triangle. He picked it up and held it for inspection. "Suffering Mother of Jesus."

HOUSE IN THE WOODS

Bone's Thing was parked in front of a small rustic natural stone house with a green metal roof—nestled in a copse of trees. He was sitting on the hood and staring at the front door of the small house. The light of a waxing gibbous moon cast odd shadows across the yard.

Suddenly, the wind blew through the trees and the numerous wind chimes, hanging from the limbs, swung to and fro in the moonlight, making eerie tinkling sounds. Bone stood up and took a deep breath, walked up onto the porch and entered the front door without knocking.

He stepped into a room which was a combination kitchen and living room. The walls were solid book shelves—wall to wall, floor to ceiling—with books ranging from the classics like Plutarch, Plato, The Complete Works of Shakespeare and The Odyssey to all eighty-five novels of Edgar Rice Burroughs—many leather bound first editions. There were also mounted fossils and reproduction paintings by the masters and an up-to-date computer with a thirty-two inch flat screen monitor.

Across the room a white-haired man with a full white mustache and matching bushy eyebrows stood at the stove stirring a pot. "You took your damn sweet time coming in...Take your hat off in my house.

Bone shook and then jerked his cap off. "Yes, sir. You... You sensed me, Padrino?"

He looked up with a wooden spoon in his hand and stared at Bone for a moment. "No, you can hear that piece of junk you drive for miles, boy."

He put the spoon on a holder, dipped some chili into a bowl, walked over, placed it on the table, pulled out a chair and pointed at it—Bone sat down.

"Coffee?"

He nodded. Padrino started back toward the stove, but was stopped short by the look on Bone's face.

"What is it?"

"Padrino...I need to...I..." He hesitated a moment and then stretched his arms out straight in front of him, palms down on the table and bowed his head.

The elderly man turned back and looked at him with a strange warmth. Bone remained still with his head bowed and arms out in front of him. The old man strode to the table, sat down across from him and stretched out his own hands to touch his fingertips to his.

"Speak to me from an open heart."

I have two things, my Godfather...First, I am seeing and being visited by the spirit of a murder victim."

"Does this spirit come to you in a dream?"

"I'm not sure…I don't think so…I…Tonight she left me this." He looked up, their eyes met and Bone fished in his pocket to bring out the triangle straw. He placed it on the table.

"Is it magic?"

Padrino looked at the triangle and pushed it back to him. "Magic is merely science not yet understood."

"I just don't understand why I am seeing her."

"Do not look for a logical explanation to every occurrence. Even the still wind has a voice…As I have told you many times before, you must look at nothing, but see everything."

Bone looked sharply at him. *That's what she said.*

"The answer you seek lies within your own spirit. The blood of the Nasca kings flows in your veins."

Bone looked at him and picked up the triangle. He placed it in his pocket and started to speak when Padrino interrupted him by holding up his hand.

"What is the second thing?"

"The captain and I were out bird hunting the other day…"

In a few moments, Bone finished his story of meeting Lucy. "…and both times, when I touched her, Padrino, I had visions of a lavender sky with two suns and a triangle shaped silver craft...want to say...a space craft...with two small gray beings inside...fighters and giant green globular ships. I saw a windmill and a flash of light..."

Padrino got up from the table, walked to the counter and poured himself a cup of coffee. "Those were not really visions, my son...You were seeing her memories...You must take me out to meet this woman."

Bone nodded. "I told her of you and she wants to meet you too...I'll set it up."

"Now you must bring what you promised."

Bone suddenly looked at him with obvious confusion.

"Where's my beer?"

***

CHAPTER FIVE

LORAINE'S DRIVEWAY

Bone was waiting in his Thing when she came out of her house and got in the car.

"Okay, what's going on?"

He handed her a DVD he burned from his TIVO. "You're not going to believe it, but our vic's doin' a car commercial on this.

"And you're sure it's her?"

Bone gave her his look. "Does a hobby horse have a hickory…"

"Why don't we take a minute, go inside and take a look at it on my player."

"Pard, that would be like a dog barkin' at a knot hole. If you remember, you didn't get much of a look at her…I doubt if you could ID her if she was sittin' in the back seat."

Bone realized what he had just said. He glanced at the rearview mirror that showed the empty back seat.

"Point." She blushed slightly as she remembered the autopsy.

He backed out of the drive and headed for the King's Row Car Dealership out on Hwy 82.

Bone and Loraine were met as they exited his Thing by a smarmy individual with slicked back hair—dressed in bright blue Dockers, a cream shirt, and a loud polka dotted tie. He half hid a snicker as he looked over at Bone's vehicle.

The salesman extended his hand and showed a mouthful of capped too-white teeth. "Well, what a nice looking early-bird couple…My name is Trent and I'm going to do whatever it takes to make you and the little missus a couple of happy campers."

"Well, Trent, there *is* something you could do that would just tickle me and the little missus to death."

"Yes, sir, and what would that be?"

Bone held up his badge and police ID for him to see. "Tell the owner of this fine establishment that Detective Bone and Inspector Rodriguez from Cross PD would like a word with him...In private."

Trent somehow lost his smile, he glanced around nervously. "Uh, I'm sorry Mister....uh, Detective Bone, but Mister Petrov is in Houston for a car show."

"How long has he been at this car show?"

"Uh, I'm not sure...four or five days as far as I know. I could let you speak with Mister Finestien...our general manager."

"Fine, Trent. You just trundle off and get him for us."

He scurried off toward the glass enclosed showroom floor where he approached a heavyset man in a light green suit—Les Finestien, the general manager. Trent spoke to him and pointed in the direction of Bone and Loraine.

Finestien ambled out the door of the showroom to the awaiting officers. "I'm Les Finestien, general manager." He did not extend his hand. "How can I help you...officer?

"I think you have a female working for you."

"Yes, we have several. We also employ a number of blacks and Hispanics...Equal opportunity, you know."

"We're just interested in one. A very attractive strawberry blonde...She does your TV spots."

"Yes, you're speaking of Beverly Farmer. She's our television spokesperson."

"Mister Finestien, would you happen to know where she is right now?"

"Yes, as a matter of fact, she's at the auto show in Houston with the owner, Marcus Petrov."

"You're certain about that?"

"Of course. She's also Mister Petrov's personal secretary...Accompanies him on many of his out of town trips."

"Would it surprise you to know that Miss Farmer was found murdered yesterday?" Bone asked.

"What?" Finestien exclaimed, obviously shocked.

"Her body was discovered in the old Pioneer Cemetery," added Loraine.

"That's impossible."

Bone took out a crime lab close-up photo of the DB and handed it to Finestien. "This isn't a great shot of her, but I think you may be able to make a positive ID from it."

Finestien stared at the photo, losing some of his surliness in the process.

"Is that her?"

He nodded slowly. "Yes…That's Beverly, all right."

"Mister Finestien, can you tell us how her body might have turned up in the cemetery when she was supposed to be in Houston?"

"I…I swear…I don't have a clue."

In the background, the dispatcher could be heard calling Bone on the radio. "Kilo Twelve-thirty-six. This is dispatch. You copy, Bone?"

"Partner, would you get that and see what the hell they want."

Loraine went to answer the radio as Bone continued with Finestien.

"How long has Miss Farmer worked here?"

"I don't know…Four or five months maybe."

"Do you know of anyone who might have more than a business relationship with her?"

"Definitely not. Like I said, she was also Mister Petrov's private…"

"Stock?"

"I assure you, Officer Bone…"

"Never mind…When is Petrov due back?"

"Uh...Late this evening or first thing in the morning...It depends on how the show move-out goes."

"Driving or flying?"

"He'll be coming into Cross City Field in his private plane..."

Loraine returned and interrupted, "Bone, we were told to report in right away."

"The Captain will just have to hold his horses."

"This comes from the Chief...He says now."

"Well, kiss my ass. Let's just put all the cop work on hold while I go into the office and compare Johnsons with the Chief!" Bone took out one of his department issued business cards and handed it to Finestien. "Here, slick, if anything comes to you, text me. My number is at the bottom...I'm open nearly every day."

"Yes, sir."

"And if your boss comes in ahead of schedule, I want to be notified immediately. Got it?...Oh, and just so you know...I'm the last guy on the face of this earth you want to piss off."

Finestien looked up at the big man, nodded and stared at the card while Bone and Loraine entered their vehicle and drove out of the lot.

CROSS POLICE DEPARTMENT

Bone and Loraine entered the front door and came face-to-face with an upset Captain St. John.

"Damn you, Bone, did you forget how to check in?"

"Sorry, boss. You told us to devote all of our time and energy to this case."

"I apologize...Dumb ass ol' me forgot to tell you the part about keepin' my rusty butt informed."

"Cap'n, I swear, we were en route to brief you when we got the call."

"Yeah, and if frogs had wings they wouldn't bump their asses every time they hopped! And..." Captain St. John stopped mid-sentence when he saw the Chief come out of his office headed their way. "Oh, fuck me runnin'..."

The balding, portly man in his late fifties strode up as if he expected to be saluted. "Someone want to tell me why I haven't been briefed on this Pioneer Cemetery murder?"

Bone handed him the DVD. "Sorry, Chief. My partner and I were out before anyone was in the office this morning...The vic's name is Beverly Farmer."

"Really?"

"Yes, sir. She was employed by Marcus Petrov at his King's Row car dealership...The reason she hasn't been reported missing is because everyone at the dealership thought she was in Houston with Petrov at the car show."

"I see...Go on."

Captain St. John stared at Bone and listened openmouthed, not believing his ears.

"At present, we have been unable to contact Petrov. But, according to one Mister Les Finestien...the general manager, he's due in late this afternoon or early in the morning in his private plane...We plan to greet him at the terminal."

The Chief glanced at the DVD. "Uh, huh...And where did you come up with this information, Detective Bone?"

"I knew I had seen the vic somewhere before, but I was unable to make the connection until last night. On a hunch, I reviewed this DVD and recognized her from a previously recorded commercial for the dealership."

St. John stared on in total disbelief.

"Remarkable," commented the Chief.

"To be absolutely sure, early this morning I met with my partner at her residence. After an extensive review of the recording, she was able to confirm my suspicions. We then proceeded to the King's Row dealership to investigate. We were *in the process* of interviewing Mister Finestien when we were called in to the station."

Chief Froman looked at Loraine. "Do you have anything to add, Inspector Rodriguez?"

"No, sir." She glanced at Bone. "That's uh…pretty much where we stand at this point."

The Chief turned to St. John. "Captain."

"Yes, sir?"

"You have two fine investigators here."

"Yes, sir…I was just telling them that."

"I suggest their time can be better spent on the street." He turned back to Bone and Loraine. "Carry on officers…Keep up the fine work."

"Yes, sir...."

"Thank you, sir."

"Captain, my office."

"I'll be right in, Chief."

He waited until Froman was out of hearing and turned to Bone, shaking his head in amazement. "Bone, I just watched you shovel more horse shit than the groundskeeper at the Fort Worth stock show."

"Actually, boss, I stuck to the spirit of the truth…mostly."

"It's amazing. Just A…freekin'mazing."

"What is that, sir?"

"I called you two in expecting to give you a royal ass-chewing. Instead, my ass is about to be chewed…Now I wonder why that is?"

"Well…Bone happens."

"Damn you, Bone. Shut up. Just shut the fuck up and get your asses back on the street."

Bone grinned and turned on his heel. "Laterbye."

He and Loraine headed for the hallway. They were almost out of harm's way when the Captain added, "By the way, I want a long detailed supplement on my desk when I get in tomorrow morning…comprende?"

"Yes, sir." Bone turned to leave again and then paused to speak over his shoulder, "Do you want that report before or after we meet Petrov's plane?"

"Out! Dammit, out!"

The two detectives drove out of the police parking lot and onto Commerce Street.

Loraine giggled and clapped her hands. "Bone, you are one fast-talking son-of-a-bitch...I won't be surprised if we come out of this goat roping with a commendation."

"I'll be majorly disappointed if we don't."

His cell phone dinged with a text message. He handed it to Loraine.

"What's it say?"

She looked at the screen. "Petrov will be landing at Cross City Field, 8:30 in the morning...Where are we headed now?"

"I was thinking I'd drop you off by your house so you could rest up and get ready for the big night tonight."

"Bone, it's not even eleven o'clock. If we're going to have the Captain's report finished, we'd best get our butts in gear."

"Pard, when you're right, you're right...Tell you what, I'll make you an offer even you can't refuse."

"Uh, huh...and what's that?"

"There's no need for both of us to get stuck doing all the mundane grunt work. How about I go ahead and drop you off?"

"But..."

"Just wait and hear me out. I'll do all the leg work and you can whip out the reports en route to the airport in the morning...Deal?"

Loraine hesitated. "Okay...deal"

Bone pulled into her driveway, she got out and stood outside the passenger door.

"I still feel guilty about leaving you with the shit detail."

"You owe me one."

"Promise you'll call if anything changes."

"Promise...Besides you need to call...Bob...and find out where we're meeting."

"I'll let you know as soon as I know...What's your first stop?"

"My house."

"Why?...You forget something?"

He started backing out of the drive as he spoke, "Nope, I'm just going to kick off my shoes, pick up the phone and let my fingers do the walking...Laterbye."

Bone backed into the street, cut the wheels and chuckled as he drove away with Loraine screaming at the top of her lungs.

"Damn you, Bone!"

DIVERSO'S RESTAURANT
LAKE TEXOMA

It was a little after eight when Bone pulled into an empty space near the entrance next to a classic burgundy 2001 Hundredth Anniversary Spirit Indian motorcycle and parked. He got out, did a complete walk-around of the spotless mint classic bike, grinned, shook his head and entered the restaurant.

The attractive brunette hostess in a black formfitting dress looked up as he came through the ornate double doors. "Good evening, sir, welcome to Diverso's. Do you have reservations?"   He spied Loraine at the far wall seated alone at a window table overlooking the lake. "Yeah, I see my party...I know the way, thanks."

The entire side of the exclusive restaurant that faced the giant lake was all glass, giving a beautiful panoramic view across the water—especially at sunset.

"Hey, darlin', come here often?"

"On a cop's salary? You've got to be kidding."

"That your Indian out there?"

"Yeah, saved for three years to get it…It was so nice out today, thought I'd ride it up here to the lake."

"Any chance of gettin' to take it for a spin."

"Sure…When you can get into a size zero tutu."

"Ouch!…Well, you're probably right anyway not to let me get on it."

"And how's that?"

"Probably wouldn' stop 'til I ran out of money."

"Woman's intuition…"

"Oh, yeah…right." Bone grinned and glanced around the place as if looking for someone. "Where's your escort…Bob?"

"Actually, he's running a little late. He said he would meet us here…" She noticed Ashworth coming toward them from the front door. "…about now…Uh, about the autopsy…"

"Say no more. I'll make you look good." He halfway rose and extended his hand to Ashworth when he reached the table.

"You must be Bone…Loraine's partner in crime…so to speak."

"And you'd be Bad Bob."

The waiter walked up to the table as the two finished their handshake.

For the first time since he arrived, Ashworth acknowledged Loraine's presence. He leaned across and gave her a peck on the cheek.

"Hi, baby. How's the prettiest girl I know?"

"Famished."

"May I get you all something from the bar?"

"Do you have a good Beaujolais?"

"Yes, sir. Would you like a glass?"

"Just bring a bottle…And be sure to open it so it can breathe…Wine all right with everyone?"

"Fine."

"Whatever you recommend, Bob," said Loraine

"Of course, sir." The waiter walked back to the bar.

"So, my sweetie was telling me about your trip to the ME's and that poor woman's autopsy."

"Yeah, every so often we have to sit in on them…I've never been able to get used to watching one, though."

"I can imagine."

"Anyway, I was doing okay 'til good ol' Doc Fisk opened up the corpse like a coin purse and started digging around to see how much change was inside."

Loraine commented through clenched teeth, "Bone, why don't we save the rest until later?"

"No, this is fascinating. Please, go on, Bone."

"Where was I? Oh, yeah…So your lil' darlin' sees I need a little fresh air…She tells the ME that she'd get the rest from his final report and gets my happy ass outta there."

The waiter returned with the wine, showed the label to Ashworth, who nodded. He then proceeded to pour a supcon into Ashworth's glass. Bob swirled it and savored the bouquet before tasting…He nodded again.

Loraine gave Bone that look of hers that would crack granite.

"Would you care to order now?" the waiter asked.

Bone finished his story, "Anyway, once we got outside, I began to feel a little better…That is until she mentioned lunch. As soon as I heard her say, *Chinese food*…I thought I was going to puke up a lung." Bone addressed the waiter as he checked the menu. "Tell me, garcon, do you have any fresh raw oysters on the half-shell?"

All the color drained from Loraine's face.

"I'll go check, sir."

As the waiter walked away, she rose to her feet as did Bone. After a beat, Ashworth followed his lead.

"Please excuse me. I have to go powder my nose."

"Are you okay?" Ashworth asked.

"Yes, of course. Please sit…I'll be right back."

The two men settled back into their chairs and watched as Loraine crossed the room and disappeared into the lounge.

"That's some lady."

"All right, let's knock off the crap…Bob…I think you're using her and I don't much care for the idea."

"I assure you, Bone, that woman means a lot to me."

"Well…Bob…let me tell you who that woman really is…She's my partner. I watch her back and she watches mine."

"Sounds like someone has the hots for her."

"Hots?…Hots? Oh, I'll show you hots, you scum suckin' little turd."

"You dare to threaten me?"

Bone leaned over into Ashworth's face and said very softly, "Believe this…sunshine and carve it in stone…When I get pissed…it ain't a pretty sight…"

Loraine returned. This time Ashworth was first to his feet, followed by Bone. He gave her another peck on the cheek and held her chair while she sat.

The big man remained standing. He picked up his drink, gave a mock salute and drained it. "Well, you two lovebirds enjoy."

Loraine looked up surprised. "Where are you going?"

He looked at his cell and slipped it back into his shirt pocket. "Just got a text from one of my chippies. Her car's broke down on Grand Avenue and she needs rescuing." He winked.

"Why don't you at least come back for some cappuccino?"

"Well, don't know how long I'll be. With a little luck, she may want to show her gratitude."

From the look on her face, Bone sensed that Loraine was disappointed and perhaps a little hurt. "Besides, I never drink anything I can't spell and three's company...and all that stuff." He and Ashworth exchanged looks.

"It's a shame you can't stay," said Ashworth.

"Oh, I'm sure we'll see each other again...soon...Bob.

They shook hands. Bob grimaced and bent slightly at the knees at the force of the man's grip. Bone smiled. "Laterbye."

BONE'S THING

Bone and Loraine were headed west out Hwy 82 to the small city airport.

"I meant to ask. How did it go last night?"

"Un....believable! And yours?"

"Same," Loraine replied. There was a long pause before she continued, "Actually, I went straight home...Alone. You didn't really get a text last night...Did you?"

"No."

""I'm glad," she said sotto.

"You say something?"

"Never mind...How will we know Petrov?"

"I told Finestien to have him meet us at the terminal, without fail."

"What if he doesn't show?"

"I don't think we'll have to worry about that. Not with his family background."

"What do you mean?"

"I did some research when I got home last night...Ever hear of a hood named Blackie Petrov?"

"The name's familiar."

"He's an old time Russian mobster from the Will Fritz and Jack Ruby days in Dallas. Racketeering, money laundering, gambling, prostitution…you name it. Right now, he's doing life in the joint."

"Any relation to Marcus Petrov?"

"Marcus is his son. And before you ask…our boy is squeaky clean. He's never been handled."

Bone parked the car and they walked to the open air portico on the side of the terminal.

He pointed at a twin engine blue and white 680S Aerocommander near the terminal. "Looks like his plane has already landed."

The door under the high wing opened and a tall well-dressed man with silver-haired temples deplaned and approached them pulling a rollaboard. "You must be the officers wishing to have a word with me."

"Yes, sir, I'm Detective Bone and this is Inspector Rodriguez. We just have a couple of questions. First, do you know a Beverly Farmer?"

"She is, or shall I say, was my private secretary. What happened to her was most unfortunate."

"You could say that…My next question is, why was her body found in Cross when she was supposedly with you in Houston?"

"Well, actually, I fired her a few days ago and booked her a flight back to Dallas."

"May we ask what the reason was?"

Petrov looked around as if someone might be listening in. "Look, I'm sure you've seen what an attractive woman she is, or was."

"Uh, huh."

"As a man, surely you understand how easy it is to fall under the spell of such a beautiful young woman." He looked at Loraine. "No offense."

"We don't offend easily, Mister Petrov."

"Anyway, she tried to make more out of it than it was. And after all, I'm a family man...I just felt it was time to end it."

"So you put her on a Southwest plane back to Dallas and that was the last time you saw her alive?"

"That's correct."

"Of course there will be a record of her being on the flight."

"I don't know why there wouldn't be...You can check."

"Oh, we will...Trust me," Loraine stated.

"By the way, how's your dad?"

Petrov's eyes flared for a moment. "I see. Just because of my father's checkered past, I'm a murder suspect. That correct...Detective?"

"Now you're the one getting offended, Mister Petrov," said Loraine.

"Damned right I am. The next time you speak with me it will be with my attorney present...Good day." He snatched up his bag and headed to the parking area.

"I think we pissed good ol' Marcus off a tad."

"Yeah, Bone, his eyes and mouth didn't match...Something is rotten in Denmark, my gut says."

"Always go with your gut..."

"What now?"

"Back to the station. You have a report to do."

"I trust you have all the information handy."

Bone fished in his pocket and came up with a micro recorder. "Verbatim."

"Damn you, Bone!"

DOWNTOWN CROSS

Officers Stella Johnson and Joel Newman were on patrol and had an old pickup pulled over.

They got out of their unit and assumed their positions. She stood just back of the driver's window. He went to the passenger side.

"License and insurance, sir," said Stella.

"What'd I do?" the driver asked as he handed her his cards.

She glanced at them. "Mister Crawford, you were all over the street, you were speeding and you don't have your seat belt fastened...Have you been drinking?"

"What?...Uh, just a couple of beers."

Stella looked in the passenger floorboard and saw three empty quart beer bottles. "Yeah, and just how big were those beers?"

The driver's hand crept over to the passenger side toward a ballpeen hammer lying in the seat.

"Step out of the vehicle, sir."

He wrapped his hand around the handle of the hammer. Newman watched him grab the hammer from the open passenger window and drew his weapon.

"I'd hate to put an early end to such a promising career as a stunt driver. But, it ain't smart to bring a hammer to a gunfight."

Crawford looked to his right and was startled to see the muzzle of the SIG 229 pointed just inches from his face.

Stella stepped to the side and drew her weapon also. "Go ahead, Einstein. He hasn't shot anybody since he joined the force...Now, I'm only gonna say this nicely one more time...Get your dumb ass out of the vehicle!"

She stepped further back as Crawford released his grip on the hammer and opened the door. Newman came around to the driver's side, still pointing his weapon at the man.

Stella holstered her Glock. "Hands on the hood! Spread 'em!"

She patted him down and grabbed her cuffs, pulled his arms behind him forcing him to put his face on the hood and snapped the shackles around his wrists. She pulled out her laminated Miranda card and read very rapidly—in staccato fashion. "You have the right to remain silent, anything you say can and will be used against you in a court of law. You have the right to talk to a lawyer and have him present with you while you are being questioned. If you cannot afford to hire a lawyer, one will be appointed to represent you before any questions, if you wish. You can decide at any time to exercise these rights and not answer any questions or make any statements…Do you understand these rights I have explained to you?"

"Huh?"

"Close enough."

Just then Bone and Loraine pull up beside them.

"Everything under control?" she asked.

"Yeah, this drunk inbreed tried to bring a hammer to a gunfight. We're taking him to the station," Newman answered.

"Time and effort will take care of ignorance, but stupid is forever. Carry on, kiddies…Laterbye." Bone grinned and nodded.

As he pulled away, another car passed in the opposite direction. The driver looked like the victim, Beverly Farmer. She looked directly at Bone with her pale green eyes.

"Did you see the driver of that car that just passed?"

"No, why?"

Bone took a deep breath. "Never mind." He glanced into his rearview mirror—nothing.

CROSS POLICE DEPARTMENT

Captain St. John stood just inside the front door as Bone and Loraine walked in. He held a pad of blank supplement forms which he handed to Loraine.

"Partner, I'll get the coffee. Looks like we'll be here a while," said Bone.

"You can bet your sweet asses you will," responded St. John.

Stella and Newman followed them in, escorting the cuffed Crawford. They continued on to the booking desk in the back.

As Bone poured two cups of coffee in the break room, he heard some commotion from the reception area. He stuck his head back out into the hall see a news camera crew as they came through the door. *Shit.*

The on camera reporter, Lisanne Adamson, said something to Lacy and she pointed back in the direction of Bone. The attractive brunette headed in his direction.

Before Bone had a chance to say a word, the cameras started to roll.

The reporter faced the camera, her mike in her hand. "This is Lisanne Adamson, with a Channel 10 News Update. In a bizarre murder case which has had the police working feverishly around the clock, the identity of the victim has, until now, remained a mystery."

Captain St. John had moved to his office with the door open and just sat down behind his desk and picked up his phone.

"Standing here with me is Detective Darrell Bone, who is assigned to the case."

St. John dropped the phone, literally jumped over the top of the desk and rushed across to where the cameras were rolling.

"Detective Bone, I understand the victim has been positively identified. And that you are following up leads which may lead to the subsequent arrest of the suspect. Is there anything you can tell us at this time?"

The perky news woman shoved the mike into Bone's face.

St. John leapt between Bone and Lisanne just as he started to speak.

"Hell, Lisanne, I don't have a little…"

"Uh, Lisanne, I'm Captain St. John and perhaps I can answer that question for you. Or better still, I can show you a video recording which was instrumental in helping to ID the victim."

Lisanne motioned for the camera to stop rolling. "Captain, is there some reason I can't interview Detective Bone on camera?" she asked, a little surprised and suspicious.

"Oh, none whatsoever, but right now he's on a very important assignment."

"Uh, Captain, my partner is filling it out as we speak."

"Not that assignment, Bone...You know...the other one."

"Other one?"

"Yes, the one across town...You know?"

Bone hesitated. "Oh...*that* assignment." He turned to Loraine and looked at his watch. "Partner, if we hurry we can just make it."

Loraine looked up from the report she had started filling out. "What assignment?"

"Just get your gear and let's go."

She gathered her purse and headed for the door. "You want to tell me what's going on?" she asked Bone sotto.

"I'll explain en route."

The news team entered Chief Fromann's office as Bone and Loraine slipped out the door.

The Chief looked up as they entered, adjusted his tie and grinned…

***

CHAPTER SIX

SEAFOOD RESTAURANT

Bone and Loraine were seated in green plastic lawn chairs around a white porcelain table on the patio outside of Seafoodville. Loraine perused the stack of papers they had amassed earlier. There were a couple of gulf shrimp baskets and fries, now almost empty on the table along with two Texas sized plastic glasses of iced tea.

"Damn, looks like the old man was into just about everything."

Bone gathered up the trash from their meal. "I don't believe for a second that he retired just because he went to the joint." He walked over to a receptacle a few feet away and dumped the refuse.

"You think junior is carrying on the family tradition?"

Bone just gave her his look.

"Yeah…As you said, according to the intelligence reports, he's never been handled."

"It's all too neat. Right down to the fake alibi…Nope, somebody's looking out for this boy."

"So, what now?"

"It's been a long day. How about I buy you a beer?"

"Where?"

"Governor's Lounge."

"That piss-on-the-wall dive? Nothing but cops and cowboys hang out there."

"Your point being?"

"Aw, hell, let's go. I'm in the mood for some ass kicking music."

"I figured good ol'…Bob…would have you out honky tonkin' every weekend."

"Bob hates country music."

"I knew there was something else about him I didn't like."

She gave him *her* look as she put the papers back into the crime portfolio and they headed to their car."

"I been meaning to ask...I glanced at your jacket...What does the DU stand for?"

He looked over at her and grinned. "Actually my given name is Darrell Ulysses, but when I was younger, I was a little on the wild side..."

"You're kidding...I'm shocked."

"Yeah, I just couldn't seem to pass up a dare."

"Oh, you mean like shooting a full can of beer off Cal's head?"

"Somethin' like that."

"What a dumb shit, the hydraulic force could have killed him."

"Close only counts in hand grenades and horse shoes."

"I've heard...so?"

"Anyway, when I was a kid, there was this eight inch water pipe suspended across this creek..."

"Someone dared you to walk across it?"

"Walk, hell...I rode my best friend's motorbike across it."

"And you didn't make it?"

"Oh, I made it across just fine…My friends said it was the coolest thing they'd ever seen…"

She shook her head.

"…but the trip back was a bitch. Spent two weeks in the hospital and eight weeks in a cast…My buddy came in and the first thing he said was, 'Damn you, Bone…you trashed my bike!'…It's been Damn you Bone ever since."

"Why am I not surprised."

"I guess you could just say I'm impulse control challenged."

She rolled her eyes. "Why me, Lord?"

GOVERNOR'S LOUNGE

When Bone and Loraine walked in to the '60s style bar, the lights were so dim that it took a minute for their eyes to adjust.

Ginny Mac had just finished *All the Man I Need* on the tiny little stage. Everyone applauded and called for more.

Thank you, thank you. You're wonderful…We're gonna take a little pause for the cause. Back in ten."

Ginny stepped down from the stage—the dancers headed toward their respective seats. She approached the big round table with Cal, St. John, Stella, Ashworth, Peach, Stanton and Newman sitting around it.

Ashworth patted his lap. "I've got a seat here for the prettiest gal I know."

"Aw, Bob, I bet you say that to all the girls," she said as she sat on Ashworth's lap and put her arm around his shoulder.

Next to Bob, Peach glared first at him then at Ginny.

The owner, Vertis Jolley, approached Bone and Loraine as he removed his jacket and hung it on a coat tree.

She looked at his side-arm. "Are you off duty, Bone?"

"I'm here aren't I?"

"We've had this little chat about wearing your gun in my bar off duty."

"Vertis...I'm a cop."

"I know, but isn't it dangerous to wear a loaded weapon in a bar?"

Bone just looked at her, stepped back to the door, pushed it open, drew his weapon and fired all five rounds into the air. "Not loaded now," he said as he holstered the S & W 500.

Vertis looked at him, shook her head and walked away.

Everyone in the place heard the gunfire—they all looked at Bone and Loraine at the door.

"Glad there's not an awning," commented Stella.

"Wouldn't have mattered," said St. John, resignedly. "Last time he put all five rounds through the *O* in the Stop sign down at the corner."

"What about where the rounds went after the sign?" inquired Stella.

"Asked him that very question myself."

"And?"

"Just said he didn't care...I've worked with a lot of people in my life and I can say that Bone's the only guy I've ever met that honestly and truly...just didn't give a damn."

"That might change one day," she observed.

"Don't count on it."

Bone glanced around the bar and saw the group. He noticed Ashworth with Ginny sitting on his lap. "Tell you what...the noise and smoke are already giving me a headache...Why don't we find a quieter place?"

"Nice try, Bone…Already saw his sorry ass."

"We ain't gonna have a killin', are we?"

"You've got to be kidding…But, then again, the night ain't over yet."

"Just askin' if you need another mag."

Cal called to them, "Hey, Bone. Why don't you and Loraine come over and join us?"

"Maybe later, Cal."

"Come on. I'm not going to let that SOB spoil my evening." Loraine grabbed his arm.

"Whatever you say, partner."

The two of them moved across the room and pulled up a couple of chairs. Loraine was careful to put Bone between her and the inebriated Ashworth.

"Hey, darlin'…How's the prettiest gal I know?"

Ginny cut a sharp glance at him, then seeing the look on Loraine's face, eased off his lap.

"Uh…I think I'd better get ready for my next set."

Loraine leaned across Bone so Ashworth could better hear her. "Go fuck yourself…Darlin'."

A chorus of "Oooooooohhh's," rose from the table.

"Baby, I'm here doing research on the thing I told you about…Oh, yeah, we never got around to that part." He elbowed Bone and winked knowingly. "Anyway, I'm going to do a story on the murder you guys are working on…Just think of it. I'll be in on it first hand from start to finish…My publisher loves the idea."

"Well, anything I can do to help…Bob…just feel free to kiss my ass."

"Now, now, Bone."

Peach leaned over to Stella. "Bless his heart, Bone has such a way with words."

"Well, anyway, can you at least tell me about that stir straw thing?

Bone cut his eyes sharply to Loraine. "Your pillow talk is none of my business…partner, but you ought to leave our case out of it."

"Just screw you, too!"

There was a second chorus of "Ooooooohhhh's." as Loraine started to leave.

"Wait, I'll give you a ride home," Bone offered.

"Don't bother, I'll walk." She got to her feet, grabbed her purse and headed out the door.

"If she didn't discuss this case with you, jerkwad…who did?"

"Ah, cops, priests and news hounds have a right to protect their sources."

Cal tried to ease the growing tension and waved at Vertis. "Nurse, bring ol' Bone here a bottle of Shiner Bock."

"I'll pass," he said as he got up.

"Hey, Bone? You're not leavin' are you?"

He leaned forward and put both huge hands on the table. "Yeah, think I'll turn in early for a change...Before I hurt somebody."

The table went deadly quiet—they all knew Bone.

BONE'S BEDROOM

He was still asleep—and dreaming. *He saw Ashworth standing before him, nude, wet, with a folded stir straw in his left hand.* His phone started to ring. *"See everything, Bone."*

On the third ring, Bone awoke with a start, jumbled it off the cradle and mumbled into the mouthpiece, "What?"

"Bone?"

He recognized the Captain's voice, suddenly he realized he had no idea what time it was. "Uh, I'm just sitting here working on that report, boss. I figured if I didn't have any distractions..."

"Knock off the bullshit, Bone. You'd better meet your partner."

"Why? What happened?"

"She found her ex-boyfriend writer dead this morning."

"Oh, Jesus! Where?"

"His turn-of-the-century home on Church Street. Just look for all the cars with flashing lights…They'd be cops."

Bone slammed the phone down and leapt out of bed. He dressed quickly and splashed water on his face. On the way to the door, he gargled with some green mouthwash and spit it out just as he opened the door.

CHURCH STREET

There were cop cars everywhere plus an EMT vehicle. Bone parked his Thing, got out and headed to the open front door of Ashworth's house. Inside, in the parlor, he found Loraine bent forward on the couch obviously upset.

"Hey, girl, you okay?"

Loraine just nodded.

"What happened?"

She looked up at him. "I was still pissed this morning when I got up. So, I gathered up some his personal items and was going to return them along with a piece of my mind."

Stella came in with a glass of water and handed it to her. "Thought you might need this."

Loraine took a sip. "Thank you…" She turned back to Bone. "He didn't answer, but I knew he was here, so I came on in. I was half expecting Little Miss Tits from the Governor's Lounge to be here. I looked all over and I finally…found him."

It was obvious that she was too upset at the moment to continue.

"He's back here, Bone," Stella said. "He has an antique tub on his deck. He was taking a hot tub soak…Looks like an accidental electrocution."

"You don't say?"

Bone followed Stella toward the rear of the house. She motioned toward a door opening onto the deck. He went through first, and then Stella followed.

Ashworth was lying naked in the antique claw-foot tub. The now cool water was within four inches of the top.

Stella began to explain the situation, "There was an old time reproduction radio on the shelf next to the tub with his candles and a bottle of brandy...From the amount of booze left in the bottle on the shelf, I'd say he was pretty wasted...Plus with what he had at the club...Looks like he accidentally knocked it off when he reached for a towel."

"Stella, for future reference, all deaths are homicides until I can prove they're not...Anyone disturb the scene?"

"No, sir. Just to determine if the vic was actually deceased. We did unplug the radio. It kicked the breaker when it hit the water...We haven't even dusted for prints."

Bone looked around and made a mental note of the deck area and pecan tree filled backyard.

She moved back to the door. "If you need anything else, let me know...I'll be just inside."

Bone nodded and continued his investigation. There seemed to be nothing out of the ordinary except water and broken glass on the deck. He slipped on a pair of blue latex gloves and started to pick up the radio out of the tub by the cord to put it back on the shelf when something occurred to him."

"Stelladarlin', would you ask my partner to step out here a sec?"

"Yes, sir."

In a moment, Loraine appeared at the door and came on out.

"Partner, I know this is tough on you."

"It's okay."

"Look at the radio."

She studied it closely. "And?"

"Look at the station it's on."

"A country station?" She looked back up at him.

"You did say he hated country music."

"With a passion...He's into classical."

He leaned down over the body and inspected it. He started to visualize: *Ashworth is soaking in the tub, listening to Mozart on a classical station, working on a snifter of brandy in his right hand and studying a folded stir straw in his left.*

He hears footsteps on the stairway to the deck and glances back over his shoulder as his hand goes under the water.

"What the hell are you doing here?

The intruder leaned down. "You're getting a little close to the house, writer boy."

"What do you mean?"

The intruder's gloved hand reaches across the tub and changes the dial on the radio to another station. "Why don't you listen to some good music?"

Ginny Mac was singing 'Dancin' on the A', a western swing song, on the radio.

The intruder drags the radio to the edge of the tub.

"Hey, hey! What are you doing?"

The radio falls into the water.

Ashworth stiffens, gags, drops his snifter to the deck and thrashes his legs.

Bone shook his head and looked at Ashworth. The corpse had something clutched in its left hand. With some effort, he was able to unbend his fingers—already stiff from rigor mortis—and retrieve the object. He held it up for Loraine to see.

"Oh, Jesus!" she exclaimed.

Bone held a red stir straw folded neatly into a triangle.

"My God, then he was the one all along."

He pulled out his cell and hit St. John's speed dial number. "Captain?"

CROSS POLICE DEPARTMENT

By the time they arrived, two investigators—both in dark gray suits—from IAD were on hand. A grim-faced St. John and the Chief were there to meet them.

The first words out of Bone's mouth were, "Where is he?"

"Interrogation room," St. John replied.

"Detective Bone, what…"

Bone held up his hand. "Later, Chief."

He and Loraine put their pistols in the lock box and went into the interrogation room.

"Hey, pard."

"Hey, Bone," replied Cal Mitchell—there were circles under his eyes. He was wearing department issued blue sweats and white running shoes. "I suppose you have some questions."

"You could say that…"

"Hell, before I start, better get out your recorder."

Bone opened his hand, which already had the tiny device in it, placed it on the table and hit the *on button*. Loraine sat in silence, glaring at Mitchell.

"By the way, I already been Mirandized and they brought me a breakfast burrito…Everybody knows your system."

Bone nodded. "So, tell me about it."

"Yeah." He stared at Loraine for a moment and then back to Bone. "Well, you know I like to gamble…a lot."

"Uh huh."

"And guess who my bookie is?"

"Marcus Petrov."

"Bingo…" He took a deep breath. "Anyway, I got into him for a few bucks."

"How much we talking about?" Loraine asked.

"Give or take…a little over 50K."

"Christ, Cal," Bone commented.

"Anyway, he said he'd cut me a deal…Hell, anything would have been better than lettin' Ruth Ann and the kids know what I'd done."

"What kind of deal?"

"Aw, you know…I take care of the split-tail and he forgives the debt."

"What did she know that Petrov wanted to keep quiet?"

"Hell, Loraine, it wasn't that she really knew anything…it was that she was three months pregnant."

"You worthless egg-suckin' bastard," she hissed through her teeth.

"Just doin' what I had to do, Loraine."

Bone continued with the questions. "So, it didn't have anything to do with the old man…Petrov just didn't like the idea of breakin' up the family home or givin' away half of his net worth."

"Naw, this was all personal."

"Tell me about the Houston trip."

"Well, that just happened to work out, see…She went to Houston with Petrov thinking everything was hunky-dory…that they would have a nice little weekend of grab ass, you know?…Then he sent her back on the pretext of picking up some important documents."

"And you were at the airport to pick her up?" Loraine asked.

"Uh, huh…I was waitin' for her in the lounge…Now, here's the funny part. When I was in the Army, I got in the habit of keeping up with my drink tab by making chains out of straws. One link, one drink. Saves a lot of arguments with the bar wench…I hooked the chain of three straws over my pen…Guess it fell off at the cemetery."

"You didn't kill her there, did you?"

"How did you know?"

Bone just stared at him.

"Yeah." He nodded and grinned to Loraine. "Your partner is a regular one man CSI…" He turned back to Bone. "I did it at the airport almost as soon as we got in the car. Waited for a jet to cover the sound and, pop, base of the skull…I drove straight to where I dropped her…I never did have any luck."

Bone reached into his shirt pocket and took out the evidence he picked up at Ashworth's murder scene. He held it up so Cal could see. "You still don't, pard."

"Damn, I saw good ol' Bob palm it at the Governor's Lounge last night. Right then, I realized he knew…because he had smoozed Peach in forensics for info…Where did you find it?"

"Good ol'…Bob…was holding onto it for you."

"Figures…Pard, do you think you could get me a cup of coffee before the goon squad transports me?…For old times sake."

Bone hesitated a moment, nodded and stood up. "Loraine, you hold the fort down for a minute?"

"With pleasure," she said.

He knocked on the door and one of the IAD investigators opened it from the other side. Bone crossed over toward the coffee pot. St. John motioned to him.

"Did he give a statement?"

"Yeah. Better send a unit to pick up Petrov…" Bone glanced through the door into St. John's office where Mitchell's pistol and badge lay on the desk. He turned sharply in almost a panic mode to St. John. "That Mitchell's gun?"

"Yeah."

"Who searched him?"

"IAD, why?"

"Where is his back-up?"

They looked toward the interrogation room where they could see Loraine being held as a shield in front of Mitchell. They were pressed tightly against the wall and he held his small .22 mag five shot revolver against her neck.

"Fuck…Let me handle it."

"You sure?"

"Yes, dammit!"

The Chief started to say something, but the look in Bone's eyes made him think better of it.

He edged up to the door and talked to Mitchell. "Cal? I'm coming in."

"That's your ass talkin', pard. Your mouth knows better."

"Look, I don't have anything on me. You know I have to cover my partner's six."

Bone took Mitchell's silence as a yes. He edged his way inside the interrogation room, holding his hands in plain view.

"I screwed up bad, didn't I, pard?"

"We'll work it out."

"Work it out, hell! I am royally hosed...Bone, I can't go to the joint. You know about ex-cops and cons."

"And you know they don't keep ex-cops in the general population."

"Pard, I can't put Ruth Ann and the kids through this. I just can't...I just can't, man." Cal edged back toward the door, still holding Loraine around the neck. "Just stay put, Bone...Okay?"

"Come on...This ain't the way, Cal."

"It's the only way."

Mitchell moved into the hall, still keeping Loraine between himself and everyone else. No one moved.

"Cal, let's talk about this," said St. John.

"Nothin' to talk about."

He moved down the hall, through the lobby and out the front door.

Just outside, Loraine made her move. She grabbed Cal's thumb, bent it backward, rolled out and side kicked him hard in his ribs just under his arm. He wheezed and went down to one knee as she took a kung fu defensive stance.

Cal pointed his handgun at her, then shook his head and looked around. Crawford had just been released after sobering up in the drunk tank and was getting in his beat-up truck. He started the engine.

Mitchell spun and sprinted to the pickup. He opened the driver's door, grabbed Crawford's arm and slung him to the pavement.

"Hey, what are you doin', man?"

"Police business."

"What?"

Cal put the truck in reverse and backed out. He shifted the stick shift to first and dug out.

Bone, St. John, the Chief and the others charged out of the station.

"Baby, are you okay?" Bone asked.

Loraine nodded.

"Where'd the hell you learn that move?"

"I'm a ninth degree black belt…Kung Fu."

Bone licked his finger and touched her shoulder. "Wow, who knew?" Then, he put his arm around her, pushed past the two IAD investigators glaring at them. "You assholes need to go back to school." He and Loraine ran toward his Thing.

"Can you catch him in this?" she asked as she grabbed the door handle.

"Watch me…Better buckle up, grasshopper, this could get hairy."

Loraine had that *oh, shit* look as they jumped in. Bone cranked the engine, backed around and tore out after Cal.

Mitchell exited the parking lot almost hitting Stella, in her personal car as she pulled in. He turned the corner as Bone pulled out of the lot. Three other patrol units were just behind him, lights flashing.

The Chief jumped in the passenger side of Stella's car. "Go, go!" he shouted to the totally confused rookie.

Cal ran a red light getting onto Hwy 82 and headed east out of town. Bone was fifty yards behind him, with the patrol units following suit—lights and sirens going. Cal turned on farm road 121 south.

Bone and his entourage followed, they were soon joined by a Sheriff's car and then joined by a Highway Patrol unit.

Mitchell took a left onto a smaller county road, sliding sideways as he made the turn. Bone was still close behind him, his bumper almost touched Cal's as they flew down the narrow blacktop road.

Without warning, the blacktop ended and the road turned into a caliche gravel road. White rock dust boiled up behind Cal, virtually obscuring any view.

"And you had to have the top down," Loraine groused.

"Sorry, didn't know we were going to be chasing a rabbit... Reach behind my seat and get my *go bag*. It's got my other weapons in it."

She reached behind his seat, grabbed a black leather shooting bag and unzipped it. Loraine pulled out an exact duplicate of Bone's regular side arm, a S&W 500 .50 cal revolver. She opened the cylinder, saw that it was loaded, snapped it shut and handed the powerful weapon to him.

"Why do you carry a .50 caliber?"

"'Cause they don't make a .60."

"You got anything smaller?"

"Yeah, there's a .45 in there too."

"That's more my style."

She pulled out a S&W 1911 .45 semi-auto pistol and racked the slide to check for a chamber.

Cal approached a T intersection a little over a hundred yards ahead—the road dead-ended into another county road. There were patrol units coming down the other road from each direction.

Bone rose up over the top of the windshield, squinting against the dust. "Hold the wheel."

She grabbed the wheel with her left hand and kept the Thing steady in the road, just about twenty feet behind Mitchell.

He aimed at Cal's right rear tire and fired. The tire on the old truck literally exploded. He fishtailed twice, crossed the intersection, hit a ditch embankment on the far side and went airborne, rolled in the air.

When his vehicle hit the ground on its nose, flipped end over end several times ejecting Cal. It finally landed on its top in a cloud of dust, wheels still spinning.

All the pursuers slid to a stop. Bone was first out of the Thing, followed by Loraine. They sprinted toward Cal lying where he was thrown. Captain St. John, Stella, the Chief and the other cops followed behind them.

Bone ran up, slid to his knees and checked Cal's pulse—Mitchell was bleeding profusely.

"Jesus, it rolled right over him...is he alive?" asked St. John.

Bone nodded. "Barely...Cal..." He cradled his former partner in his arms. "Cal, why, why?"

His eyes fluttered open, and then focused on Bone's face. "You know why...pard," he managed to choke out.

"You could have come to me."

"I made...my...my bed..."

His eyes rolled up behind his lids and his last breath came out in a rattle. He was gone.

"Aw, Jesus, Cal..." Bone closed his eyes with his finger tips. "Go with God." He pulled his friend's head to his chest.

CROSS POLICE DEPARTMENT

Bone and Loraine walked out of Captain's office. St. John was coming toward them from the rest room.

"Ah, there you are...By the way, boss...That report is going to have to wait one more day."

"Where are you going?"

"Lucy has invited my partner and me to bring my horses out to her place for a ride. Been feelin' bad that we've been neglecting her, but now that we got that case put to bed…need to make amends…When do you expect to hear back from the Rangers on Global Energy?"

"In the morning…Lucy didn't invite me?"

"Well, actually she did, but I only got two horses…Didn't much think you'd want to jog alongside while we rode Lucy's hills."

"I appreciate the consideration, Bone…My office, first thing in the morning."

"Laterbye."

He turned into his office as Bone and Loraine headed to the front door.

The Captain grabbed his coffee cup to go and get a warm up. It had been super glued to his desk blotter. "Damn You, Bone!"

He turned and saw Bone and Loraine suddenly being swarmed by Lisanne Adamson and her camera crew as they charged through the front door. The lights came on and the reporter said something to the camera.

Observing through the glass in his door, Captain St. John could not hear what was being said, but he knew what was coming. Perky Lisanne shoved her microphone in Bone's face, who said a short phrase.

The camera lights immediately were turned off and the shocked anchor woman covered the microphone with her hand as Bone and Loraine disappeared out the front door. St. John retired to his chair with a chuckle.

"Bone, you're terrible," said Loraine as they walked down the sidewalk.

"I know." He looked down the walk and saw what appeared to be the murder victim, Beverly Farmer, approaching them. He froze in his steps and whispered to Loraine, "Do you see her?"

"Well...yeah."

The beautiful strawberry blond woman stopped in front of them. "Excuse me. Are ya'll police officers?"

Bone just stared, unable to speak.

"Yes, I'm Inspector Rodriguez and this is Detective Bone, may we help you?"

"I here to check on the status of Beverly Farmer's murder case."

"And you are?" Bone asked, finally able to speak.

"I'm Brenda Farmer, Beverly's sister. I'm also an attorney, licensed in both Arizona and Texas, I'll be handling her estate."

"I'm sorry for your loss…Uh, how long have you been it town?"

"I just arrived this morning from Arizona. Why?"

"Oh…nothing, just curious…Twins?"

"Yes."

"Ask for Captain St. John inside, he'll fill you in," Loraine offered.

"Thank you," she said as she continued her way.

Bone and Loraine exchanged glances as they watched her walk away.

Brenda opened the door to meet Vernon coming out after just being released. He looked at her and his eyes got big as saucers. He stumbled, and then turned and backed away from her, stammering. "No…no…no!"

Loraine wrinkled her forehead. "You think?"

"Nah…Say, Pard, you know the difference between a bucket of chicken and sex on a blanket?"

"No…and I'm afraid to ask."

"Wanna go on a picnic?"

Loraine backhanded him across his chest.

***

CHAPTER SEVEN

LUCY'S RANCH

Bone pulled up in front of the white picket fence surrounding her house. He and Loraine got out of his 2006 silver Dodge Ram four door pickup and headed to the small gate. Lucy and Tyrin stepped down the steps from the front porch and walked up to greet them as they came into the yard.

"Hey, Lucy, this is my partner, Loraine Rodriguez...Pard, this is Lucy."

"I've heard so much about you, ma'am. I'm really happy to meet you," Loraine said as she held out her hand.

"I'm very pleased to meet any friend of Bone's…and you are just as pretty as he said you were." She took her hand in both of hers as Loraine shot a glance at Bone. "And this is Tyrin."

The muscular dog lifted his right paw. Loraine knelt down, took it and ruffled his ears as he smiled for her.

"Well, aren't you something?"

He jumped up, spun around, sat back down and kissed her hand.

"All right, Tyrin, that's enough. It's apparent he knows you're a friend of Bone's and has completely accepted you."

"What he doesn't know won't hurt him." She grinned.

"He's a very good judge of what's in a person's heart…Bone, you two can ride as long as you like. I see you're both wearing your police weapons."

"Yes, ma'am…never know when we might come across a snake…of one kind or another…We solved that case I told you about and my partner and I…well, kinda need a bit of a break… Hope you don't mind."

She smiled and nodded. "Of course not. You're welcome anytime...Do you need me to tell you which way to go?"

"No, ma'am. Pulled up a satellite photo of the property and the surrounding ranches...Got a pretty good idea of some of the nicer places."

"When you're done, I'll have refreshments and a snack..."

"Oh, Lucy, you don't have to go to all that trouble, we..." Loraine started to say.

"Now you hush...it's no trouble. I would enjoy doing it. As I mentioned when Bone and your Captain were out, I don't have many guests...Except for those...people."

"Yes, ma'am." Bone turned to Loraine. "You heard the little lady, missy...Time ta...saddle up...wa-hah."

"Jimmy Stewart, right?"

"Just go." He pointed to the silver two-horse Featherlite trailer hooked to the back of his truck. "We'll be baaak," he said over his shoulder.

"My God..." Loraine shook her head. "...don't give up your day job."

"You just don't appreciate talent."

"That's the problem...I do."

He surreptitiously flipped her the bird and then unlatched the drop ramp on the trailer—the top doors had been removed for summer time—and unsnapped the rubber-covered butt bars. "Back up you guys…back…back," he said to the two horses and stepped to the left.

On cue, the well-trained Quarter Horses simultaneously backed out the thick rubber-layered metal ramp and stopped once they were completely on the ground. Bone grabbed the blue braided nylon halter lead rope draped over the copper sorrel's neck nearest to him. "Take the mare and hitch her to your side of the trailer on that D ring. I'll tie him off and come around and get her saddle out of the front compartment."

"Can do," Loraine said as she led the chocolate mare to the right side. "What's her name?"

"Two-Eyed Tippy. Grand daughter of Two-Eyed Jack, the leading sire of World Champions in all of Quarter-horsedom."

"I'm impressed."

"Just stay out of her mouth or you will be impressed…She'll put your butt in the dirt."

Her eyes widened at that thought.

He came around to her side, opened the front storage compartment and pulled out a cutting saddle and blanket. He placed the thick pad with the front over the mare's withers, flipped the saddle on top and lifted a bubble in the blanket up into the gullet.

"Why'd you do that?"

"Well, when I tighten the cinch, that extra room keeps the saddle from pinchin' her," he said as he gathered the latigo from the other side, looped it twice through the large O-ring in the girth, pulled it tight and buckled it off.

"Oh."

"We'll have to tighten it back up a bit when she lets her air down."

"You say that as if I actually know what the hell you mean."

Bone grinned as he reached in the compartment, lifted a single-ear headstall with attached reins out and looped the leather ribbons over her neck. He unbuckled her halter, let it hang down, placed his thumb in the corner of her mouth and gently slid the short shank snaffle bit into her mouth—being careful not to bump her teeth—and then placed the top of the bridle over her poll and pulled her right ear through the leather loop. "She's ready to go."

"Please don't say *go* like that."

"Give me your foot and grab the saddle horn…wussie." He lifted her easily up into the saddle. "Now walk her about in a circle a bit while I put a saddle on Scooter…She'll be a touch fresh, so keep your heels out of her side."

"Now you tell me."

"Just follow my instructions and she'll be okay."

"And if I mess up?"

"It won't be pretty."

"Wonderful."

After Bone had repeated the saddling procedure on his gelding, he mounted and trotted over to Loraine, still walking Tippy in a large circle.

"All right, Pard…don't wear her to a nub before we even get started."

"But you said…"

"Never mind…let's head out." He waved at Lucy and Tyrin sitting on the porch and she waved back. Tyrin lifted a paw.

Lucy watched them ride off, and then glanced at a gold-linked bracelet on her left wrist. "Oh, dear…We have trouble, Tyrin."

Tyrin looked back up at her and cocked his head.

"Let's mosey on down to that creek over yonder. The horses could probably use a drink after bein' in the trailer for over an hour. Besides, it'll put us out of sight of that hill off to the left...Looks like her friends are back. We're being watched...You can look, but act like you're not looking."

"What?"

Bone eased his mount down the embankment to the clear, shallow limestone-bottomed creek with Loraine right behind him. He stepped Scooter out into the knee-deep water and stopped. He could see bream and a few catfish flit away from the strange horse's legs that invaded their domain. "Loosen her reins and let her drink...Folks say that you can lead a horse to water, but can't make 'em drink...Can if they're thirsty."

"Is that another of your Boneisms?"

"Damn, gotta remember that one, Pard...that's almost as good as your Igor comment."

"Bite me."

Bone grinned as heard slight sucking sounds from both horses. He gave them enough time to get a gallon or so and then lifted his reins. "They've had enough, let's head downstream. This creek curls around that hill those yahoos are camped on. We'll come up on the back side."

They followed the slowly moving water south and then back to the east as the creek meandered its way toward the Elm Fork of the Trinity River. The fifteen to twenty foot depression the waterway followed was lined with towering cottonwoods, sweet gum and pecan trees and kept the two well hidden from the visitors. Fox and gray squirrels gathering their winter stores of the abundant nuts available, chattered their displeasure at the pair for interrupting their daily foraging as they rode past.

Nearing the base of the hill next to a limestone outcrop, they pulled rein to a stop.

"Tie 'em up here and go the rest of the way on foot. Never have been able to teach these guys how to tiptoe. They sound like a herd of horses coming."

"What?"

"Nothin', just tie her to that black gum tree limb."

"That will hold her?"

"No, but she thinks it will. Besides, she won't leave Scooter and he'll stay where I leave him. It's called ground tying…If I drop the reins to the ground, that's where he will remain."

"That's neat."

"Old Indian trick."

"Really?"

"Yep…Learned it from an old Indian."

"Damn you, Bone, I never know when you're serious."

"Funny you should say that…I never know when I'm serious either."

She just shook her head, dismounted and tied Tippy to the branch.

"Check your weapon…we may be going amongst the Philistines."

"Seriously?"

The big man nodded. "Now, I'm seriously serious."

He silently opened the five round cylinder on his .500 Smith and Wesson, checked the loads and rotated the crane back until it snapped closed. Loraine racked her 1911A to chamber a round, thumbed the safety up to the engaged position and returned it to her paddle holster. Bone slid the big wheel gun into its custom leather and led the way.

Slowly, they eased up the hill, taking advantage of the available cover from the scattered brush and scrub oak. Near the top, he was able to make out two individuals. *Hmm, different boys this time...Maybe they take turns.*

He motioned her to stay hidden and stepped out from behind a nine foot cedar. "Guess you two honyocks didn't get the word."

The strangers were standing behind a device on a tripod that resembled a surveyor's scope and spun around at the sound of his booming voice.

The larger of the two individuals was dressed in light tan coveralls. He threw a sharp glance at Bone. "You are making a mistake, primitive."

"Primitive?...Wow, been called a lot of things, but don't think I've ever been called that before. Need to write that down...Have been known to make a mistake or two...but not today."

"Leave."

"No, pal...you and your friend there are the ones that are gonna be doing the leaving."

"You have been warned," he said as he pointed a silver tube at Bone. A greenish beam reached out...

CROSS PD

Stella set a fresh cup of coffee on St. John's desk. The captain looked up from the stack of papers he was working on. His collar was unbuttoned, his shirt looked as if he had slept in it, his blue tie was loosened and hung askew.

"Oh, thanks...Think I really need that."

"Noticed the face you made taking a sip from that cup on your desk and my developing detective skills told me it was probably cold."

"Yeah, it may take me ten days to wade through all these supplementals from last week...and that's not even counting the one Bone and Loraine will bring in tomorrow on the cemetery murder."

"If you'll pardon my saying so, sir...you look like you've been rode hard and put away wet...Maybe you need to take a break like they did or like your Chickasaw buddy..."

"Heard about that, did you?"

"It's a small department, sir."

"Right."

LUCY'S RANCH

"Gun!" Bone shouted as he leapt from the green beam's intended path. The laser beam nearly caught his midsection as he dove for the ground, but it sailed past in a blinding streak of energy that hit the ill-fated cedar tree squarely. From the center of the trunk, a greenish force spread out like lightning to the tips of all the branches and the tiniest of the verdant leaves.

Bone heard a hiss behind him as the tree vaporized in a couple of milliseconds. He didn't bother to turn and look back. By the time he landed hard on his left side—he had his heavy stainless pistol out—he rolled over once more where he could scramble to a knee.

Loraine drew her Kimber and stepped out from behind her cover in one rapid motion. *Holy crap! What was that?* She didn't wait until she could answer her own question. She triple tapped the man with the laser tube weapon.

The echoes of the three rapid-fire shots were dwarfed by the tremendous roar of the .500 Smith. "Jesus H!" Bone exclaimed as he fired three .50 cal rounds.

There was a brief shimmer in the air surrounding the man, as, just for a instant, he changed from a normal looking human being to a scaly green reptilian creature—with a head resembling a cross between a snake and an alligator, a thick rotund body with legs like tree trunks and four huge fleshy arms.

As quickly as the grotesque reptilian creature appeared, it changed back to human form, glanced down in surprise at the six holes in his chest for a moment. It then looked back at Bone as they began to weep a grayish viscous fluid.

They watched unbelieving as the man, instead of falling, reached over and touched a control pad device on his arm, and then he merely appeared to dissolve into a tenuous vapor.

His companion grabbed the tripod, turned and quickly leaped in the opposite direction. Bone centered his front sight on the man's back, when suddenly, the area beyond him began to shimmer and there appeared a large iridescent green metallic ball some thirty feet in diameter. Bone watched with his mouth open as the man cleared the space in one jump and dove into an open round hatchway. It hissed and slammed behind him.

Almost immediately, the orb began emit a strange pulsating sound then started to rise into the air. Bone snapped off his remaining two rounds at the closed doorway as Loraine fired her final five. Seven small holes appeared in the four foot circular hatch seemingly at the same time.

The craft continued to rise more rapidly leaving a faint green vapor trail coming out of the tightly grouped holes. In a few seconds the streaking globe was completely out of sight. Far in the upper atmosphere, a small flash sparkled like a fourth of July starburst and then quickly disappeared.

Loraine stood only ten yards from Bone. She turned and just looked at him curiously. "What the *hell* just happened?"

"You saw what I saw and ain't neither one of us even been drinkin'...yet." Bone opened his mouth wide and worked his jaw in an unsuccessful attempt to get some relief for the ringing in his ears. *Earplugs would have been helpful.*

"He fired at you with something that looked like a Romulan disrupter from Star Trek." She pointed at the still smoldering very short stump sticking out of the ground behind him. "But that's damned sure not play-like."

"Yeah, woulda left a bit more than a mark, I imagine."

"Woulda left nothing at all…What do you think? Aliens?"

He nodded. "That'd be my guess…You saw that thirty foot leap the other one made like superman…Huh, guess it's like Arthur Conan Doyle said in Sherlock Holmes…'Once you eliminate the impossible, whatever remains, no matter how improbable, must be the truth.'…As they say, 'We are not alone'."

"Know anybody that's going to believe us?"

"Only one."

The two cautiously moved forward as each reloaded. There in the short grass where the creature had vaporized, lay the silver tube. Bone started to reach for it.

"You're not going to just pick it up are you?"

"What? You think I'm gonna call the Homeland Security assholes and have them lock us away somewhere while they bury any trace of this encounter?"

"Really think they'd do that?"

"Is a bullfrog waterproof?"

"Uh-huh."

"Well, there you go." He knelt down and gingerly lifted the tube.

"Watch it! You don't know how that thing works!"

"Calm the hell down, Pard...I know that I don't know what I don't know."

"What?"

"It is what we think we already know that often prevents us from learning."

"Huh?...Who said that?...Confucius?"

"Nah...some fortune cookie I got at the Taiwan Chinese Restaurant...I wonder what this little button does?"

Loraine's face contorted into a mask of fear. "No! No!...Don't!"

Bone grinned. "Had you goin'...didn't I?"

"Bone, you big dumb..."

"You really can't tell when I'm kidding, can you?...That is so cool."

She gasped for breath a couple times as a tinge of anger flushed her face. "Bastard...Really, what are you going do?... Who we gonna call?"

"Ghostbusters?" he said with a hint of a grin. "Or maybe their new division...Alienbusters."

"Damn you!"

"Okay, okay…only know one other person I truly trust…Padrino."

Bone slipped the silver alien weapon into his saddle bag when they got back to the horses. Loraine swung aboard Tippy as he crow-hopped up into the stirrup and was mounted in a flash. They scanned the terrain to insure no one else was watching and rode back down the creek. They kept a sharp eye on the sky above, as well as their six o'clock position all the way back to Lucy's house.

Tyrin ran outside the large house to greet them. He circled around, but did not bark, as if somehow he knew not to scare the bigger horses.

Bone was the first to step down and helped Loraine as she swung her right leg over the mare's rump. He placed his hands under the brunette's rib cage and lifted her light as a feather out of the stirrup and set her gently on the grass.

"I can get down by myself. I'm not helpless, you know."

"Never said you were…I've seen you shoot! Remember?"

Her frown disappeared as quickly as it came. *Okay...if the big galoot wants to be chivalrous, who am I to deny him?* The sight of Lucy walking out the front door with a tray of fresh baked blueberry muffins and three glasses of lemonade caught her attention. "Why Lucy, you really didn't have to go to all that trouble," she said as Bone tied Scooter to the trailer and loosened his girth.

"Oh, hush that silliness. It's nothing at all...I just whipped it up in a jiffy. You all are back a lot sooner that I expected. Did you two get some target practice in? I thought I heard gunshots in the distance."

The two cops exchanged glances, and then both spoke simultaneously. "Yes." "No."

Lucy looked somewhat perplexed. Bone was the first to break the awkward silence.

"Miss Lucy, we ran into a couple guys up on the hill watching your place." He looked at Loraine for backup.

She nodded and looked worried as she inquired, "Were they from Global Energy?"

Bone began to nod his head and then quickly shook it. "No ma'am...can we go sit down at your picnic table and we'll tell you all about it?" He tied off his partner's horse as Lucy led Loraine over to the shade.

"So you see why we don't want you to go telling everybody about this little run in, now. Don't you?" Bone said after they filled Lucy in with all the details they could recall.

She placed both hands over her mouth for a second and looked each in the eye. "That's the wildest thing I ever heard in all my days. If I didn't know better I'd say you both had been drinking..."

"I know. I can't believe it myself and I was there," Rodriguez said.

"There's no proof they were even here, save the burnt stump and somebody could claim it was hit by lightning," Bone added. "The last thing we want is to draw more attention than those jakelegs from Global have been giving you. The feds get involved and they'll be here with a whole army of scientists in hazmat suits."

"Oh, my...That would never do...I, uh, enjoy my privacy far to much."

"That's what we figured riding back here. Loraine and I will just keep this to ourselves for the time being...Keep a sharp lookout, Lucy. I don't have a clue what those...whatever they were...were interested in, but they certainly tried to blast me to smithereens just for challenging them."

"Big mistake on their part, it appears. Thank you from the bottom of my heart. I don't know how ever to repay you."

"How 'bout one more blueberry muffin and we call it even?"

"Bone!" Loraine shot him a look.

"You can have as many as you want, my knight in shining armor."

Bone grinned as he peeled back the aluminum foil from the bottom of the muffin. "These are low calorie, right?"

Lucy waved as his truck and trailer rolled out of the yard. She knelt down and scratched Tyrin behind the ears. "There now, my four legged friend. It would seem our old enemies, the Reptoids somehow monitored my emergency signal. We have to check the transmitter to see if it is still operational." She slid the bracelet up her wrist and rubbed the skin under it as they walked out the gate.

Tyrin scouted across the hilltop as Lucy walked around surveying the damage to the cedar tree. *It's as bad as they said. The evil creatures used their pulse laser. Bone was either very lucky or very quick.* She knelt beside the small pyramid shaped device and turned it over in her hand. A tiny LED light showed blue on the ELT, meaning it was still functional. She carefully placed it back in the ten inch tall grass and stood up. Lucy scanned the countryside for any more unwanted visitors and called to Tyrin. "Come on, boy. Nothing else for us to do now but wait and see."

He woofed and ran to her side. She slowly made her way down the hill and back into her house.

Bone's truck and trailer stirred up a cloud of caliche dust as they headed toward Lucy's front gate over a half mile from the house.

"Why didn't you tell her about the tube you picked up?" Loraine asked.

"Thought it was better not to. She doesn't need to be compromised any more that she has to...Tough lady, but I'm not sure she could handle it."

"Right...To tell you the truth, I'm not sure she really believed us."

"Would you?"

***

CHAPTER EIGHT

DIAMOND S RANCH

The rolling hillsides of the Diamond S ranch teemed with deer, turkey and quail in the cross timbers area of the county. It spread across four sections of land and was home to a cow-calf operation as well as six hundred acres of dryland wheat farming. To the north, a person could see down into the Red River valley and the state of Oklahoma beyond its sandy banks.

To the west, lay the small town of Saint Jo, one of the small communities with visible ties to the last of the great cattle drives of the middle of the 1800s. The famous Chisholm Trail from Texas to Abilene, Kansas crossed the Butterfield stage route in Saint Jo. The town square still sported an active concrete water trough for cowboys passing through as they rode their horses from one smaller ranch to another, or just stopped by en route to the Dairy Queen, the only eating establishment still left open.

To the east, between the Diamond S and Cross lay the 640 acres belonging to Lucille Wilson.

The owner of the spread was a fourth generation Texas rancher who worked as hard as his hired hands. Buck was a no-nonsense cattleman who loved his land with unbridled passion. He was operating one of the ranch's Caterpillar D-8 bulldozers pushing down a small copse of western cedar trees from the bottom of a steep sandy draw. The shallow root systems offered little resistance to the nine foot blade.

Buck skillfully pushed the half-dozen *trash trees*, as he called them, into the growing pile of brush, *Make a good bonfire.* He looked at the four acres he had cleared for the small water conservation lake. *That ought to about do it. Start on the dam tomorrow mornin'.*

He judged the wind by looking at the direction the diesel exhaust drifted out of the stainless steel stack and drove the smoke belching behemoth upwind a bit over fifty yards and pulled to a stop. Once the brakes were set, he shut it down and unbuckled the dirty seat belt.

Buck stepped down onto the left track and reached back behind the operator's seat and grabbed the two and one-half gallon polymer container of diesel fuel. He turned and jumped down the three feet to the red sugar sand, wincing as his sixty-five year old spine protested the sudden stop. *Hells bells. I know that dozer ain't gettin' any taller.* He stretched, and then twisted his lower back, attempting to work out the kinks from four straight hours in the seat. *One of these days, they're gonna figure a way to put shocks on these big boys.*

He strode up the brush pile and dowsed an area six foot square with the green-dyed off-road diesel. He reached into a shirt pocket and withdrew a silver cigarette lighter—one carried only for situations like this one. Buck lit a small dry branch, set it alight and carefully touched it to the fuel soaked brush. Almost reluctantly it sputtered, caught fire and spread slowly to the rest of the huge pile and sent a greasy gray column of smoke heavenward.

High on the limestone studded ridge to the south, two men lay prone watching the action through binoculars. "Got himself a heck of a bonfire there. Too bad it's way down in a hole where nobody else can see it."

"You sure that's the owner? Old buzzard's been working all by himself...You'd think he'd have some young stud drivin' the equipment. The report said his net worth was several million..."

"Maybe that's why he's still got the dough...skinflint won't pay anybody else to do what he can do himself."

Buck watched the fire expand to its zenith, then backed away and climbed back onto the Cat, fired up, lifted the blade and spun it around, heading south. He quickly ran through the four forward gears and began clanking up the creek bed like an Abrahms tank. After a couple of hundred yards, he turned up a roadway he had cut earlier into the side of the ravine.

"Let's head back to the Jeep...we'll drive up about the time he gets to his pickup on the rim of the canyon. Boss wants this place as much as the old lady's and Ken Farmer's cattle ranch on the other side. We'd best get something under contract or the son of a bitch will fire our asses," said Hollister of Global Energy.

"Heard that...He's wound up tighter than dick's hat band. And don't seen to be in a any kind of a mood to take no for an answer," added Jeffers.

They got to their feet, dusted off and slipped away in the oak brush and redbud trees.

It was only a little after 4pm when Buck brought the dozer to a stop near the trailer-mounted fuel tank. He pulled along side and shut it down with the rear end of it, close to the hose on the three hundred gallon diesel tank. He stepped out on the right track and moved back to the Caterpillar's fuel tank and unscrewed the large industrial grade cap. He let it hang by its internal chain as he crossed over to the two and seven eighths inch tubing pipe railing around the sixteen foot trailer.

He unhooked the fuel nozzle from its cradle and began to fill the big cat's tank. A twelve volt battery powered pump made the transfer quick and painless. *This beats the hell out of those old hand cranks on a fifty-five gallon drum.*

He finished the operation, stowed the handle and made his way to his Chevy pickup. He stopped short of the driver's door, slipped off his oil-stained work gloves and pulled out the orange earplugs he had worn all afternoon. Buck took off his straw Stetson, the shantone weave was completely covered in a fine red sand, courtesy of the Caterpillar's tracks. He slapped it twice against his Wranglers to knock off all but the damp ring circling the sweat band. Buck took the slightly cleaner hat and secured it upside down in the spring-loaded wire rack mounted in the center of the truck's interior roof.

He stowed his aviator style sunglasses in the case kept on the dashboard and noticed his reflection in the rear view mirror. *Ain't you a sight. Have to hose off the big chunks before you can walk in the house.*

His hat kept his forehead and hair clean, but below that, the sand had caked itself like a redneck version of a spray tan. His eyes were clean, thanks to the glasses, but the overall effect was almost comical. His chambray work shirt, jeans and neckerchief were coated in reddish brown.

He heard the sounds of a four wheel drive vehicle coming up behind him. He got out of the truck and as he turned, a dark green Jeep Laredo slid to a stop. He stood sideways looking at the unwanted visitors.

Unseen by them, Buck's hand went to the H&K USP pistol holstered on his right side.

Two men stepped out of the SUV. He noted the logo for Global Energy on both front doors. *Here we go again. Bastards don't seem to pay attention to the No Trespassing signs.* His suntanned face was lined with concern and his full beard showed his displeasure in the form of a frown as the two approached.

"Mister Stienke, we'd like a moment of your time to discuss a business proposition," Jeffers said as he extended his hand.

Buck's own hand stayed on the butt of his forty-five. "Gents…whatever you're peddlin', I don't need…Get back in your vehicle and get the hell off my property."

Hollister stood up a little taller as he pressed in closer. He was almost as tall as the much older man and perhaps twenty pounds heavier. "No need to get grumpy, old man. We're here to make you a generous offer from Global En…"

"I read better than you listen." Buck snatched the USP from the Yaqui slide holster and thumbed the hammer back to full cock.

Hollister froze in his tracks as the handgun rose only slightly higher than the rancher's waist. At the close range, he could see the gun's sights were aligned precisely with his right eye. The dark muzzle seemed to grow to a full inch across as he spoke in a direct manner, "You're not the only one with a gun, mister."

"Go for it…if you got the guts. Talk's cheap…Don't need…or want your oil money…and I'm not one to engage in idle chatter. If you're still here when I count to three, I'm gonna do what I have to do and burn your sorry carcasses in the bonfire."

Jeffers began backpedaling unsteadily as he signaled surrender. Hollister's hands clenched into fists—his face reddened, and veins bulged in his thick neck.

"Come on…it ain't worth it!" Jeffers hollered.

Hollister swallowed hard as he tried to stare down the recalcitrant rancher. His mind raced as he judged his limited options.

Buck's dark brown eyes narrowed and showed no hint of mercy.   "Two," he said without blinking.

"What the hell happened to one?" Hollister asked as he started to step back, uncertain of what was going to happen next.

"Get in the car!" Jeffers screamed.

Hollister tripped as he stepped back. He fell hard on both elbows as the .45 discharged and sent a 230 grain Federal Hydroshock into a red oak behind him. The burly thug scrambled back to his feet and lunged for the door handle on his SUV.

He snapped a quick glance at the silver-haired landowner as he hopped inside and fumbled for the ignition. Once the engine started, he floored it and slammed the shift lever on the console into reverse. It fishtailed, straightened up, and then lurched back in the direction from which it came—kicking up a small cloud of red sandy dust.

"Three," Buck said as a hint of a smile came to his face.

After traveling a couple of hundred yards in reverse, Hollister braked hard and swung the back end of the Jeep around. He slammed the shifter into drive and raced down the one lane ranch road and exited over the big cattle guard in the main gate.

"Damn that hardass old sumbitch! If he hadn't got the drop on me, I'da popped his ass and tossed him down the canyon."

"Hollister, that's a load of crap and you know it...I saw you backpedalling a fast as you could..."

"Bullshit! Tripped on an root or sumpthin'."

"Says you...What are you gonna tell the boss, anyway?"

"Gonna say it's high time we bust a cap or two in this hick county...These local yokels don't know what's good for 'em...need to make examples outta a couple and the rest will start to fall in line PDQ."

"Hope you're right. The boss is gettin' mighty testy these days, with those two drillin' rigs sitting idle. All comes out of the bottom line and 'sides...cuts our own profit sharing bonus."

"Tell me somethin' I don't know...ain't gonna let any old timer get between me and my Benjamins. Got things to do and people to see," he replied as he grinned and flexed his massive knuckles around the steering wheel.

Buck wheeled into his parking spot and pressed the remote on his garage door opener attached to his truck visor. The massive rollup steel door clanked shut as he shut off the vehicle's diesel engine and climbed out.

He walked into his ranch style home sited on a bluff overlooking the Red River and hung his Caterpillar hat on a set of bull elk horns mounted English style on a walnut plaque. He checked his messages on his home office phone and deleted a couple from Global Energy without even listening to them. *Thank God for caller ID*. He headed to the laundry room located near the entrance from the garage.

Buck used a black cast iron boot-puller fashioned in the shape of a cockroach to step out of his Larry Mahans. The retired world champion rodeo star was a neighbor only a couple of miles away just across the line in Montague County.

Leaving the custom caiman boots on the laundry room floor, he stripped off his filthy work denims, left them on a pile of dirty clothes and wandered to the bathroom where he climbed into the shower and turned on all four pulsating heads. Rivulets of reddish-brown ran down the drain as he soaked away the stiffness in his muscles.

Several minutes later, he stepped out of the custom designer bath and slipped on a white light cotton bathrobe. He ambled back into his office and sat down in a high-backed padded saddle-leather chair and reached for his cell phone. He swiped a finger across the face to open the home page and deftly tapped on the telephone icon. Once the contacts list appeared, he scrolled down to the *Bs* and selected an old friend's new cell number.

After three rings, a booming voice came over the other end. "We gave at the office…It wasn't me and I got witnesses proving was out of town at the time of conception."

Buck grinned. *Some people never change.* "Cut the crap, amigo…We need to talk."

"Sure, old buddy, old pal. It's your dime…"

"When is the last time you even saw a pay phone?"

"Now that you mention it…it musta been back when you had brown hair…"

"Your ass, Bone. Anyway, You ain't gonna believe what just happened out here on my place…"

After the lengthy blow-by-blow description of Buck's encounter with the men from Global Energy, Bone walked to the fridge and grabbed another Shiner Bock. "Hang on a sec, Kemosabe. Gotta put the phone down for a minute."

He laid his cell on the kitchen counter, untwisted the top and took a swig. *Better.* Bone picked the mobile and said, "Back with ya."

"Am I boring you to death over there?"

"Naw…The thing is…get thirsty when I'm mad."

"Thought I was the one that was pissed off…"

"That may be how it started out…but I get that way too when thuggy bastards get heavy-handed with me or my friends. You're not the first one to get the strong-arm treatment from those jackwagons."

"Really? No surprise there."

"Tell you what…how 'bout if Loraine and I run out to the rig in a day or so and have a little face time with those two?…Somebody has to keep 'em in their place."

"If anyone can teach them a few manners, I would think you can…Appreciate it, bud. I don't mind double tapping their arrogant asses, but sometimes a grand jury tends to take a dim view of that these days…Know what I mean?

"I do…Laterbye."

**CROSS PD
PARKING LOT**

Bone parked his Thing near the west entrance and got out. He moved over to a line of patrol cars close to the east side, quickly checked out the parking lot to

208

see if anyone else was around and opened the black and white driver's door.

He reached into a small brown paper sack and took out a very realistic looking rubber snake and coiled it in the floorboard on the driver's side. After propping the head on top of the coils facing the seat, he closed the door, looked around once more, grinned, and walked into the Cross PD headquarters.

CROSS PD

"Mornin', Bone," Lacy, a twenty-five year old heavyset black receptionist said as she buzzed the inner security door open and he stepped inside.

"Mornin', Lacy, how's your day?"

"Can't complain."

"Well, don't get cocky...ain't over yet."

"Heard that."

"Any calls?"

"Nope, you're clear."

Bone nodded and headed toward the break room.

Peach, Stella and Joel Newman were on break, getting coffee, nuking bagels or eating donuts as he entered.

Peach held up the coffee pot. "Hey, Bone, need some caffeine?"

"How old is it?"

"I think it was made the end of the graveyard shift."

"Wow. Fresh coffee."

"It'll put hair on your chest," said Stella.

"Speaking from experience, little bit?"

"You'll never find out."

"Never say never," he said with a grin.

Peach poured Bone a cup. "Cream, sugar?"

"Nah, Darlin'…don't want to ruin it."

"How could you tell?" cracked Newman.

Bone nodded and headed to the detective's room. Loraine was at her semi-cluttered desk finishing the complicated supplemental report on the Pioneer Cemetery murder case. A pair of black-rimmed reading glasses were perched on the end of her nose—she looked over the top as he came in.

"Where's mine?"

"Peach is making a fresh pot. They're gonna use what was left of the last for paint remover…but I can bring you a cup before they start."

"Pass. I'll wait on the new batch."

He grinned and sat down at his desk and clicked the Google page on his computer.

"Think we should say anything about yesterday?"

"Nope. Who would believe us anyway. Hell, I'm still not sure it happened...there was no evidence and considering my reputation..."

"Yeah, but what about mine?"

"You were with me, right?"

"Point." She turned back to the paperwork. "Why is it I get to do the grunt work?"

"You know what the captain said about my penmanship."

"I think you do that on purpose..." She noticed he had accessed Google. "What are you doing?"

"Oh, just a little research I've had to put off for the last week."

"Right...Well, stay off the porn sites."

"The captain blocked 'em."

"I know."

Bone pulled up a copy of a newspaper article from the nineteenth century.

DALLAS MORNING NEWS, April 19, 1897.

E. E. Haydon

SPACE CRAFT CRASHES NEAR AURORA, TEXAS

PILOT KILLED

Aurora, Wise County, Texas, April 17, 1897

About 6 o'clock this morning the early risers of Aurora were astonished at the sudden appearance of the airship which has been sailing around the country. It was traveling due north and much nearer the earth than before. Evidently some of the machinery was out of order, for it was making a speed of only ten or twelve miles an hour, and gradually settling toward the earth. It sailed over the public square and when it reached the north part of town it collided with the tower of Judge Proctor's windmill and went into pieces with a terrific explosion, scattering debris over several acres of ground, wrecking the windmill and water tank and destroying the judge's flower garden. The pilot of the ship is supposed to have been the only one aboard and, while his remains were badly disfigured, enough of the original has been picked up to show that he was not an inhabitant of this world.

Mr. T.J. Weems, the U.S. Army Signal Service officer at this place and an authority on astronomy gives it as his opinion that the pilot was a native of the planet Mars. Papers found on his person -- evidently the records of his travels -- are written in some unknown hieroglyphics and cannot be deciphered. This ship was too badly wrecked to form any conclusion as to its construction or motive power. It was built of an unknown metal, resembling somewhat a mixture of aluminum and silver, and it must have weighed several tons. The town is today full of people who are viewing the wreckage and gathering specimens of strange metal from the debris. The pilot's funeral will take place tomorrow.

Bone scanned the article then looked at his watch, got up and headed toward to door.

"We all still on for Shooter's tonight?" Loraine asked.

"Far as I know."

"I gotta work out the soreness from all that riding we did out at Lucy's yesterday…She's so nice."

"Sore, huh?"

"Oh, my God, you wouldn't believe…the inside of my thighs…see why cowboys walk bowlegged."

"Want me to kiss and make it all better?…Or I can give you a hiney massage."

"Nice try, Bone…swear to God I'm going to kill you."

"Hey, don't jump to conclusions…you might like it."

She threw her stapler at his head. He leaned back, caught it with his left hand and set it back on her desk. "Dropped something."

"Damn you, Bone…Wear your dancin' shoes…"

"Thought we were goin' boot scootin'?"

"Get technical…Boots then."

"That'll work fine…since I don't own a pair of shoes."

He headed for the captain's office and passed Sergeant Richard Hung in the hallway. The Malaysian immigrant of Chinese descent had his usual stern game face on.

"Mornin' Dick…Got day duty, I see…Goin' huntin' for bad guys?"

"I have patrol duty, if that's what you mean, Detective."

"Pretty close…Well, kick ass and take names."

"Take names?" Hung had a very puzzled look on his face.

College boys. Bone just shook his head and entered St. John's office as Hung walked out the front door. He sauntered in and took a chair across from the captain. "Did you hear back from the Rangers on that Global Energy bunch?"

St. John leaned back in his well-worn simulated naugahyde chair. "Well, some. There've been numerous complaints about their...uh, more than heavy-handed tactics in the acquisition of leases."

"Heavy-handed?"

"Yeah, talked to Ranger Carmichael down at Weatherford. He told me about a couple cases of personal threats and harassment and three cases of suspected arson."

"Any direct evidence tying it to Global?"

"Nothing hard, so far...They're even buying some apparently abandoned properties outright for taxes...There've also been reports of unexplained accidents and..."

"Got a call from big Buck out on the Diamond S. He had a visit by a couple of the knuckle heads from Global yesterday evening. The usual kind of crap...veiled threats..."

"Buck ain't one they want to threaten...he'll shoot first and not bother asking questions later."

"One of the reasons we get along so well." Bone chuckled. "Reckon Loraine and I should go out and have a talk with those nabobs before they do something stupid and get..."

Just then, they both heard the sound of twelve rapid fire shots from outside.

St. John jumped up. "What the Sam Hill?..."

"Sounds like somebody's startin' a war."

The captain grabbed his side arm and paddle holster, slipped it on his belt, and charged to the door followed closely by Bone.

Loraine, Peach, Newman and Stella moved quickly down the hallway in the direction of the front door—weapons in hand.

Moomer, the department armorer, and Wanda stepped out of the armory.   He was—a big man, with a slight speech impediment—carried a M-4 carbine and wore a kevlar vest. Wanda had an M-16.

"Are we under attack?" he asked.

"Don't know, but I got your six, Moom," Wanda said.

"What in the world's going on out there?" asked Loraine.

"I would say Bone had something to do with it, but bless his heart, he's here in the station...So, I suspect that's out," Peach commented as they rushed toward the door.

"I wouldn't make bet on it," said Stella.

They met St. John and Bone coming out of the office and all looked at the big man.

"What?"

The group streamed out of the building on a shuffling run—Bone brought up the rear. Everyone carried their weapons at the low tactical and were looking around—except for him.

Across the street, they spotted Hung standing beside his open driver's door, pointing his 9mm sidearm inside the vehicle—the slide was locked back.

St. John and the rest approached the still shaking sergeant.

"Snake, snake, snake!" he stammered.

The captain approached the open door and looked inside to see multiple holes in the floorboard caused by the twelve rounds of rapid fire. There was also the untouched rubber snake coiled in the floor mat. He reached in and picked up the movie prop, turned back to the group holding the fake Copperhead head high for everyone to see.

Hung took a step backward.

"Uh, Sergeant, it's a *rubber* snake...and out of twelve rounds...you didn't hit it once...Think you need to spend more time at the range..."

He was interrupted by the sound of an engine starting. They all turned in time to see Bone departing in his Thing. He waved back to them.

"Damn you, Bone!" Hung screamed and shook his fist at the rapidly retreating gray boxy vehicle.

Stella leaned over to Peach. "Told you."

Newman added, "Glad I didn't bet." He turned to Loraine. "How in the hell do you work with him?"

"I keep my eyes closed most of the time."

He turned south on I-35 and was laughing to himself. "Bone, you are so bad." At Denton, he took the I-35W split toward Fort Worth. His cell phone rang. He answered on hands-free. "Hey, pard, what's up?"

"You are in deep ka-ka, Bone. The captain wants your ass."

"It's so nice to be wanted...and the best part too...Don't worry, he'll get over it." Bone chuckled.

Loraine was back at her desk in the office. "You're gonna have to pay to fix Hung's unit."

"You mean there's something wrong with Hung's unit?...Tell him to try Viagra."

"Damn you, Bone! I'm trying to be serious."

"I am serious...Viagra should help the boy."

"Oh, you're hopeless, good bye."

"I'll call if you need me…Laterbye."

Bone glanced at the grassland sprinkled with mesquite. He had been driving through it since he turned off I-35W onto Hwy 114 shortly after he had passed the giant Texas Motor Speedway. The tiny hamlet of Rhome was in his rearview mirror as he approached a city limit sign.

AURORA
City Limit
Pop. 376

"Damn…Glad I didn't blink."

He located the cemetery on his GPS—pulled up outside the ornate gateway set between four foot tall, two foot square concrete columns. Just right of the entrance was an official State of Texas Historical Marker. Bone stopped to read the plaque—he paused near the center.

…This site is also well known because of the legend that a spaceship crashed nearby in 1897 and the pilot, killed in the crash, was buried here…

"I'll be damned."   Bone immediately saw the gnarled oak he had seen in his previous two visions only now, much bigger, older and much more gnarly. He sat down cross-legged underneath the thick

L-shaped branch on the trimmed Bermuda grass. His hand rested on the ground beneath the limb.

He began to see images, some were the same that he saw when he touched Lucy. *A triangle shaped silver craft—a city with silver towers under a lavender sky with two suns—a small gray woman and a small man in a type of cockpit—a space battle that put the special effects of Star Wars to shame—an old fashioned windmill coming fast in the cockpit window—a flash of light—townspeople gathered around flaming wreckage—an elderly man and a woman approaching the debris and finding a small body—There is a funeral with a small casket being lowered into the ground under the oak tree by four men with ropes—a small silhouetted figure watching from the shadows nearby.*

He shook his head, got to his feet, exited the cemetery and drove to the site of the crash—the old Proctor homestead.

Bone walked around with a high-tech metal detector. He had laid out a grid and had spent the last hour working the pattern. He had been picking up numerous hits, but all of them had been some old piece of farm metal, including a piece of a water pump from an old poppin' Johnny, better known as an early John Deere tractor. He was on the next-to-last line near a small limestone outcrop—the unit buzzed with an extra strong signal. Bone looked at the display identifier—*AU*—Gold!

He laid down the detector, unfolded a GI shovel he had stuck in his backpack and started to dig at the base of the outcropping. He heard a slight *clink*. Placing the shovel aside and carefully using his hands, he cleared the rest of the dirt from a circular object.

Bone picked it up, took out his handkerchief and began gently cleaning the encrusted soil away to see that it was a bracelet—a very small bracelet like a child's.

As he continued, he was able to determine that the unusual adornment was indeed made of gold as indicated by his detector. He took out his dome magnifier and studied the unusual symbols—almost rune-like characters—inscribed in gold on turquoise insets in the thick gold links. The unique hieroglyphics were unlike anything he had ever seen. He noticed the clasp on the bracelet latch was broken…

***

CHAPTER NINE

SHOOTER'S CLUB

Captain St. John, Stella, Bone, Loraine and Peach sat around a large table drinking beer—Bone leaned over.

"Little Bit, your hair reminds me of that movie star…"

"Oh, really! Who?"

He leaned back and away. "Lassie."

Newman returned to the table from going to the head just as Stella tried to backhand Bone—he ducked. She hit Newman in the crotch.

He bent over and then squatted down. "Ahhhh!...Damn, Stella! What'd you do that for?"

"Oh, my God, Newman!...I'm so sorry. I was tryin' to hit Bone...Oops, I mean...aw, hell, you know what I mean."

"Well, you came close. Gonna have to start wearin' a cup around you."

"Do they make 'em that small?" she asked.

"Bite me, Johnson."

"Ooh, now he's getting romantic."

Newman moved to his chair as he glared at her. "Pay backs are a bitch."

St. John pushed back from the table and stood up. "Ya'll excuse me. Be right back." He turned to walk away.

When he was out of sight, Bone took the salt shaker on the table, unscrewed the top and poured half of the contents into St. John's beer, replaced the lid and wiped off the top of the bottle. All the others at the table just looked at him.

He looked up at the stares. "What?"

"One of these days, your jokes are going to backfire on you," Loraine commented.

"I guess I'm just impulse control challenged...'Sides, it'll be funny...Wanna dance?"

"Why not?"

Bone and Loraine got up and joined other couples on the floor, dancing to Texas swing.

Captain St. John returned to the table. He grabbed his beer as he sat down and took a big swig. He gagged and spit it on the floor. "Damn you, Bone!"

As they danced past the table, Loraine looked at Bone and started laughing.

"Told you."

The song ended—they started walking back to the table through the other couples on the floor. Another song began to play on the jukebox. Williams—one of the men from Global Energy—walked up to Loraine just as they reached their table.

"Hey, pretty lady, how about a dance?"

She stopped, turned to the well-built dark-haired man. "I don't think so. Got a cold beer waiting...Thanks anyway."

"What's the deal? You too good to dance with me?"

"No, I'm just danced out right now. Maybe some other time."

Williams grabbed her arm. "Come on, it's a slow dance."

"She said no...Slick."

He turned to face Bone. "I don't remember asking you."

"Why don't you ask me if I care what you remember?"

St. John and the others at the table tensed up—they knew what was coming.

"Oh, shit," the Captain muttered.

Williams started poking his finger in Bone's chest. "What are you big man...her guardian?"

Bone looked down at William's finger then back to his face and grinned.

St. John leaned in to the others. "Uh oh, big mistake." He started to remove his watch.

"I really wish you hadn't done that," Bone said.

Loraine moved Williams hand away. "I can handle this, Bone."

Farlow walked up behind Bone.

"See, big man, she says butt out." Williams pulled Loraine toward the dance floor.

She grabbed his hand, twisted it into a wrist lock and drove her knee hard into his thigh—he hit the floor, holding his leg.

Farlow grabbed Bone's right shoulder with his left hand to spin him around as he cocked his fist.

Without even looking Bone threw a quick right-handed back-fist into the man's face. Farlow staggered back and fell to his butt, holding his nose, blood oozing out between his fingers.

Someone on the dance floor yelled, "Fight!"

Farlow got to his feet and charged Bone.

Williams also scrambled up and took a swing at Loraine. "Bitch!"

She ducked and placed a spinning roundhouse kick in his ribs. He staggered toward St. John who popped him in the face on his way by—Williams hit the floor again.

Bone grabbed Farlow by his collar and threw him over their table. Stella, Peach and Newman were trying to keep the crowd back.

A couple of drunks came up to Bone and took swings at him. He held up his own fist, one guy hit it—there was a audible *snap*. The drunk dropped to his knees, holding his wrist.

"My hand! You broke my hand."

The second drunk's head was down, plus he was very short and his fists struck him in the chest. Bone looked down, grabbed the brim of his cowboy hat and pulled it up where he could see the little man's face. He let go and threw a short forearm shiver to his forehead. The drunk's eyes crossed, rolled up in his head and he fell backwards to the floor.

Bone grabbed Loraine, threw her over his shoulder and started to make his way out.

St. John worked his way through the combatants and blocked several roundhouse punches with vertical arm blocks. A tall guy threatened him with a pool cue. The captain executed a spin kick to his face and—as the man fell forward—he snatched the stick from his hands.

Loraine was livid and started kicking her feet up and down and slapping Bone on the butt. "Put me down, you big galoot, before I beat you to a pulp!"

Bone saw a couple of other guys coming at him and he spun slowly around and let Loraine's feet knock their hats off and send them into retreat—then he sat her down.

"Sorry, Pard, I just didn't want to see a little gal like you get hurt."

"I'll show you some hurt, you big dummy."

A heavy-set drunk held a folding chair over his head and rushed to strike Bone. Loraine jumped between them and delivered a quick strong snap kick to the his crotch. He stopped, his eyes crossed and as his hands came forward, he dropped the folding chair, which landed on his head. He grabbed his testicles, mouthed a silent *Ow*, fell slowly to one side on the floor and curled up in the fetal position.

Bone's mouth opened in surprise and then he grinned. A skinny guy took a roundhouse swing at him and missed. He lost his balance and spun around 180 degrees facing the opposite direction. Bone grabbed him by the scruff of the neck and seat of the pants, lifted him up over his head and tossed him into a crowd of drunk fighters, sending the lot of them all to the floor.

St. John broke the pool cue in two pieces over his knee and started spinning the pieces like a nunchuk. He worked his way close to Bone and Loraine and signaled to Stella and the others.   "Time   to   go boys   and   girls.   Sheriff   Brennan's   deputies   are probably on their way. Let's get the hell out of Dodge."

"Good idea," shouted Stella.

The captain pitched the pieces over his shoulder, twirled a finger and pointed to the door.

"Yeah, probably wouldn't do to have a bunch of Cross's finest put in the county hoosegow," offered Loraine.

"I just don't want to read about me in tomorrow's paper... besides Sonjua'll kill me," added the Captain.

They all headed to the door with sirens wailing ever closer in the background...

CROSS POLICE DEPARTMENT
PATROL BRIEFING ROOM

Sergeant Hung strode into the room with his usual air of authority, he carried his assignment clipboard under his arm like Patton carried his swagger stick. He immediately began to brief the night shift.

Seated were Officers Dale 'Moomer' Anderson, Juan Sanchez and six others. Several small talk discussion were going on across the room.

Wanda Stanton entered the room in a rush. "Sorry I'm late, but Lauren was telling me she heard over the radio from county there's a riot out at Shooters!"

"Think they need our help?" asked Juan.

"I doubt it...Bone, Loraine, Stella, Newman, Peach and Captain St. John were all going out..."

They all exchanged knowing glances.

Wanda looked around the room and grinned. "Oh, yeah... right." She took her seat.

"Okay, people, settle down…Welcome back to the night shift."

There was an immediate chorus of groans.

"Take it easy, you'll be back on days next week. We have a couple of velly important things to cover. First, the motor pool has released two of the new cars for patrol duty tonight!"

Another chorus erupted from the room, this time in 'Yeahs'—there was also a smattering of applause.

Three officers raised their hands. "I'll take it!" shouted Juan.

"Give it to me!" said Moomer.

"It's my turn!" chimed in Wanda. "Time in grade."

The three got in to a minor squabble among themselves as to who should get the first new cars in a year.

"All light, all light! Quiet! I'll decide who gets to drive the new units.

There was a undercurrent of mumbling and grumbling throughout the room.

"As lanking officer, I should get one, of course, since my legular unit is in the shop curtesy of Detective Bone."

There were numerous muted snickers.

"And I'll assign the second to Wanda Stanton as a leward for her superior wok in the area of leports. The leports for the Pioneer Cemetery murda were outstanding," said Hung.

All the other officers looked at Wanda and she blushed.   Juan threw a wadded up sheet of paper at her. "Brown nose," he muttered just loud enough for her to hear.

She countered with a middle finger salute.

"In my expert opinion, our department luns on paper. Therefore the quality of our police wok is leflected in the quality of our supplemental leports. Neatness, punctuation and spelling are the hallmark of every good cop."

All the other officers look at each other and surreptitiously rolled their eyes.

"Secondly, the chief has asked me to lemind you of the enhanced potential for nefarious activities this evening. For those of you who don't know, tonight is the second Flyday in the month and, as such, is payday for many of our good citizens. There also is a full moon tonight, which has historically shown to exacerbate the activities of certain classes of miscreants. These two factors...when combined with tonight's date...the 13th, are often taken by the superstitious among us, to be a bad omen. In the stock market, it's called tliple witching hour…We'll just call it 'Bad Moon' night.

All the officers again exchanged looks.

"Exercise lequisite pludence. That is all…Dismissed."

Everyone stood to leave. Juan grabbed Wanda's arm. "What did he just say?"

"He said, "Triple witching hour and ya'll be careful out there.'

Juan looked confused. "Oh…Why didn't he just say that?"

CROSS PD PARKING LOT

Several cops were checking out Wanda's new patrol car. Sergeant Hung hopped in his unit, started it and drove away.

Wanda got in hers.

Juan stuck his head inside the window. "How's the seat?"

"Nice, very nice."

"Wow, it even has that new car smell."

"Same radio and computer monitor?" asked Moomer.

"Yeah, all the comforts of home! It's just like your unit, Juan, except nobody has puked or peed in it..."

They all laughed.

Juan countered, "Yet...I hope you enjoy it, you..."

He was interrupted by the sound of tires screeching and then a car crash very close by.

Everybody snapped their heads in the direction of the sound.

"That wasn't far, we better go check it out," said Juan.

Stanton started her unit. The other officers all jumped into their vehicles and exited the parking lot in sequence, lights flashing.

Only one block away, Sergeant Hung had run a stop sign and T-boned a beater car driven by a little old lady.

His car was buried in the passenger side of the older Pontiac and his air bags were deployed. Several of the other units pulled up and around his vehicle.

Wanda got there first and stood on the driver's side of the wrecked vehicle and called to the others. "She's okay! How's Hung?"

The look on his powder-covered face said it all when Juan checked on him. "Still Hung…just a few bruises to his pride."

All the assembled cops cracked up.

"He is who he is," said Moomer.

"The Chief is gonna love this."

CONVENIENCE STORE

A young black man, Ronnelle Washington, was sitting in car in the parking lot of the store. He finished wrapping his head with gray duck tape for a mask, picked up an Airsoft pistol from the car seat and got out of the vehicle. He walked across the parking lot and entered the front door of the store.

Bobby Wilson, a large middle-aged black man, was working behind the counter when the robber entered.

Ronnelle leveled the plastic gun at him and announced his intentions. The duct tape was so tight around his jaws that his speech was severely impaired. "Thish ish a stish up! Gimme all yo money."

Bobby threw his hands up until he got a good look at the gun and realized what it was. He dropped his hands and yelled at the would-be robber. "You jackass! That's not even a real gun!"

"Yeth it ith! It weal!"

Bobby reached under the counter and pulled out a baseball bat. "Well this is a real baseball bat too...asshole!" He started around the counter and the man pulled the trigger on the Airsoft. A yellow plastic B-B bounced off Bobby's chest and fell to the floor—he looked down and watched it bouncing across the tile. "You stupid son-of-a-bitch!"

Ronnelle turned and ran for the door. In his panic he tried to go out the *IN* door, hit his head on the glass, bounced back stunned and fell to his butt.

Bobby started beating him on and about the head. The robber tried to fend off the bat and dropped the Airsoft gun. "Sucka come in here and try to rip me off!"

"Ow! Thop! Thop! Ow!" Ronnelle yelled.

"Plastic B-Bs...punk ass, dumb mother..."

"I gif up. Ow, king's x!"

Bobby picked up the pellet gun and threw it over the counter, grabbed the robber's arm, yanked him to his feet and walked him into a corner behind the counter. "Sit! You move one muscle, I'll make you wish your momma was still a virgin."

The terrified would-be crook complied and sat down on the floor while Bobby picked up the phone and punched 911.

Bone and Loraine were still laughing about the fight at Shooter's.

"The look on the guy's face when he dropped the chair on his head was priceless," said Loraine through giggles.

"And dumb ol' me was trying to protect *you*!…Shoot, you and St. John could put on a martial arts demonstration all by yourselves…Hey, if you don't mind I need to stop by Bobby's and pick up some beer."

"No problemo. It's still early…I need a six pack for the house, too."

Bone's pulled in the lot, drove up near the door, parked, went in and headed straight to the cooler.

Bobby was still behind the counter with the portable phone to his ear. "That was fast, Bone. Damn, you're good."

"Why, thank you very much, Bobby. What am I good at…in particular?"

"I just called 911 ten seconds ago…I'm still on the phone."

"For what?"

"Attempted armed robbery. I got the jaybird chillin' out over here." He pointed behind the counter.

Bone looked over the counter and cracked up. "All out of pantyhose at the Stupidville Wally World, sunshine?" He turned to Bobby. "Be right back." He headed out the door and walked back up to his Thing.

"Don't tell me they're out of Shiner."

"Nothing serious as that...grab my *go bag* from behind the seat, please. Come on in...You'll want to see this."

A confused Loraine grabbed the black leather bag from behind the seat and handed it to Bone. He removed his S&W 500, badge and cuffs and they headed back into the store.

Bobby had the man on his feet and was holding the bat in one hand, the pellet gun in the other. "Dumb ass comes in here with a Airsoft pellet gun and tries to rob me...an inactive Marine!"

Bone turned the suspect around and cuffed him. Then he bumped fists with Bobby. "Semper Fi, brother!" He looked at his prisoner. "What's your name, dummy?"

"Wonnelle Wahthington."

"Just a sec…I can't understand you with all that duct tape."

Bone started to unwrap his head. As he got to the skin layer, the tape stuck and he pulled harder. Skin started coming off with the tape.

Ronnelle protested, "Ow, ow, ow…Watch it, man! That hurts!"

"Oh, I'm so sorry, sir…just this one…little strip…"

Bone grabbed the last piece and yanked like he was starting a chain saw.

Ronnelle screamed. "Ow! Po-lice brutality! I wants me a lawyer!"

Bone looked at the tape. It had two full eyebrows attached—he cracked up. Then he showed the tape to Loraine who broke up as well.

The hapless robber's face was red, bloodied and bruised. He had no eyebrows and his nose appeared to be broken.

Bone regained his composure somewhat. "Let's try this again. Now, what's your name?"

"Ronnelle Washington. My fren, dey call me Ron."

"Short for Mo-ron," Loraine said sotto.

"I din't do nuthin'."

"Of course not...Ron. I'm just thinkin' that just might be your gun."

"Dat's not a real gun."

"You said it was real ten minutes ago," said Bobby.

"Dat wuz jus to makes you gives me da money."

Bone and Loraine broke again into a fit of laughter.

"I din't do nuthin'. Ossifer, I wants to press assault charges against dis man. He be tryin' to kill me wif dat der bat."

"Well...Ron, that probably is not a happenin' thing...tell me about the duct tape...that's a new one on me."

"Dat's not my duck tape!"

Bone, Loraine and Bobby all cracked up again.

A police cruiser pulled in front of the store. Officer Wanda Stanton got out and entered. "Hey guys, looks like you beat me here...didn't catch your call in."

"We just stopped in for some beer. I'll swap cuffs with you and you can take Einstein here for an all expense paid trip to the steel motel."

"It's Washington," Ron said.

"Whatever," Bone responded with a grin.

Wanda took it all in. "Thought I'd seen everything..."

LORAINE'S DRIVEWAY

Bone pulled his Thing halfway up the drive and stopped as he saw Loraine already coming down her front porch steps. She opened the passenger door and got in. He handed her a cardboard cup of coffee from 7-11. She took it and popped the drinking opening down.

"Thanks…So, what is it we're doing again this early in the morning?"

"Going out to visit some yahoos in the oil patch."

"Do what?"

"You'll see."

It was slightly after 9:25am when Bone and Loraine pulled up at the Global Energy rig number 12. A dozen assorted pickups and 4WD SUVs, belonging to roughnecks working there, were parked in the caliche lot off the newly-made gravel road leading to the drilling pad site. A handful of SUVs just like the one Buck had encountered on his ranch were parked near the rig, including a dark green Jeep Laredo with a Global Energy logo on the driver's door.

"Well, that looks familiar," said Bone.

"What do you mean?"

"Means I've had truck with it before...or one like it." He pulled up beside the dusty SUV, parked and got out. "Looks like a herd of turtles swarmin' round the platform. Must be a deep one...considerin' the stack of drill stem sections...Hm, making a trip."

"To where?"

"It's what they call pulling all the pipe out so they can change out the black-diamond studded drill-bit."

"Black diamond drill-bit?"

"I think that's what I said."

"Why would they use diamonds?"

"The cones of the big drill-bits have black or industrial diamonds embedded in the surface. They have to drill through some pretty hard stuff down fifteen thousand feet."

"Wow, who knew?"

"Me."

"Smart ass...You would." Loraine glanced over at her partner. "You ever work on a rig like that?"

"Sure, brought me my beer money when I was in college."

"What are all those big engines for..."

"Engines to turn the rotary table and mud pumps….Big Waukesha diesel motors hooked up with hydraulic pumps to help lubricate the drill bit and flush the ground-up rock particles to the surface…See that retention pond over there?"

She turned to see where he was pointing. "Uh huh."

"They bring in water in tanker trucks and store it there until they need to send it down-hole. One of the sheds has drilling mud in bags to be mixed as needed with the water for later use."

They watched as the derrick man pulled over a section of drill stem and slap it into what the hands called the cow's cock on the block. The huge diamond-shaped steel pulley eased the pipe out of the stack, lifted it up and a roughneck aligned it with the hole in the rotary table.

A floor hand slung a chain around the bottom end and it wrapped itself around the pipe four times counter-clockwise. As the 40 foot long section was lowered into the upper collar of the preceding pipe, another roughneck threw the slips around the pipe, locking it into the table and nodded at the driller.

"Watch this…They are gonna spin that new length of pipe onto the down-hole section."

The driller pushed a control lever and the chain was pulled tight by the spinning Kelly on the side of the near engine, causing the section to screw itself down into the cylindrical coupling until the two pieces were securely locked together.

"Looks kinda dangerous. Does anybody every get hurt on that contraption?"

"Sure...fingers, toes...sometimes hands or heads. Cain't be sleeping on the job. That's for sure...Come on, the folks we want to talk to are inside...up there. What you are looking at are the hired hands." He drove near the small square steel building attached to the side of the rig floor and parked. "Stay loose, pard."

"You got it."

Jeffers glanced out as the movement of the VW Thing caught his eye. He saw Bone towering over the diminutive vehicle. "Crap...It's that big sumbitchin' cop again and he has some split-tail with him."

Hollister looked up from his seat on the sofa. "We better get down there. He probably found out we went over to the Diamond S and put pressure on that old man...You guys cover for us."

Field Operations Manager Williams, glared back at him. "I might be able to buy you two a few minutes,

243

but I guarantee you'll need to come up with a more permanent solution to these pesky small town yokels…Catch my drift?"

"We'll think of somethin'." Hollister grinned as he and Jeffers stepped out of the crew dog house and down the twenty-five foot steel stairway to the ground. They approached Bone and Loraine.

"Well, well, look who came for a visit, Jeffers. Man Mountain himself."

"And he's got his lady with him too…Extra protection, you think?" Hollister laughed.

"You got a habit of going out of your jurisdiction, big man," challenged Jeffers.

***

CHAPTER TEN

GLOBAL ENERGY RIG #12
County Road 432

Bone pulled back onto the blacktop and ran through the gears. The wind noise almost masked the sounds of his 1600 cc four cylinder engine.

Loraine removed her sunglasses from her small Dooney & Bourke purse and slipped them on. "How many squirrel power does this jalopy have back there anyway?"

"Would you rather walk? That can be arranged…"

"Sounds like mating season in a pecan tree."

"Philistine…No appreciation, I see, for classic automotive engineering…but you'll have to tell me about mating in a pecan tree sometime…Sounds like fun." He leered at her with a purposeful grin.

She backhanded him across the chest. "Sex! Is that all you think about?"

"Until somebody invents somethin' better, it'll do…"

"Yeah, right…How do you think it went back there? Don't think they fell for the good cop-bad cop routine…They didn't look very intimidated to me."

"Pard, when you been in this business as long as I have, you'll be as old as I am and come to understand the wisdom of my superior intellect…"

"Crap."

"Potty time already? I thought you went back at the sta…"

"No, dammit! Check your rearview…they're following us."

Bone glanced at his side mirror. "Ah-ha…the plot thickens, me thinks…Can't tell if they are actually following us yet or not. We'll hang a left up by Buck's and run past the Diamond S."

"We can drag their sorry asses into the city limits if we circle back east from there...They won't think of that."

"Probably not...but I already did. The road going out to the old landfill is the dividin' line."

"He's turnin' north, away from town," Jeffers said.

"I ain't blind. There's nothing out there but a few ranches...Won't be no witnesses," replied Hollister.

"I love it when a plan comes together." A big grin came to his face. "Get your piece ready. I'll pull alongside and you can take 'em out."

"A double tap of Federal Hydroshocks oughta do the trick." He pulled the Beretta 92FS out of his cross-draw holster and held it in his lap.

"They're closing in on us."

"Yep, looks like it...better check your weapon, Pard." he said, glancing at the rearview. "While you are at it, grab my backup out of the floorboard behind me." He slammed the accelerator to the floor. The lightweight open-top car responded with a slow but steady acceleration down the long winding grade.

"He's trying to rabbit…nail it!" Hollister barked as his pulse began to race. "Come on! Ain't got all damn day…"

"I got it, I got it. That piece of junk can't do over eighty." He stomped the gas pedal, causing the transmission to downshift as the engine RPM built up. The in-line six cylinder whined as the Jeep surged ahead in response.

The road dipped down to a low water crossing and then turned sharp to the left as the two vehicles raced past at almost 70 MPH. Bone downshifted and then punched the throttle as the Thing drifted perilously close to the shoulder in the narrow curve of the two-lane county road. Loraine's eyes grew wide as she held her breath—the shoulder harness pressed hard against the right side of her neck.

The Jeep's tires screamed in protest as the heavier vehicle's rear end slid wide in the tight turn and gnawed at the gravel on the edge of the asphalt. "Keep it between the ditches, dipstick!" Hollister yelled at Jeffers.

Climbing up the far side of the valley, the two cars—only sixty yards apart—roared passed the entrance to the Diamond S ranch and kept going.

Bone grinned as the Thing went airborne over a rise and chirped the tires as it settled down past the crest. "Are we having fun yet?"

She shot him a look that would melt steel as he downshifted for a ninety degree right turn. "Fun!...Son of a bitch! You call this..." She screamed as a 9mm bullet whizzed past his head and punched a hole in the windshield—spider cracks circled the half inch hole and radiated out for several inches. A second shot ricocheted off the outside edge of the windshield frame.

The big man's eyes narrowed. *Sorry mother...* "Hey, Pard. You can shoot back anytime, you know."

She didn't need any further encouragement. Loraine spun around and tried to aim at the Jeep, but the newly installed shoulder harness was too restrictive. She punched the lap belt buckle release and brought her Kimber 1911 up to arm's length and fired quick three rounds at the driver.

Jeffers swerved to the left after the second one crazed the safety glass but did not penetrate. The third hit just under the rear view mirror and left a pockmark with a two inch scar on the outside. "They're shooting at us!"

"No shit...Einstein. What was your first clue? Get me in closer. That SOB keeps weaving back and forth..."

"My .45s are bouncing off the windshield!"

"Told you...Not enough velocity. Use my .50...Shit! Tractor!..."

He yanked the steering wheel to the left and took to the unpaved left shoulder of the road. The mammoth John Deere 4440 air-conditioned cab tractor with wide duals mounted on the rear axle took up over most of the roadway. He looked at the thick steel axle protruding past the outside wheel rim and swerved even farther—off the shoulder and down into the infrequently maintained ditch.

The bare bumper on the Volkswagen began to shred the woody stalks of the sumac and persimmon saplings at 45 MPH—bits of leaves and branches thrashed the vehicle's slanted hood and covered the windshield.

Bone braked hard as a bulldozed erosion control cut in the ditch loomed up ahead. Vivian fell forward against the dash and slumped down over his hand atop the stick shift as he yanked the wheel hard to the right. The little primer gray sports vehicle went airborne and landed ten yards in front of an astonished farmer moving his turbo-diesel tractor from one field to another.

Jeffers braked to a panic stop as he realized they were momentarily pinned in by the big John Deere. As soon as the tractor was past the erosion preventative cut in the ditch, he swung back onto the pavement and floored the Jeep.

"Don't let 'em get away!" Hollister yelled as he pointed at the Thing disappearing over a rise.

"Shut the hell up! Just be ready when the time comes."

DIAMOND S RANCH

Buck was on his way to his mailbox when the sound of several handgun shots from the direction of his north property line caught his attention. *Dammit sounds like some asshole shooting at road signs again. If I catch 'em, I'll put a knot on their heads.* He drove out his entrance and turned north, the exhaust of his big dually blowing dark gray diesel smoke under the acceleration.

"Loraine! Loraine! You hit bad, baby?" Bone slid his massive hand off the shift knob, turned his palm up and lifted her.

"Get your hand off my tit!" She pushed herself erect and turned around to sit down. "Where the hell did you learn to drive? Can't you keep it on the damn road?...I dropped my gun..."

"Dammit...I said use mine...They're still back there...but closing fast."

She glanced over her shoulder and then grabbed Bone's *go bag* from the floorboard. Quickly unzipping the ballistic nylon case, she pulled out the monster wheel gun. The four inch .500 Smith and Wesson had the exact same bone-shaped logo inlaid in its rubber grip. "Your backup is just like your carry gun."

"And your grasp of the obvious is exemplary...It's loaded. Get busy."

She turned around again and put her knees in the seat. Drawing the hammer back to full cock in single action mode, she placed the black partridge style front sight on the driver's silhouette and centered it in the white outline of the rear sight.

Bone yanked the wheel and took the VW into the left lane as he saw the shooter in the green SUV extend a handgun out the passenger side window.

Loraine rocked to the left as the hammer fell. A horrendous blast rocked both of them as a 275 grain solid copper hollowpoint exited the big gun at 1,665 feet per second.

The bullet punched through the jeep's windshield like it was Saran Wrap, leaving a inch and a half hole, disintegrating the rear view mirror and shattering the rear glass completely. Tiny shards of glass peppered both men inside and left small lacerations on their faces and necks.

"Whoa! That was close!"

"Shoot, damn you, before she tries again!"

Loraine held her hand up to her left ear—it didn't stop the ringing at all. "Jesus! That's loud!"

Bone shook his head. "What?"

A rapid-fire string of 9mm bullets impacted the rear of the VW and one whistled through Loraine's blouse sleeve before it blasted though the windshield. Bone saw the impact and reacted immediately. He downshifted and turned left onto a narrow dirt road.

Loraine fell hard against the passenger side door and had her right wrist hooked around the top of the seat back. Her torso hung over the side from the *G* force of the unexpected turn.

"Hey, girl! Quit horsin' around!" He reached over, dropping two fingers inside her waistband, and hauled her back inside.

"Get your hands out of my pants, jerkwad!"

"What?"

"We got 'em now," Hollister yelled. "Reload."

Dust boiled up behind the Thing in front of them as it accelerated away. He floored the Jeep once more as a trail of smoke began to emanate from the VW's engine.

"Look! I got 'em!…I got 'em!"

"Keep shootin'…We're in too deep to stop now."

Loraine glared at Bone for a second before the cloud of white smoke churning up from the back of the car got her attention. *Oh crap…Not now!* She pounded on his right shoulder.

He looked over at her and shrugged. His ears—particularly his right one—rang and still hurt a bit. *What the hell does she want now?* he wondered as he tried to keep the vehicle in the rutted roadway. Grass grew up almost a foot high in the seldom used abandoned road. At one time, long past, it led to a toll bridge across the Red River—before it was made obsolete by the construction of Interstate 35. The approach and pilings were still there, but the wood and iron bridge itself were distant memories—victims of time and flood waters.

She mouthed the word *smoke* twice and pointed behind them.

He glanced in the side mirror and took in the bad news. *Aw, hell!* A second glance inside at the oil pressure gauge told him what the smoke meant. The needle was low and bouncing erratically. *Oil cooler, cylinder or crank case...and I just got this sumbitch running like I wanted to! If we can only make it another 800 yards...*He looked ahead to the area where the road dipped down out of sight.

"Cain't see shit in front of us!" Hollister complained.

"Fire at the smoke...they gotte be up there."

He had to agree with that logic. Whatever was smoking in that VW was still kicking it out like a mosquito fogger. He could taste the burnt oil spraying on to the hot exhaust system. He leaned out and dumped another fifteen rounds into the greasy dust cloud.

Two bullets hit the Thing. One pinged off the bumper and another dug into the rear quarter panel. "Get down! I don't want you to get hurt…" Bone yelled.

"Screw that!" Loraine fired three rounds at their back trail. "Two can play at that game."

Bone grinned. *Salty little shit…I like that.*

One of her rounds sliced through the Jeep's hood and tore into the air cleaner—not doing much mechanically to slow them down. The slug then demolished the SUV's radio and CD player when it slammed into the fire wall and tumbled like a miniature buzz saw inside the electronics. Continuing on, it punched a hole in the rear door with a resounding *blang*.

"What they hell are they shooting at us? A twelve gauge?"

Loraine turned around to face forward for a second. Her eyes grew big at the river up ahead. She glanced at the speedometer and saw it was pegged at 70 mph.

She pounded on Bone shoulder again. "No bridge! No bridge!"

He turned to her, grinned and nodded. "Uh huh."

She scrambled for her seat belt as they barreled down the slope.

The buckle's metal tip barely clicked into the receptacle when Bone slammed on the brakes and turned the steering wheel sharply to the right. The little car entered a controlled slide off the roadway and down into the deep river sands lining the banks and stopped abruptly.

Bone flipped off his seat belt and stepped out even before Loraine could begin breathing again. His hand flashed to his holster.

The stainless .500 carry piece did not look nearly so big in *his* hands, she remembered thinking as he turned to face the smoke and dust trail they had left in their wake.

The view through the oil-smeared windshield suddenly cleared. Both oil company paid musclemen were astonished to see water ahead of them and a huge pissed off lawman standing off to their right with an equally huge hand-cannon pointed at them.

Jeffers tried to brake, but it was instantly apparent that his effort was far too little and too late to keep them from going off the bridge abutment.

Bone fired the big bore handgun double action—three shots rang out as they rocketed past. Two closely spaced holes appeared in the front passenger side door. A third round went into the exposed fuel tank as the front end of the Jeep nosed over—the vehicle's roof impacted the exposed concrete pilings and exploded in a huge fireball.

"Bonus time...Extra crispy...no additional charge."

Loraine stepped out of the car, still slightly shaken. Black smoke continued to pour from the burning wreckage as the Jeep sank in ten feet of the slow moving Red River. She walked around the front end of the Thing and stared at the bullet holes in the glass.

"You okay, Pard?"

His voice shook her from her thoughts of their close encounter with death.

"Damn you, Bone! You sorry son of a bitch!...You planned this didn't you? Almost got us both killed..."

Sounds of a heavy diesel pickup driving slowly through the dissipating smoke caught his attention. He raised his revolver and pointed it south.

Loraine reached into the Thing and recovered her Kimber from the floorboard. She dusted it off and assumed a Weaver stance.

The truck eased forward until both could recognize the driver. He brought it to a stop and stepped out. "Bone, old buddy. Ya'll all right?"

"We are now, Buck…Thought I was gonna have to carry my little partner back to town. My ride has had the biscuit, and cell phone reception sucks down here by the river…What the hell are you doin' here? Fish ain't biting this time of year."

Buck grinned. "Heard the shootin'. Came a runnin'. My neighbor, Rick Hess…told me you came blowing by his tractor at the speed of heat…Ain't too many cars like yours on the road anymore."

"Maybe one less after today."

"Is that who I think it is in the river?"

"Yep…Loraine here got 'em all pissed off at us and they commenced to start a war."

"That's not even close to true, asshole," she protested.

Buck laughed. "Aw hell, you say it was and I'll testify to it." He winked at her. "At least you two knew how to end it...Hop in...give ya'll a ride to town. Oh, yeah...Diners's on me."

"Appreciate the kind offer, amigo, but we'll be tied up this evenin'...There's gonna be a officer-involved-shooting inquest, not to mention gettin' a wrecker and the ME out here to recover the stiffs before the catfish and turtles gnaw 'em up beyond recognition."

"And a stack of paperwork this high," added Loraine, holding her hand up above her waist.

"Too bad...Feel sorry for ya'll already."

The fire had extinguished itself by the time the convoy of police vehicles, fire trucks, EMT wagon and wreckers arrived on the scene. Captain St. John bent over, placed his hands on his knees and looked at the bullet holes in the back of the VW.

"This is the one that got your oil cooler...Motor lock up from oil starvation?"

"Nope, but I bet the bearings are history...Probably smoked 'em good. Same for the pistons, jugs and rings...Hope the crank is salvageable."

"Too bad...It was fun for off road."

One of the young patrol officer, Joel Newman, had changed into a bathing suit and swam out to the rear end of the charred wreckage sticking out of the water. He was carrying a steel cable with a hook on it. The other end was fastened to the powerful wench on the wrecker's upright A frame. He hooked the line around the hitch assembly of the SUV and swam clear. "Take it up!" he hollered as he clambered up the sandy embankment.

The operator engaged the winch and slowly the cable became taut, pulling the Jeep backwards until its weight caused it to settle back on its wheels and sink from view.

Bone, Loraine, Peach, and St. John looked on as the water flowed around the high test steel wire, making a V in the surface of the river as it flowed past.

Doc Fisk, the county ME drove up and parked. He joined the others as the blackened rear end cleared the water's surface. "What have we got here? Insurance fraud? Somebody burn it and dump it in the river?"

St. John turned around. "Hey, Doc…You haven't heard the story yet?…Bone and Rodriguez got into a runnin' fire fight with two men in that Jeep…Somehow they ended up in the river on fire."

He raised an eyebrow and looked directly at Bone. "Why does that not surprise me?"

Bone shrugged. "What?"

The wrecker sucked down slightly on its rear suspension as the Jeep's front wheels lifted off the riverbed and all its weight—plus the water inside—hung from the cable. The operator—using a remote controller—walked to the edge of the bridge approach and rechecked for any obstructions that he might have missed. He kept the winch turning and soon had the vehicle dangling almost to the top on the A frame's pulley. A torrent of muddy river water drained from the tiny spaces where once there were windows and a windshield.

He picked up two large steel hooks—like barbless fishhooks for killer whales—and connected them to the rear axle close to the drive wheels. Once the heavy chains attached to the hooks were securely locked down on the wrecker's bed, he hopped inside and pulled forward fifteen feet until the Jeep was upright. Two tiny streams of water poured out of a pair of closely spaced holes in the passenger side door.

St. John leaned over and inspected the obvious bullet holes. The green paint was missing for an inch around the half inch openings. He place his index and middle fingers over them to staunch the flow of water for a second, and then glanced over his shoulder at his largest detective. "Your handiwork?"

Bone shrugged and nodded.

"Nice group." The captain lifted his hand and wiped it off on his jeans. He looked inside and studied the two crumpled bodies, barely visible through the gap between the door and the rooftop. "We're gonna need the Jaws of Life to get these doors open."

"Mind if I give it a try, Cap'n?"

He looked at Bone for a second as he tried to judge the ramifications of allowing him to touch the vehicle. "Sure, but use gloves…prints."

"But of course." Bone walked down the his vehicle and collected a pair of work gloves from the glove box.

As the wrecker operator prepared the hydraulic lift to tow the Jeep to town, Bone stepped up to it and placed his left hand on the door jam and his other on the handle. "Here goes nothing."

With one mighty yank—with the high-pitched screech of twisted metal-on-metal—the door popped open a foot. A flood of river water soaked his boots and a single six inch juvenile sand bass flopped around on the deteriorating concrete. It was washed over the edge of the bridge and dropped into the water barely missing the sandy bank.

"One lucky dude," Bone quipped as he stepped back from the torrent.

"Luckier than that guy," Fisk said as he stepped closer and looked inside. "Took two to the rib cage."

David St. John looked troubled. "I was afraid of that."

"Afraid of what?" Loraine asked.

"Afraid your partner here actually hit what he was aiming at."

"That's a problem?" Bone asked before the realization hit him. "Son of a..." He slowly drew his S&W and thumbed the cylinder latch open. Placing his middle and ring fingers inside the frame, he dumped the two loaded and three fired cartridges into his right hand and offered the unloaded weapon to St. John. "Here you go, boss. OIS...SOP."

Loraine looked perplexed. "What's going on?"

"Give the man your weapon, sugar britches."

She glared up at him. "Don't call me sugar...SOP? I don't understand..."

"Officer Involved Shooting...just the department's standard operating procedures. We have to turn in our weapons until the inquest is complete."

"I'll get them back to you as quick as I can...Ain't nothing wrong, as far as I can see."

"Thanks, Captain." Loraine dropped the magazine from her Kimber and cleared the round from the chamber. "I never shot at anybody before."

"Be glad...You'll see why after you fill out the reports...In triplicate."

"I'll vouch for that," Bone added. "Hey, I just thought of something. That guy in the passenger seat was the shooter...Gotta see if I can find the weapon. Probably on the floorboard." He took a step back toward the Jeep, but St. John put a hand on his chest. "Hold it there, buddy. Not you...Peach, get over here."

Bone and his captain locked eyes for a second. St. John shook his head and Bone finally nodded and then stepped back.

"Peach, honey, can you see if you can find a weapon or fired cases in here? You'll need to wear gloves, of course."

"I'll get my kit, Cap'n."

Bone stepped back and turned to look at the river. It peacefully flowed as if nothing had happened at all.

Loraine walked up beside him and placed her hand around his waist.

"You okay?"

"Yeah...I'm fine. Getting suspended from a case is not what I was plannin' on."

"You mean we are suspended?"

"Light duty...not the same thing, but we can't investigate ourselves very well, can we?"

"Guess not." She hugged him.

"What was that for?"

"For your keeping us alive. I'll never complain about your driving...never again."

"Really?"

"Not 'til you scare the pants off me again."

He grinned. "Uh...What's it take to do that...exactly?"

When she finally figured out what he had said, she doubled up a fist and slammed it into his belly. He doubled over slightly.

"Oooff...Jesus, girl...can't you take a joke?"

She smiled. "Some folks can tell 'em...and some can't."

Peach got to her feet and turned around. "Sorry, Captain. I couldn't find any weapon and if there's any fired brass aboard, it may be washed up underneath the dashboard." She looked at Bone and Loraine and mouthed the word, "Sorry."

St. John looked perplexed. "I know those holes in that Vee Dub didn't get there by themselves."

Bone stepped closer. "Cap'n, the shooter was hanging out the window when he fired. Stands to reason, the brass ejected to the right and wouldn't be inside the vehicle."

"I'll buy that…but, where is the weapon?"

Bone closed his eyes for a second and relived the last few seconds of the encounter.

St. John watched his eyes moving beneath his lids. Bone's head slowly turned and his hand went down to his holster and came back up as if he was firing at the Jeep. When his body stopped turning, he opened his eyes.

"The guy had it in his right hand…up there by the A pillar. It was still there when I fired. He let go after the second shot."

"So that puts it in the river?"

"Exactly."

"How do you do that…that thing you just did? Is it like self- hypnosis?"

"It's a gift."

"Okay…Newman! Did you bring SCUBA gear?"

"Yes, sir."

"Get suited up…Got a little job for you."

He disappeared to the back of the Cross PD tactical unit.

A few minutes later, he returned wearing a single US Diver's tank and regulator over a full wet suit and booties. A weight belt, dive knife and buoyancy compensator completed the outfit. He carried a stake and a fifty foot length loop of yellow poly rope in one hand and his swim fins in the other. Newman walked to the water's edge and set up for his search, starting by driving the stake into the ground and attaching the rope.

"What's the rope for? The current is not all that strong here."

"Not about the current, Pard," Bone replied. "He'll do a series of concentric arcs, each only a foot or so apart. Visibility ain't all that great down there when he gropes around in the silt."

"Learn something every day."

A few minutes later, Joel breached the surface with a Beretta 92 in his hand. He spit out the SCUBA mouthpiece and yelled, "Found it!"

St. John bumped fists with his friend. "Bone, I think you oughta buy the kid a beer."

"A beer? Hell…A case is more like it…Hey, if you need us, we'll contact you…been a long day and a dry one at that."

GOVERNOR'S LOUNGE

"Hey, Vertis…another round."

She nodded. reached into the cooler, began to grab Shiner Bock longnecks and set them on a round cork-lined tray. Smoothing her hair back with her free hand, she headed to Bone's table.

Ginny Mac opened the side door and blocked it with her guitar case. She set another heavy square case inside and picked up the guitar.

Bone, sitting with his back to the wall, and saw her struggling a bit. "Hey, Joel. A pretty lady needs your manly assistance." He nodded toward the doorway.

The good looking twenty-six year old patrolman, turned and jumped to his feet when he saw her.

"Let me give you a hand there!" He hurried to her aid.

"And they say chivalry is dead," Stella observed.

"Not when hormones are involved, they're not."

Loraine stomped on Bone's foot under the table.

"Ow…What was that for for?…Ow." He said when she did it again. "What did I do?"

"You're setting a bad example for these young officers. Chivalry is something that should be appreciated…I know I do."

Bone crossed his arms. "Women are like bacon…They look good, smell good, taste good…and kill men slowly."

Vertis set out the round of beers and popped him on the back of the head as she sashayed back to the bar.

St. John chuckled. "Bone, I suggest you quit while you're behind."

***

CHAPTER ELEVEN

RED RIVER BOTTOM
Cross Timbers County

A large brown hairy creature knelt down in the forest near the river. His fingers dug around a very small pecan seedling until he succeeded in digging the tiny tree up, root system intact and encased in the surrounding leaf mulch.

Nearby at a stream, a similar creature—a female—curled a piece of cottonwood bark and dipped up fish eggs from the water with it. She stood, held the bark close and peered closely at the collection of the tiny milky white gelatinous globes.

CROSS POLICE DEPARTMENT

Bone got up from his desk. "Goin' to get a cup of coffee. Want any?" he said to Loraine.

She looked over the top of her computer glasses. "Why not, haven't had a cup in almost thirty minutes."

"Right back."

Bone headed out the door, stopped at the break room, hesitated, turned, continued down the hall to St. John's office and stuck his head in the door. "Hey, Cap'n, busy?"

He had his head buried in a stack of supplemental reports and did not look up. "What do you want, Bone?"

"Just got a wild hair since you put us on light duty…thinkin' about goin' campin' and doin' a little fishin' this weekend on the Red…You game for it?"

St. John looked up. "Damn, that does sound good. Need to get out of this man killin' office for a while…Sonjua's takin' Damarcus to see the grandparents this weekend, anyway."

Bone stepped on in the office. "I'll see if Loraine wants to go."

"Bet not."

"Probably get her feelings hurt it if we don't ask."

"Waste of time, but she is a woman…Whatever you think they're gonna do…you're usually wrong."

Bone nodded and stepped back out the door and walked back down the hallway passing Stella. He smiled at her.

She stopped and put her back to the wall.

"Hey, little bit."

"What are you up to, Bone?"

"Now, why would you think I was up to something?"

"You're breathing, aren't you?"

He just grinned, shook his head and continued to his office.

Loraine glanced up as he entered.

"Where's my coffee?"

"Oops."

"Bone, you'd forget your head if it wasn't stapled on."

"Well, had a thought on the way to the break room."

"Uh oh…That's scary…Better check my insurance.

"No, really, just talked to the Cap'n and we're goin' campin' and doin' some fishin' this weekend. Got nothin' else to do…Wanta go?

"My idea of camping out is the Holiday Inn…I don't squat in the bushes…plus there's bugs, poison ivy and the humidity.

"Is that your way of sayin' you don't want to go?"

"Wow, Bone…you're good. May not have to send you back to finishing school after all."

"Smart ass…I'll just ask someone else then."

"What about my coffee…Oh, never mind, I'll get it myself…Don't trust you."

"Moi?"

She got up and headed out the door as he walked over to his desk, took out his cell and hit speed dial.

"What?" Padrino answered. "I'm busy cleaning the horse stalls that you failed to do this morning."

"Oh, yeah, that…Say, the Cap'n and I were talkin' bout goin' campin' and doin' a little fishin' this weekend…What do you think?

"What time we leavin'?"

"Figure we oughta head out before dark, so's we can set up camp and maybe have time to run some trot lines."

"I'll start packing up the gear and grub. We can pick up the beer on the way."

"Sounds like a plan. Check the battery on the boat, too. We'll be there shortly...Laterbye." Bone turned off his Galaxy 4 as Loraine reentered with her coffee.

"Gonna miss a great adventure."

"I'll suffer in silence...while I'm snuggled up in my nice comfy bed with a glass of wine and a good book."

"Each his own."

RED RIVER BOTTOM CAMPSITE

Bone and St. John were busy erecting the dome tents in a semicircle around a rock-lined campfire. Padrino had unpacked the supplies and built the fire. The camp was on the river bank, their flat-bottomed outboard fishing boat—with an electric trolling motor up front—was tied to a nearby willow sapling.

The three men sat around the campfire on camp stools after dinner, drinking beer. The sounds of frogs, crickets and the occasional bass slapping the water with his tail increased as darkness fell on the deep woods along the river.

"Now, this is the life...can't get no better'n this," said Bone as he opened another Shiner.

"Steaks were good, but I'm just about ready for some grilled catfish," added St. John.

"I expect the trot line will yield us some nice channel cat. I've been curin' that stink bait for six months," said Padrino.

"I know, damn near rubbed the hide off my hands gettin' rid of the smell."

"You're supposed to use a stick to push the sponge down in the jar, Bone...not your fingers," offered the captain.

"Knew I was forgettin' somethin'." Bone blew beer out of his nose as a roaring high-pitched scream emanated from the blackness of the woods. "Jesus!"

They all looked around at the darkness.

"What the hell was that?"

"Didn't sound like no panther," said Bone as he wiped the foam from his chin.

"Sounded a little like a howler monkey, but too deep and throaty," added Padrino.

"Maybe we got a Bigfoot in the area."

Padrino looked over at him. "Haven't heard of any sightings on this side of the Red. Mostly from up in the Kiamichi Wilderness in southeastern Oklahoma."

A second scream echoed throughout the dense woods.

"Whatever it is…it's damn spooky," said St. John as he patted down the hair on the back of his neck. "But I don't believe in Bigfoot or Sasquatch…whatever you want to call 'em."

"Well, that's what a lot of folks say about aliens and flyin' saucers…Maybe I'll tell you girls a spooky campfire story later."

Padrino looked at Bone, cocked his eyebrow and grinned.

"Right," said St. John as he shook his head.

RED RIVER BOTTOM
SHACK

A ramshackle clapboard unpainted cabin sat nestled in a copse of trees at the end of an old logging road. It had a full width front porch—the door was propped open with a chunk of firewood. Smoke curled from a metal chimney and dissipated in the light early-morning breeze. An old faded green '90 Dodge pickup was parked near the shack.

In the deep shadows of the heavy woods, something very large watched the cabin.

Inside the spartan, weather-worn dwelling, were several rickety tables with drug-making paraphernalia and supplies scattered about along with a couple of old ladder-back chairs. Against one wall were two World War II army type cots. Each had a dirty pillow and wadded up sheets on top.

Two ne'er–do–well rednecks, Chaz Brison and Willie Parmalee were cooking meth on an old cast iron wood burning stove. The stench permeated the small room and was overpowering—both wore surgical masks.

Willie spoke through the covering, "Man, this stink is about killin' me."

"Me too…I'll lower the fire and let's git outside fer a spell," Chaz said as he closed down the damper on the stove pipe.

"Works for me...Let's see if we can pop some squirrels for supper." Willie pulled off his mask.

Chaz joined him. "Waitin' on me, you're backin' up."

They grabbed their weapons—Chaz a .22 Stevens and Willie his bolt action .410 shotgun and headed to the open door.

Outside, they both took several deep breaths as they stepped off the porch.

"Oh, man, oh, man...fresh air's good...Let's head down toward the river," said Willie.

"Yeah, be squirrels everywhere around all those native pecan trees."

They walked west in the direction of the Delaware Bend of the Red and into the heart of the bottom.

The large shadow watched them, and then it moved off deeper into the woods.

Chaz turned. "What was that?"

"What was what?"

He pointed off to his right. "I thought I saw something move over thataway."

"I don't see nothin'."

"Swear I seen a shadow move."

"You just breathin' too much of that meth."

He stared a moment longer into the dark undergrowth. "Yeah...could be."

RED RIVER BOTTOM
CAMPSITE

Padrino stirred the mixed bacon and eggs in a cast iron skillet at the campfire. A blue and white speckled graniteware coffee pot sat on a flat rock close to the fire. St. John relaxed on a camp stool, having his morning coffee when the big man strolled back into camp.

"Where you been, Bone?" Padrino asked as he looked up.

"Markin' my territory."

"Glad you went downwind," commented St. John.

"Breakfast is about ready...ya'll grab a tin plate."

Bone and St. John ambled to the camp table and each picked up a graniteware plate.

"Fill 'er up, Padrino. We gotta go run the trot line before the turtles start eating on our catch."

St. John dished a heavy helping of the scrambled egg and bacon mixture on his plate. "You're assuming we have a catch."

"I guarantee that stink bait will have us some monster channel cat and maybe some blues," proffered Padrino. "Got the recipe from my grandfather in southern Arkansas…Guaranteed to catch monsters…'course it might get an alligator snappin' turtle or two along with 'em."

"Sure drew flies around Bone," cracked St. John.

"Flies like honey, too."

"And horse's asses."

Bone slipped him a early morning single finger salute.

WOODS
RED RIVER BOTTOM

Chaz and Willie eased through the timber—walk hunting squirrels. They were separated by about fifteen feet, so they could see each side of a tree—squirrels are good at hiding behind a tree when hunters are near. They stepped softly, studying the branches and listening for their barks.

Chaz whispered, "I know there's squirrels in here…They's always around."

"Yeah, should be chatterin' like crazy…Shhh, there's one." Willie spotted a fox squirrel, raised his .410 shotgun and fired—a clean miss.

Bone, Padrino and St. John heard the report of Willie's shot.

"Squirrel hunter."

"Yeah, Padrino, sounded like a .410."

"Not too far off, either," said St. John.

Willie looked through the bare branches of the big pecan tree for the squirrel.

"Missed, dickwad…How kin you miss with a shotgun?…Way to go."

"Didn't see you shootin' when it ran to your side of the…" Willie turned and saw the female Bigfoot about fifteen yards away. "Jesus H. Christ!" He started firing his bolt action .410 as fast as he could at the huge creature.

Chaz joined in and started pumping shots from his .22.

The Sasquach stretched both arms out and roared at the two rednecks. She was hit by both weapons, screamed in pain, turned and ran off into the woods.

"My God, Willie…did you see that thang?"

"Well, yeah. I was shootin' at it...wadn't I?"

"Yeah. Better get the hell outta here...You know what they say about wounded animals."

"It may be comin' back this way...Go, go!"

They spun around and started running in the opposite direction as hard as they could.

"That was a Bigfoot!" Chaz shouted as he ducked a limb.

"No shit, Sherlock!"

RED RIVER BOTTOM WOODS

The male Bigfoot heard the scream of the female in the distance and started running in that direction, tearing through the undergrowth like so much tissue paper.

The three fishermen heard the fusillade of shots, followed by the scream.

St. John jumped to his feet. "What the hell?"

"That was panic shootin'," said Bone.

"But what was that scream?" asked Padrino.

"Sounded somethin' like the one last night." Bone glanced at the others.

The female Bigfoot ran through the brush, but after a distance, she started to stagger, fell, got back up and stumbled on. She stopped at the edge of a small opening and held on to a nearby tree. Bleeding from multiple wounds, she lost her grip and slid to a sitting position at its base—the giant creature collapsed to the ground.

She shimmered and morphed into a tall woman in a gray formfitting body suit with a utility belt that had various electronic controls—she had long snow-white hair and aquiline features. There were multiple holes in her chest—all weeping blood…

CAMPSITE
RED RIVER BOTTOM

Willie and Chaz burst into the campsite, panicked and out of breath.

"Help us!…Bigfoot!…Bigfoot!" Willie stammered.

Bone got to his feet. "Whoa, there boys. Calm down."

The two rednecks simultaneously turned and looked back the way they came.

"We shot a Bigfoot!…It's wounded!" Chaz added.

RED RIVER BOTTOM
WOODS

The woman slowly raised her hand to her chest, then lifted it up in front of her unlined face. Her fingers were covered in blood. She struggled to get to her feet, but collapsed back to the ground and drifted into unconsciousness.

CAMPSITE
RED RIVER BOTTOM

St. John pointed at their weapons. "You shot it with those?"

"Yeah, didn't have no big guns," Willie replied.

Padrino just shook his head. "Uh, oh."

"You boys stay here, we'll backtrack and try to find it," said Bone as he checked the weapon on his hip.

"It's huge, man…Must be eight or ten feet tall," Chaz added.

"And you idiots shot it with those pop guns…Brilliant," commented St. John.

"We was scared," Willie said, trying to be defensive.

Bone turned to St. John and Padrino. "Let's go…Double check your sidearms."

They started out in the direction Willie and Chaz had come from.

"There's coffee by the fire, help yourselves," Padrino said over his shoulder.

"Did ya'll smell those rednecks?" commented Bone after they had penetrated the woods a short distance.

"They reeked," agreed Padrino.

"Yeah, been cookin' meth," added St. John.

Bone noticed an anomaly underneath a large juniper, he walked over for a look—a large bird nest with ten eggs.

"Interesting…turkey eggs. Don't see their nests too often."

The two rednecks poked around the campsite. Willie opened the cooler.

"Hey, now we're talkin'…Beer."

RED RIVER BOTTOM WOODS

Bone stopped again and knelt down, rubbed a finger in a spot on the ground, held it up and sniffed. "Well, they hit it…Leads this way."

He led off, following the blood trail, passing broken branches along the way.

Padrino pointed at some disturbed leaf mulch. "Running here…staggers."

"Must be hit pretty bad," said St. John.

"Yeah, fell here, got back up…staggered on," added Bone.

They moved through the brush and then came to the female, lying at the base of the tree.

"Holy Mother of God! They shot a woman!" St. John exclaimed.

They rushed up to her.

"What's this she's wearing?" Padrino looked at the gray rubber looking suit, and then knelt down and checked her pulse. "Faint pulse…Irregular."

Bone shook his head. "I don't get it. The tracks we were followin' were definitely Bigfoot...Musta been sixteen inches long."

St. John walked a large circle around the tree. "There's no tracks continuing. This has got to be who...or what we were tracking."

Without warning, the male Bigfoot burst out of the brush, roaring...

CAMPSITE
RED RIVER BOTTOM

Willie and Chaz sat on the ground next to the dead campfire, each with a beer. They were surrounded by numerous empties.

Chaz took a big slug from the longneck. "Beer was a better idea than coffee...Whole lot better."

"Figured they had some."

"You notice the guns those guys were wearing?"

"Yeah...What about 'em?"

"Think they're cops."

Willie nearly choked on his beer. "Oh, crap...We better get the hell outta here...We left the meth cookin'."

Chaz had a sudden look of panic. "Shit a brick...You can smell that stuff for miles!"

They guzzled the remaining beer down and pitched the bottles to the ground next to the other empties and headed quickly back to the cabin.

RED RIVER BOTTOM WOODS

The three men drew their weapons and aimed at the huge creature, but Padrino lowered his .45 and held up his hand. The hairy beast stopped. "Put your weapons away." He directed his voice to the Sasquatch. "It's all right, we're friends."

The Bigfoot shimmered and morphed into a tall man wearing the same gray formfitting body suit—he also had long snow-white hair and heavier aquiline features.

"How did you know, Padrino?" asked Bone.

"He told me...at least I think he did...Hell, I don't know, but I knew...Understand?"

"No."

"How are you called?" Padrino asked the being.

"I am called Vesta. What has happened to my mate, Rania?"

"She has been shot by a couple of hunters who feared her."

"We must do something quickly...I need you and the big man..." He pointed to Bone. "...to help me."

"What do we need to do?"

"Kneel with me and place your hands on my hands. You have a altered state, you term your Chi...you must go there and give your energy to me."

Bone looked at Padrino—they nodded at each other and knelt down on both sides of Vesta and placed their hands on top of his on either side of her chest.

"You must know we have two hearts. One for each lung. Visualize the tissue healing...It is very similar to your own."

Padrino and Bone's breathing slowed as they entered into their Chi state of deep meditation. A blue glow flickered slowly and grew stronger as the three focused their healing energies into the injured woman. Their faces began to perspire and soon Bone, Padrino, Vesta and Rania were all enveloped in a bright blue glow.

The punctures in her chest began to close and the blood absorbed back into her body until the wounds completely disappeared. All that was left were the small holes in her suit.

Vesta weakly staggered to his feet as Bone and Padrino both collapsed and fell over unconscious...

WOODS NEAR CAMPSITE

"We should have grabbed a roadie," commented Willie as they moved through the woods.

"Yeah...We're not far, let's go back and get a couple."

"Right, we got time...Amazin' how brilliant minds think alike."

RED RIVER BOTTOM
WOODS

Rania stirred and opened her eyes. Vesta knelt down beside her and caressed her face.

"What happened to Bone and Padrino?"

He turned his head slightly from her to St. John. "They were drained by the healing process. They will be all right in a moment. Your species is not used to using that capability…"

"Vesta! What…"

He turned back to her. "It is going to be all right, my dear. These humans are friends…These two beside you saved your life."

Bone and Padrino stirred and sat up, both looked somewhat confused.

"I feel like I've been run over by a truck," Padrino said as he shook his head.

"Heard that." Bone blinked his eyes several time.

Rania looked over to them. "Thank you, my friends…for my life."

"Glad to help, but Vesta, how did you know we could assist you?" asked Bone.

"I sensed it when I entered this small clearing. Just as I sensed from your elder you were friends."

Rania got to her feet and inspected her suit. "I'm glad we have spares."

"Who are you and where are you from? I thought the *Grays* were supposed to be small," Padrino asked as he rose also.

"We are the Aldebarian…distantly related to the smaller *Grays*, as you call them. We evolved to a larger size on our planet in the Aldebaran system."

Rania glanced at her mate, he nodded. "Our planet, Aldebara, was hit by the outer edge of a gamma ray burst from a distant supernovae. As you may or may not know, a gamma ray can be very deadly...It destroyed almost half of our ozone layer and all the lower forms of life on our planet went extinct in just a few of your years. It took our scientists ten cycles to finally reestablish our ozone shield."

Vesta took over, "We have been coming here to Tellus...your Earth...for many years collecting seed stock of your flora and fauna to repopulate our world. It will take many more of your years as there are hundreds of thousands of species we must collect. We have already reestablished the micro-biotic ecosystem which we had to do before reintroducing the higher forms..

"We can only collect seed stock because mature flora and fauna would not survive the transfer."

"Anything we can do to help?" St. John asked.

"Our collection bins are almost full for this trip. However, we haven't been able to locate turkey, owl or hawk eggs as yet," said Rania.

"Well, I think we can help you out a little here. I spotted a turkey nest while we were looking for you…Musta had ten or twelve eggs in it," offered Bone.

"Wonderful. We'll only need six. We don't want to overly upset the hen," said Vesta.

"Why the Bigfoot disguise?" asked St. John.

"In our research of your planet, we found out about the almost universal belief of a mythical creature you call Bigfoot or Sasquatch," replied Vesta

"We felt that if we were seen, that no one would believe the witnesses," added Rania.

"How did you do your research?" asked Bone.

The two Aldebarians glanced at each other and smiled. "Your television signals."

St. John guffawed. "That's a scary thought."

"Where is your spacecraft?" Padrino interjected.

"It is cloaked a few hundred meters from your camp," replied Rania.

"Familiar with that cloaking stuff," said Bone.

"How do you mean?" she asked.

"Had a little business with some ugly mothers…sort of a cross between an alligator and an elephant. Their ship was cloaked. One of 'em tried to burn me with some tube, but didn't count on my partner and I being armed. Killed one…The other jumped in his sphere and took off...with about six holes in his door...I might add."

"Reptoids," Vesta and Rania said together.

"What were they doing?" she asked.

"Spying on some little woman."

"Annuna," they again spoke simultaneously.

"Excuse me?"

"The Tyranians, that's the smaller versions of us, have been looking for one of their missing people...her name is Annuna...They traced her damaged ship to a crash site near here and saw many years later on a television show from your History Channel that the locals had buried only one body..."

Vesta interrupted, "I fear the Reptoids will be back."

"Know one thing, they aren't bulletproof...Neither is their ship. Tried to run us off and called me a primitive...Me!"

Padrino chuckled. "They must be very perceptive."

Bone snapped him a look.

"We tried to frighten you away last night, too," said Rania.

"Well, you damn near did," offered St. John.

"We are very happy we failed."

"It's too bad you didn't scare those two nimrods out of here."

Vesta looked puzzled for a moment. "Nimrods?...Oh, yes, they are preparing some noxious chemical in their dwelling... What is the purpose?"

Bone and St. John exchanged looks...

RED RIVER BOTTOM SHACK

The two rednecks mounted the steps to the cabin—neither was too steady. Chaz stopped, slammed the empty beer can to his forehead in an attempt to crush it.

"Ow! Ow!...Damn, that always looks so easy on TV."

"Don't you reckon that's why those actors get the big bucks?"

"Yeah..." He paused for a long moment. "We are so stupid."

"How's that?"

"You got any idee what a Bigfoot carcass is worth?"

"Uh..."

"Hunderds of thousands…millions…hell, maybe bazillions to the tabloids or one of those monster shows on cable TV."

"Say, yeah! They've all been hollerin' for a body."

"Your phone has a camera…right?"

"Yeah?"

"Let's get our hog rifles outta the truck and go make sure that ugly son of a bitch is dead…Then we'll hang it from a tree and take our pictures with it…We'll be famous."

"What about those cops?"

"Settle their hash too…Got more firepower than they do." He belched loudly.

They wobbled over to their pickup. Chaz opened the driver's door and grabbed the two rifles from the rear window gun rack, a 30-30 Winchester Model 94 and a scoped 30-06 Remington Model 700. He handed the bolt action to Willie.

WOODS

Cap'n, let's you and me go check on those two inbreeds… Padrino, why don't you show our friends here where the turkey nest is."

Padrino nodded.

Bone and St. John headed back in the general direction of the camp.

"I think camp's this way...those two idiots ran all over the woods after they shot Rania."

"You know what happens when you think, Bone."

"Would you rather I follow my impulses?"

"Is there a third choice?...Didn't think so."

***

CHAPTER TWELVE

RED RIVER BOTTOM WOODS

"Should we activate our creature holograms?"

"Probably a good idea Vesta," replied Padrino.

The Aldebarians morphed back into their Bigfoot images.

"Let's go find those turkey eggs again."

CAMPSITE
RED RIVER BOTTOM

Bone and St. John entered the campsite and looked around at the mess.

"Looks like those morons drank up most of our beer and cut out," observed the captain.

"Bet they're goin' back to their shack to check on their meth."

"No bet."

WOODS

Willie pointed toward a dark section of the timber. "There should be a blood trail over that way."

"You loaded?"

"Well, yeah." Willie eased the bolt back on his Remington to see if there was anything in the chamber, but found it empty. He quickly racked the bolt and loaded a round from the magazine. "Am now."

SHACK

"Don't think anyone's home," said Bone as they approached the ramshackle building.

"How's that?

"Pickup door's open…No guns in the rack."

"I'll check the cabin." St. John cautiously walked up the four steps to the door with his weapon at the ready, stepped to one side, reached over, turned the knob and flung it open—the toxic stench almost knocked him down. He covered his nose with his left forearm. "Holy shit!" He stumbled back from the porch and down the steps—bent over and took several deep breaths when he got to the ground.

"Guess it don't take you long to check out a cabin."

"Bite me…They're still cookin'…How do those rednecks stand the stink?"

"Even a skunk don't think he smells."

St. John coughed several times and then looked up. "What?"

"Never mind…We gotta track these yahoos, Padrino and our new friends might be goin' in harm's way." Bone stepped over to the truck, raised the hood and jerked the ignition coil wire out and stuck it in his pocket. "In case they beat us back here."

They moved back out to the woods, following Willie and Chaz's tracks.

Padrino, Vesta and Rania knelt down at the turkey nest. She reached through her hologram disguise, took out a silver cloth collection bag and carefully put the eggs inside along with dry grass that her mate had collected.

Padrino watched the care she took with the eggs. "Turkey eggs are pretty tough."

"We still must protect them until we get them back to the ship," replied Vesta.

"I understand."

The inept pair neared the area of the turkey nest. They couldn't see Padrino or Rania through the brush, but saw Vesta when he stood.

Willie whispered, "There he is…Got a shot?"

Chaz raised his iron-sighted Winchester. "We gonna be rich!"

He fired, the bullet struck a tree limb between him and Vesta, breaking it and ricocheting off into the woods.

The Bigfoot turned toward the pair and roared.

Willie hurriedly threw his Remington to his shoulder. "He's mine!" In his hurry, he jerked the shot above the creature's head. The recoil of the rifle slammed the scope eyepiece into his eyebrow and split it open into a half-moon crescent—blood flowed into his eye. He dropped the gun and fell to his knees, holding his face. "Oh, my God, they shot me! They shot me!"

Padrino reacted to the gunfire, stood and drew his weapon. "Get down!"

Bone and St. John heard the rifle fire through the woods.

"Damn!" He drew his weapon.

"That way!" St. John pointed and pulled his.

They broke into a sprint.

Padrino fired three rapid shots only inches above the heads of the two rednecks.

Willie and Chaz dove to the ground as the bullets clipped several small twigs above. Leaves drifted down around them.

"It's that old geezer with a gun!" exclaimed Chaz.

"Them Bigfoots call 911 on us?"

"Hell, I don't know...You crawl thataway and we'll cross fire 'im."

Willie tied a red bandanna around his head covering up his right eye to stop the bleeding, and then crawled over next to a tree. He tried to aim with his left eye through the scope. "I cain't see 'im!"

"You idiot! You cain't shoot right-handed with your left eye!"

"I know...but, cain't see out of my right."

"Let's trade guns."

"That's a good idea...Never woulda thought of that."

"I know."

Willie crawled back over to Chaz and they exchanged weapons.

Padrino turned to Vesta and Rania. "Ya'll get back to your craft...I'll cover you." He cranked off another two shots in Willie and Chaz's direction as the Aldebarians disappeared into the brush.

Bone and St. John sprinted through the woods, jumping deadfall and dodging limbs. The big man signaled to slow down.

"Those last five shots were from Padrino's .45…He's only got four rounds left."

"We're gettin' close, want to split up?"

"I'll go to Padrino…you follow and flank me."

Willie had crawled back to his tree with Chaz' Winchester. "Wonder where those other two cops are?"

"You can bet they heard the shootin'. Probably on their way…"

"Screw 'em, we got 'em outgunned."

Bone crept up behind Padrino.

"Took your time," his godfather said without looking around.

"Hell, if you could shoot, you wouldn't need any help."

"Stuff it, Bone…They've separated."

"Got any more mags?"

Padrino shook his head. "Didn't know we were goin' to war."

"I got fifteen rounds. Captain's got eighteen in his Glock…Oughta be enough."

"They've both gone to ground…One is under that tree at eleven o'clock."

Bone aimed his .50 cal at a two inch limb sticking out horizontally from Willie's tree and fired. The limb blew apart and fell on top of his head.

"Ow! Ow! I'm hit! I'm hit!"

"Damn, they got cannons!" Chaz fired two rounds in Bone's direction.

St. John belly-crawled up to a tree. He stood up behind it and looked toward Willie and Chaz's position. "Police officers! You're surrounded! Give it up!"

Willie scrambled out from under the limb, rolled over and levered two shots at St. John.

One shot went wild and the second chipped off bark near the captain's face. He ducked, dropped to a kneeling position and double tapped in Willie's direction.

The two rounds kicked up dirt and leaves in front of his face.

Bone could see Chaz's foot sticking out beyond the tree where he knelt. Aiming carefully, he cranked a shot off, completely blowing the heel from the boot.

Chaz was rolled over from the impact of the .50 cal round. "My foot! My foot! He blew my foot off!" He looked down at his boot and saw that only the heel was missing. "Son of a bitch!…New boots."

"Let's make like a tree and get the hell out of Dodge," yelled Willie.

"What?"

"I only got four rounds left, let's git to the cabin for more ammo."

Chaz looked at his boot. "Think we're gonna need more than ammo."

They jumped up and tore off in the direction of the cabin—Chaz was running like a three legged mule.

St. John moved to another tree, peered out from behind it to see them high-tailing it through the woods. "Bone! You and Padrino okay?"

"We're good. You?"

"Yeah! Looks like they're headed back to the shack!"

"Stay put, we'll come to you."

The rednecks charged through the brush. Willie pushed a limb out of the way as he ran past it. He let go, it snapped back and caught Chaz across the throat—clothes-lining him. His feet came completely off the ground and he landed heavily on his back.

"You stupid son of a bitch! Coulda killed me," he tried to yell at his partner in a very garbled raspy voice.

Willie stopped and came back. "What? Speak up...I cain't hear you."

Chaz pointed to his throat. "Cain't...throat."

"Cane pole?...What the hell are you talkin' 'bout?"

"'Bout broke my neck, moron," Willie wheezed out.

"Broke back mountain?...We ain't *that* good a friends, Chaz...What's wrong with your voice?

"Branch."

"Dance?...I don't dance. Specially with you...Ain't got time anyhow...You're talkin' funny...Come on, we better get a move on...And watch out for them low branches."

Willie turned and moved off.

Chaz reached down, grabbed a stick almost the size of a baseball bat and threw it, striking him in the back of the head—he face-planted to the ground.

The three men joined up at St. John's location.

"Better follow those jugheads to the shack," proffered Bone.

"Suspect that's a good idea...Lead on McGruff."

"I think it's 'Lay on MacDuff,' from *Macbeth*, David." commented Padrino.

"Not in Bone's case…The mighty crime dog."

"Ah, right."

SHACK

Willie and the hobbling Chaz ran up the steps and opened the door.

"I still cain't see too good…Got double vision."

"Low branches is a bitch, ain't they?" replied Chaz, still raspy.

"Who is?…"

"Never mind. Get the ammo."

"I better get the ammo, them guys are dangerous."

"It's not them I'm worried 'bout."

"Maybe those cops want them Bigfoots for themselves."

Chaz swilled down a couple of slugs of Old Charter whiskey. "That's better."

"What's better?"

"My throat, you imbecile."

Outside, Bone, St. John and Padrino spread out and cautiously approached the shack.

"You boys best come out!…With your hands up," shouted the captain.

Willie looked out one of the broken windows. "Damn!"

"This is another fine mess you've gotten us into."

He turned toward Chaz. "Me?"

"You shot the Bigfoot first."

"Yeah, but you shot it second…and third."

"He said come out! Now," yelled Bone.

Chaz went to the window and fired the Remington in the direction of Bone's voice.

The 30-06 round creased the hood of the pickup Bone was behind. He raised up and snapped off a round from his 500. The round went through the wall and blew a leg off the table where several gallon cans of ether were sitting.

The table wobbled, tilted and slowly toppled over, spilling the containers—ether started leaking from a loose metal cap.

Willie turned when the table fell and noticed the highly volatile liquid spreading across the floor. "Oh my God! Oh my God! The ether! Run for your life!" He dropped the Winchester, ran to the door, yanked it open and sprinted outside. He slammed it behind him. "Ether! Ether! Oh, my God!"

Chaz hobbled over to the door and tried to open it—it was stuck. "Help me! Help me, it's locked!"

Bone jumped up on the porch and kicked the door in, knocking Chaz back and to the floor. He rushed in, grabbed the small man by the front of his bib overalls and literally threw him through the doorway and out into the yard—he quickly followed.

"Everybody down!" he yelled as dived behind the truck.

The shack exploded in a mighty roaring fireball creating a huge mushroom cloud that rose above the trees.

Bone squeezed under the truck as flaming debris fell all around.

St. John had dragged Chaz behind a tree and Padrino held Willie behind another—until the debris stopped falling. Bone peered out, and then crawled from under the truck. There were pieces of the shack everywhere, some of it still burning.

Padrino and St. John came out from their cover with Willie and Chaz in tow.

"Guess Sheriff Brennan will have to add littering to the drug charges," said the captain.

"But what about the Bigfoots?" exclaimed Chaz.

"What Bigfoots?" asked Bone.

"You boys must just have been high on meth fumes," said Padrino.

"You had to have seen 'em! There was at least five or six!...Regular army!" Willie added.

Padrino grinned. "A mind is a terrible thing to waste."

Chaz glanced over. "Say what?"

"See?"

"Cap'n, probably should go ahead and call the sheriff's office. I ain't hauling those stinkin' bastards in my pickup."

"Have you smelled your truck lately?"

"Pound sand...It's a long walk home, Padrino."

"But I got the keys."

The captain punched the number on his phone. "Sheriff, St. John. Sorry to bother you on a Saturday, but we got a couple of rednecks had a little, uh...accident with their meth lab...Damn near blew half the countryside away."

"Dammit, St. John, I'm in the middle of grilling steaks."

"Sorry 'bout that, Will. We'll just handcuff 'em to a tree."

"Where the hell are you?"

"Deleware Bend of the Red, 'bout half a mile off county road 121...Just follow the smell."

"I'll send a couple of deputies directly."

"Might ought to send the Fire Department with their hazmat team too."

"Wonderful."

"St. John disconnected. "Brennan said just go ahead and shoot 'em."

"No, no! You cain't do that," exclaimed Willie.

"I ain't wastin' any more ammo. You know how much .50 cal rounds cost?"

Padrino pulled his ten inch Bowie knife. "How about a knife?"

"Now that's a knoife," added St. John, in his best Aussie accent.

"Wait a minute..."

Bone interrupted Chaz. "Works for me." He pulled his big belt knife out too.

A yellow puddle formed at Willie's feet as a large wet stain appeared on the front of his pants.

"Damn, Willie, you ain't done that since we got caught stealin' them peaches," said Chaz.

"I never did get all that bird shot out of my butt."

"All right, enough fun…You boys go over there and hug a tree," said St. John.

"Huh?" Chaz looked confused.

"Don't make him say it again," cautioned Bone.

The two stepped over to a nearby black gum tree and wrapped their arms around it, facing the trunk. Bone and St. John cuffed them together.

"But, what if the Bigfoots come back before the sheriff gets here?" queried Willie.

"Tell 'em we said hi," replied Bone as he, Padrino and St. John turned and headed back to their camp.

"Didn't we see a Bigfoot?" Willie asked.

"Well, yeah…I think…Maybe."

"I told you we was makin' that meth too strong."

"Wadn't my recipe."

"Yeah but you was doin' the mixin'…Ow!"

"What?…Ow, ow!"

"Fire ants!…They's a nest in this tree!"

"You picked it!"

They stamped their feet trying to kill the ants with little to no success.

CAMPSITE
RED RIVER BOTTOM

Bone, Padrino and St. John sat on their camp stools drinking beer.

"I just want to thank you boys for inviting me on such a relaxing weekend," said Padrino.

"Don't know when I've had so much fun since Bone put the flash powder in the chief's ashtray," added St. John.

"Cap'n, would it be out of line if I put in for overtime?"

"Don't start with me, Bone."

Padrino opened up the cooler and took out a bottle. "Only one left. Those peckerwoods drank up most of our beer...What say we call it a weekend and go back to town?"

GOVERNOR'S LOUNGE

They sat at a circular table working on their second round. There were two extra long necks on the table. They watched Sheriff Brennan at the shack site on the

TV monitor. The reporter held the mike in front of him.

"This is Lisanne Adamson, Channel 10 News with a late breaking story. I have with me, Sheriff Brennan of Cross Timbers County here at the scene of a drug manufacturing operation gone bad. What can you tell us, Sheriff Brennan?"

"Well, Lisanne, we got an anonymous tip from a concerned citizen about a suspected methamphetamine lab here along the Red River. My tactical operations team arrived at the suspected drug lab moments after a explosion destroyed the facility. Quick action from my deputies enabled them to apprehend the suspected dealers."

"Have the suspects been identified, Sheriff?"

"Not yet, Lisanne. They are presently being decontaminated and are apparently still under the influence of inadvertent contact with the illicit drugs."

In the background, Willie and Chaz were being sprayed with foam by members of the Cross Timbers Fire Department.

Bone signaled to Vertis to kill the TV. "Well, anonymous concerned citizen, what do you think of that?"

"I think Brennan learned his BS from you," St. John replied.

Bone laughed. "I'll take that a compliment."

"It wasn't," said Padrino.

Loraine and Stella entered and spotted the guys at their table at the same time Bone noticed them.

"Hey, ladies, right on time. I've already ordered for ya'll."

The girls sat down in the chairs that had the beers in front of them.

"So, how was the big adventure?"

"Pard, you wouldn't believe," said Bone.

"When's the fish fry?"

Bone, St. John and Padrino looked at one another.

"Damn! The trot line!" they simultaneously said. All three jumped up and rushed to the exit.

"What the hell was that all about?" Stella asked as she watched the door close behind them.

"With that group, you never know." Loraine grinned.

They both tried to pick up their beer bottles—only to find that they've been super glued to the table.

"Damn you, Bone!" they said in unison.

WOODS
RED RIVER BOTTOM

As night fell, the two Bigfoot creatures approached a small clearing near the river. They shimmered and morphed into Vesta and Rania. The taller male Aldebarian touched a control button on his belt—an acorn-shaped golden craft materialized in front of them. An elliptical-shaped hatch opened and they both entered. It closed behind them with a hiss and in a moment, the craft began to glow blue and pulsate with a slight humming sound. After a few seconds, the frequency of the hum changed to a higher pitch and the pulse rate increased faster and faster...

CAMPSITE
RED RIVER BOTTOM

There was a large washtub full of catfish iced down next to the camp table.

Bone took a pull of his Shiner. "We gonna flip to see who cleans and filets the fish?"

"I didn't bring my knife," said the captain.

"You lose and I'll loan you mine," offered Padrino.

Bone looked off and saw a blue glow through the trees, the others turned also. They saw the Aldebarian's craft rise above the trees and then shoot skyward in the direction of Orion's belt—there was absolutely no sound. They watched as it vanished in the darkness.

"Looks like Vesta and Rania filled their quota," said Bone.

In some trees across the Red, a large hairy creature watched as the glowing craft disappeared into the stars. Bigfoot raised its face to the sky and roared his strange cry.

Bone, Padrino and St. John heard the eerie sound echo throughout the Red River bottom. They looked into the darkness across the river and then at each other.

"This didn't happen," said the captain.

Bone and Padrino nodded.

***

CHAPTER THIRTEEN

LUCY'S HOUSE

C. W. Williams and Barry Farlow got out of their green Suburban. Williams was wearing sunglasses that almost covered his black eye. Farlow had white tape across the bridge of his badly swollen nose. They approached the gate to the white picket fence but stopped when they saw her dog.

Tyrin was in the yard between the gate and the house—growling at the men—his feet apart in the stance that pit bulls take when on the arousal. Lucy came out of her house and stood beside him.

"You aren't welcome here, Mister Williams...Looks like you weren't welcome somewhere else, too."

"Miz Wilson, we just wanted to give you one more opportunity to listen to reason..."

"Or what?"

"Well...I guess you could say things might get a little unpleasant." Williams glanced at Farlow.

"I think they're already unpleasant."

Tyrin growled deeper and advanced stiff-legged toward the gate.

"Better leash that damn dog, lady. He don't seem to like us," Farlow said.

"This is his home...Maybe he feels the need to protect it...He doesn't like snakes either."

Tyrin took a few more steps. Farlow pulled out a 9mm Glock pistol and shot him. The faithful animal yelped and collapsed in a heap.

"Tyrin!..." Lucy knelt down beside him. "Why?...Why did you do that?" she asked through her tears.

"He was a vicious animal, lady...He was going jump the fence to attack us."

"Let's go," Williams said as he touched the man's arm.

The two men turned and got back in their vehicle, started the engine and left in a cloud of dust.

Lucy cradled Tyrin to her chest—tears streamed down her face.

The men sped down the ranch road, sending a tall plume of white caliche dust behind their SUV high into the air like a smoking tail.

"Well, that went perfect. Couldn't have gone better if we'd written a script."

"Yeah, got rid of her alarm system and since she don't have electricity and no phone out there all by her lonesome…We can take our time."

"You took care of the mutt…I'll buy the beer."

"Works for me," said Farlow with a sardonic grin.

Lucy still cradled the muscular blond and white dog to her chest. She began to gently rock back and forth. A soft glow of pale blue slowly encompassed both her and Tyrin. The light got brighter for a long moment—then faded away.

Lucy continued to cradle him for a few more minutes—then Tyrin stirred, looked up and licked her face. She collapsed to the ground beside him…

COUNTY ROAD

Bone drove down a tree-canopied country road on the east side of the county. A frown covered his face and he rubbed the back of his neck, and then took the bracelet out of his pocket and briefly looked at it as he drove. He rubbed his neck again, pulled over to the side of the gravel road and stopped. After sitting there for a moment, he got out, leaned over, put his hands on his knees and took a couple of deep breaths. *Damn, got dizzy there...for just a moment...No, not dizzy...Uncomfortable. Weak...Yeah, weak. What the hell?* He shook his head, got back in his pickup and continued the way he was going.

LUCY'S YARD

Lucy lay where she collapsed—not moving. Tyrin licked her face again and whined. He gently put one paw on her shoulder, lay down beside her and placed his chin on her chest.

PADRINO'S HOUSE

Bone pulled his truck into the driveway. The numerous styles and types of wind chimes—hung from limbs—played their soothing tinkling music in the soft breeze that drifted through the trees in the yard.

He got out and walked to the handmade thick plank front door mounted to the frame with wrought iron strap hinges— carrying a six-pack of beer. He entered, stepped over to the kitchen counter and set it down.

Padrino looked up from the autographed copy of *Haunted Falls* by Farmer & Stienke he was reading as Bone opened the carton and handed him one.

"Brought your favorite, Padrino."

"I hope it's cold this time," the wiry shaman said as he put a marker in the book and laid it on the end table beside his well-worn red leather recliner.

"Just picked it up."

"St. John put you back on full duty?"

"Yeah, we were no-billed...Classified it as a righteous shooting."

Padrino twisted the cap off the longneck, took a sip and then looked back at Bone. "What's the matter?"

He took a sip of his own beer and sat down on a tall stool next to the bar between Padrino's kitchen and den—and got that thousand yard stare...

LUCY'S YARD

Tyrin still had his paw on her shoulder, he lifted his head from her chest and licked her face again. She stirred, blinked her eyes several times and rose to a sitting position.

Thank you, sweet thing..." She put her arms around his thick neck and hugged him. "Are you all right now?"

Tyrin gave a short bark and wagged his tail.

PADRINO'S HOUSE

Bone put his hand to the bridge of his nose. "Don't know, just felt uneasy for the last ten minutes or so...like I was fallin' through the air or somethin'...It's passed."

Padrino got up from his chair and the two men sat down at the solid oak trellis dining table.

"You remember I told you about the little woman St. John and I met a week ago last Saturday and the flashes of visions…"

"The one Vesta and Rania think is Annuna, a missing small Gray?…I've been waiting for you to take me out to meet…"

"I know. Been kinda busy, as you recall…But I also found a newspaper article on the internet about a reported space craft crash in 1897 near Aurora, Texas…Where she said she was from…Matter of fact, the last space shuttle built in the NASA fleet was named *Aurora* after the incident."

Bone handed Padrino a printout of the article.

He scanned the paper. "I have heard of this. No military ops back then to cover up the story…"

"Interesting that the name Aurora comes from Roman mythology…means *The Goddess of the Dawn*…And somethin' else, the new top-secret hypersonic spy plane that the US says doesn't exist…kinda like Area 51…or the Black Eagle Force…is called *Aurora*."

"A lot of coincidences, wouldn't you say?"

"Yeah…don't really believe in coincidences…Now here's the kicker…Found this near the crash site in

Aurora the day before our run-in with those thugs from Global."

He handed the bracelet to Padrino.

When he touched it, he started seeing images similar to Bone's, but in more detail—*A city with tall silver towers under a lavender sky with two suns—a small gray man and woman in a type of cockpit—small hands, with the bracelet on the left wrist, flashing rapidly over a touch screen console—an old-fashioned windmill coming fast in the cockpit window—the gray figures look at each other with their large almond-shaped black eyes. They touch finger tips—a flash of light—fire.*

"Look at these rune-like symbols engraved in the stones. They're inlaid with gold."

Padrino took the bracelet to a small table that had an articulating magnifying glass. He turned on the attached light and placed the bracelet under the glass and began to study it and the symbols. "Hmm…Due to the lack of corrosion, the metal appears to be primarily gold with turquoise-like stones…May not actually be turquoise, you know…but then again they might. We would just have to have them analyzed…But the metal…"

"My metal detector read *gold*."

"Atomic number of seventy-nine and with the designation *Au*. Easy to identify…I've seen symbols similar to these before."

He went to his computer and searched *ALIEN SYMBOLS*. The first page to come up on the screen showed *ROSWELL*. He clicked on that item. A montage of symbols page came up: ⚵, <>, ⚴, ^^^, V~, ∂.

"There…These are the same type of hieroglyphics…some are even identical."

"But, how can that be, Padrino?"

He looked up at the big man. "Lucy is not of this world…I believe she is indeed the missing Annuna…Our ancestors tell of visitors who not only came regularly, but spent much time with them…They were small people who came in strange flying ships and were very benevolent and kind."

"She said…as she put it, that she had occasion to study our ancestor's culture."

"I'm sure she did."

"Somethin' else…Several days ago, my partner and I decided we needed a break after the cemetery case and went ridin' out at Lucy's…You remember I mentioned it to the Aldebarians…Now, you're not goin' to believe this, but…aw, hell, you probably will…"

"Cut to the chase, Bone."

"Right…Well, we were ridin' and I noticed we were bein' watched. Assumed it was the Global Energy folks that had been givin' her a hard time. So, we sneak up on them, so to speak. This one yahoo calls me a primitive…Me? Can you imagine?…And then points this thing…" Bone reached in his cargo pants pocket and laid the silver tube on the table. "…and a green light comes out and this big assed cedar tree just behind where I was standin', just friggin' disappeared…gone, poof…left a little smoke…Well, my partner and I took him out."

He took a sip of his beer. "For a brief instant, the guy changed to some kind of reptile lookin' thing…Ugly don't tell the half of it. Then he touched a button in a pad on his wrist and just vaporized…sorta like the tree. The other guy grabbed their gear…like I told Vesta and Rania…"

"…and then we rode back to Lucy's, loaded up and boogied…I think Lucy thought we were nuts…That's pretty much it…Wild, huh? What do you think…aliens?"

Padrino handed the bracelet back to Bone, picked up the tube and examined it under his light. "I'd say Lucy was just being coy...No question...The Aldebarians called them Reptoids." He handed the tube back to Bone. "Wouldn't touch that little button near the one end if I were you." He grinned and grabbed his cap. "Take me out there...Now."

LUCY'S YARD

Although not fully recovered, she walked unsteadily to her well, took a dipper full of water and after drinking, she offered some to Tyrin—he took a few laps. She put the dipper back into the bucket, pulled out Bone's cell, pushed *01* and held the Galaxy to her ear.

CROSS POLICE DEPARTMENT DISPATCH

Dispatcher Lauren flipped a switch and answered the incoming call.

"Cross Police Department. What's up, Bone?"

"This is not Detective Bone, but may I speak with him, please?"

"Uh, Detective Bone isn't here at this time, ma'am…Would you like me to patch you through to his radio?"

"Please."

BONE'S DODGE PICKUP

Bone and Padrino drove down a caliche road in his 2006 truck, a rooster tail of chalky dust in their wake.

"We should have taken my truck, it actually has real air conditioning."

"What?…And miss all the fresh scents of the outdoors?"

"Including that dead skunk we just pass…"

Bone's radio crackled to life.

"Kilo 12-36, Dispatch. You around Bone?"

"Kilo 12-36, go ahead, Lauredarlin'."

"Kilo 12-36, you have a phone call…It's from…uh, your cell phone."

"I know…Patch it through."

"10-4, Bone. Patching."

"Lucy…everything all right?"

LUCY'S YARD

"Well, not really, Bone…I had a couple of visitors. This time they were big shots from Global Energy…They tried to kill Tyrin…"

"I know *that* feelin'…What do you mean, they *tried* to kill Tyrin?"

Well, ah…apparently, they…Mister Farlow…wasn't a very good shot."

"Are they still there?"

"No…but, I have reason to believe they're coming back."

BONE'S PICKUP

Lucy, you stay put, I've got Padrino with me. We're on our way."

"Oh, good. I was hoping I would get to meet him before I…uh, well, soon."

"We just turned on your ranch road. Crossin' your cattle guard now…See you in a few."

She smiled at the news. "I'll make some more lemonade."

"Love your lemonade…Where'd you get lemons?"

"I have several trees out back."

"Right…I knew that."

Padrino got a wry smile on his face.

They pulled up in front of her house and got out. Bone grabbed a white butcher-paper wrapped parcel from the floorboard.

"Neat, that house was built around the turn of the century…the twentieth century, that is. Called a dog run style," observed Padrino.

"Dog run? Why?"

"There's a hallway…sometimes folks called it a breezeway, that runs the entire length of the house. It was usually ten to twelve feet wide with bedrooms on one side, dining and kitchen, more bedrooms and maybe a parlor on the other. The hallway or dog run usually had couches and chairs along the sides with doors that could be opened at each end to ventilate the entire house…With the twelve foot ceilings, it worked pretty well."

"Who'd a thought."

Lucy and Tyrin came out of the house and down the front steps off the wraparound porch. The diminutive woman was carrying a tray with a pitcher of iced lemonade and three glasses. She nodded at a tree with a picnic table and benches. "Let's sit outside here. It's so nice today."

Bone and Padrino sat on one bench, Lucy set the tray on the table and sat on the other side.

Bone unwrapped the parcel and handed Tyrin a beef knuckle. "Here you go, buddy."

The dog took the entire knee joint in his massive jaws and ducked under the table.

"That's very kind, Bone. Where…"

"Scivally's Grocery. They got the only real butcher shop left in these parts…" He looked at the pitcher of lemonade. "Meant to ask you the other day…Where'd you get the ice, Lucy? I didn't think you were hooked up to the Co-op?"

She smiled wryly. "I have my ways."

Padrino also gave a wry smile.

"Lucy, this is my Padrino."

"I've been looking forward to meeting you, Padrino."

"As I you, Lucy.'

He clasped her hands in his and got the same visions as before when he touched the bracelet. He bowed slightly. "Welcome to our world, Sky Queen…or should I say Annuna?"

Lucy's eyes widened, she removed her hands. "How do you…"

Bone interrupted, "We had a little adventure with some Aldebarians this weekend…"

"…My, I don't know those particular Aldebarians, but I was aware of their mission. I'm happy you were able to help." She looked deep into Padrino's eyes. "I understand what Bone meant now about you being a shaman…You are quite like your ancestors…both of you are. Even considering the great disparity in size…You both have the Nascian type eyes…bronze is the best description…With flecks of topaz and gold."

"I have heard many stories of you, Sky Queen."

CONFERENCE ROOM
GLOBAL ENERGY

Davis, Williams, Farlow, Harvey Reid and Nate Pelosi—Jeffers and Hollister's replacements—sat around the big glass-topped walnut conference table.

"Report," said CEO Davis.

Williams spoke up, "Farlow took care of her mutt, so we should be able to get right up to the house and barn."

"Reid, you and Pelosi are responsible for planting the incendiaries…" Farlow added.

"What about that little woman?" asked Pelosi.

Davis responded, "She'll have to worry about herself."

"I'll provide cover…Farlow, you and the rest of the boys take care of the house and barn…This should all go like clockwork," said Williams.

"How about those city cops? I'm not inclined to tangle with that big son-of-a-bitch again," Farlow groused.

"Right. Had a run in with that asshole myself…They'll probably be at a club that time of night, knocking back a few… Not their jurisdiction anyway," said Williams.

"Heard man-mountain don't seem to care about that," said Reid.

"Big don't mean he's bullet proof…If they happen to show up, we'll settle their hash too…Let's stop by the rig and pick up some of the roughnecks," Williams added.

"Yeah, right. Turn them loose on that big bastard. They'll kick their own mother's ass for a couple hundred bucks."

Davis took a big draw on his Cuban cigar and blew a cloud of blue smoke over his head, and then looked down the table. "No witnesses, no loose ends...Are we perfectly clear?"

"Crystal," responded Williams

Davis rose and walked toward the wall to the outside that was solid glass and stared out across the city from his twenty-fifth floor suite. "I'm tired of fooling around with that old bitch."

LUCY'S YARD

Bone, Padrino and Lucy were still seated at the table. Tyrin was underneath the table, happily crunching on his bone. The lemonade was almost gone.

"...and you're how old?" Bone asked incredulously.

"In your years...I'm over two thousand years old."

"You hold your age well."

"You have to understand the space-time continuum and quantum physics."

"Come again?"

"She's talking about Einstein's theory of relativity, Bone," said Padrino.

"Except that it's not a theory. He was pretty close. He was only off on one thing."

"That would be?"

"The speed of light is not ultimate."

"You see…the faster you travel, the slower time goes…and it is not necessarily linear, " Padrino offered.

"Ya'll are making my head hurt."

"My race has a life span of a little over four hundred Tellurian years, but, because we use what you term, worm holes or warps in the fabric of space and time, we can actually reach our destination within moments of departure…I have aged naturally since I have been marooned on your planet."

"Excuse me?"

"It's relative," said Padrino as he grinned.

Bone just shook his head.

GLOBAL DRILLING RIG #12

Williams and Farlow pulled up at the big jackknife deep-drilling rig platform in their Suburban. Reid and Pelosi followed in the Jeep.

Reid got out and climbed the metal stairway to the dog house and went inside. In a few moments, he came back out with four roughnecks in tow.

"You boys load up and follow us…It's party time," Reid said when they reached the bottom of the stairway.

The four crew glanced at each other, nodded and headed toward one of their personal Ford 350 crew-cab pickups.

LUCY'S YARD

"Padrino, why is it that you can talk about all this quantum stuff with Lucy, but you've never mentioned it to me?"

"You've never shown any interest before, Bone."

"Try me, I might surprise you."

"Lucy, I would really be interested in knowing more about your inertialess drive...It's almost mind boggling."

"I suppose it could be...We developed it well over three million of your years ago...It just seems very natural."

"As our internal combustion engine is to us...and it's only a little over a hundred years old...Staggering to the imagination."

"I can see the comparison...to start with, we learned how to use cosmic energy and store it in our accumulators...so we never have to actually carry fuel. Then came the inertialess drive. Without it, our bodies could not stand the rigors of space travel...the maneuvers we can perform, and creating velocities many times greater than the speed of light...relatively speaking.

"Inertialess simply means massless. In other words, once engaged, the matter of our ships and our very bodies, for all intents and purposes, ceases to have any mass and are therefore totally unaffected by gravity."

"Huh?" Bone had that deer-in-the-headlights look.

"The field surrounding our vessels, in a sense, puts everything into what could be called another dimension...so when we go inertialess, the ship and everything inside has the same intrinsic velocity...Were that not so, we would end up as so much Tyranian goo."

CROSS PD

Stella poked her head in the Detective's Room. "Hey Loraine, where's Bone?"

"I was just wondering the same thing...makes me nervous when I can't see him."

"Lauren said a woman called in from *his* cell phone wanting to speak with him. She patched her through."

"Had to have been that sweet lady...Lucy something or other. He introduced us the other day when we went riding...She owns a section of land on the west side of the county. Bone said he gave her his cell because she's totally off the grid and has been having trouble with some lease hounds...Ya'll stick around...Got a feeling..."

LUCY'S YARD

Even Padrino shook his head. "I think we're going to have to go through this in stages…starting to make my head hurt too…Lucy, do you know the Nasca language?"

"Yes, I can speak it…just haven't had the occasion to use it in…quite a while."

"I would love to spend some time and learn what you can teach me."

"I will be happy to tell you what I can. I visited the Nasca at the beginning of your first millennium when we were assisting them in creating the desert images your civilization is so fascinated with…The whale, spider, sun dial, pelican and a landing strip."

"What were those images used for?" asked Bone.

"Signals…communication signals for us…And somewhat of an homage thing. We tried to convince them that it wasn't necessary, but to no avail. They continued to look upon us as Gods…as did many other civilizations, like the Egyptians and the Maya. We finally quit showing ourselves intentionally almost a thousand years ago."

"The pyramids and Pumapunku! You used your inertialess anti-gravitational device to move those monstrous blocks of stone," Padrino exclaimed.

Lucy nodded. "We helped the Egyptians build the structures at Giza to serve as additional cosmic energy accumulators. Later, we developed more efficient methods and no longer needed pyramids for that purpose."

"How did you wind up here?" asked Bone.

"Our race has been protecting your planet for millennia. My mate, Garrin, and I came back to the Sol system in your nineteenth century with a Tyranian battle fleet to stop an invasion by a race of those malevolent Reptoids you encountered from the Alpha Draconis system..."

"We were being invaded? Why?" asked Padrino.

"The Reptoids attack planets more backward than they are for raw materials, slaves...and as a food source."

"You mean they..."

Lucy interrupted Bone. "Yes...We have been battling them since we started exploring. One of their scout ships apparently discovered my locator beacon accidentally...That's when you stumbled into them. They have the technology to disguise their horrendous bodies with a holographic image…"

"Like the Aldebarians…Shades of Star Trek all over again."

"Something like that. Although some of your indigenous species refer to them as shape-shifters…they are merely projections. "

"They were ugly son of a guns…short, squatty and legs like elephants."

"Their planet in the Draconis system has almost three times the gravity of Earth and Tyrin."

"Ah, that explains it."

"Do you think the survivor managed to get back to their world?" asked Padrino.

"From what Bone told me of the flash high in the atmosphere…I don't think so. They would have had to be well outside the outer thermosphere to activate their interstellar drive. I'm convinced the craft was destroyed by Bone and Loraine's weapons."

"Can't believe our handguns were able to bring down a spaceship."

"We, the Aldebarians and the Reptoids have protective force fields, but they are designed to protect the ship from pure energy, laser and other vibratory weaponry…not your solid high-velocity projectile devices. I'm sure the survivor was quite surprised…I fear, however, he was able to get off a message…If so, there may be more coming. They would love to get their hands on a live Tyranian."

"They have that inertialess drive too, then?" asked Padrino.

She nodded. "They developed it at nearly the same time that we did, as well as force fields…Fortunately, our beams of pure directed energy and Thorium torpedoes are more powerful than their pulse lasers and we managed to destroy the Reptoid fleet that time…We are not always as successful. But, our fighter craft was damaged in the battle…"

"You got shot down?" exclaimed Bone.

"Well, in a manner of speaking." Lucy smiled. "You see, we have a procedure that we have to go through when we go from inertialess, or free, to inert because of the buildup of kinetic energy…We weren't able to do that when we were hit by the pulse weapon of the Reptoids…That's why we were literally knocked all the way to Tellus…Earth, some fifty-seven million miles during the big space battle…"

"Like a bat striking a ball."

"Something like that. We tried to reach what is termed a Ley Magnetic line…Your planet is crisscrossed with them in perfect triangles and are sources of energy for our accumulators...One of our ships also crashed in 1947 near Roswell, New Mexico trying to reach the same line. Both Aurora and Roswell lie on the thirty-third parallel...as does the mountain where your Moses received the Decalogue or Ten Commandments. "

"Amazing," said Padrino.

"Not really. All iron-cored planets have them...We managed to make it through your atmosphere without burning up and crashed near Aurora in April of 1897...not far from here."

"That's why you said you were from there," said Bone.

"Yes, a little white lie...Garrin was too badly injured for me to restore."

"Like you did to that bird and to Tyrin and the way we helped Vesta?" asked Padrino.

Lucy nodded again. "Our species is gifted with the ability to...what you term as *heal* living tissue. Actually, it is the ability to transfer energy at the cellular level through physical contact...If there isn't too much damage."

"There are stories of some in our species that are purported to have that same ability," Padrino added.

"You all have it…to some degree…from our DNA. You just haven't evolved far enough, yet, to know how to use it on demand…Vesta sensed your latent ability, that's why he enlisted you to help restore his Rania."

"I think ya'll are way above my pay grade…How have you been able to survive here in all those years since the crash?"

"Well, I took our locator sub-space beacon, a small cold fusion power generator, some carbon crystals…ones that you call diamonds…and a supply of gold we use with thorium in creating our inertialess antigravity drive from our craft before the townspeople arrived on the scene."

"Is that how you were able to buy this property just after the turn of the century."

"No…actually I pretended I was a mute abandoned child. The Wilson family near Aurora took me in and shortly thereafter we moved here to Cross Timbers County…I learned your language and when the Wilsons died in the flu epidemic of 1918…I couldn't save them…I inherited this place…and that's when I set up the locator beacon…"

***

347

CHAPTER FOURTEEN

GLOBAL ENERGY WAREHOUSE

Williams, Reid, Pelosi, Farlow and the four crew, were all dressed in gray and black BDU camos and were checking their weapons and ammo—the roughnecks had AK-47s.

Reid loaded another magazine for his UZI. Williams and Pelosi each were snapping magazines together in spring steel adapters for their AR-15s. Farlow checked the wiring connections on two small beer-can size canisters of napalm with attached timers.

"When these things go off, all hell's goin' to break loose...no more house, no more barn...They'll go up like a couple boxes of matches," said Farlow.

"Just make sure we have enough time to get the hell out."

"Ain't my first rodeo, Williams."

"Yeah, just wanted to make sure it wasn't the last...for all of us."

LUCY'S YARD

"...and you were able to blend in?" asked Bone.

"Of course, other than my size, there isn't much difference...You see, we actually seeded your planet with our DNA over three million years ago and periodically added to it as you developed. The last two times was some one hundred thousand years ago with the Cro-Magnon and then ten thousand years ago at the end of your last ice age...This is why we watch over you...Tellus was one of the first places we visited when we developed our ability to travel on an interstellar basis. The Sumerians referred to us as the Anunnaki...It means 'seed from the sky'."

"You're our ancestors?...That would blow the creationist's skirts up."

"Well, not necessarily...You see, it's written on the Great Obelisk..."

"The what?" Bone asked.

"It's what we call the Great Obelisk...you can compare it to your Bible or Torah...if you wish. It's inscribed upon it that our destiny is to populate this galaxy with the human species...which we have been doing in increments for millennia...Divine guidance, if you will. When we found a suitable humanoid form...of which there were quite a number...our instructions from the Holy Entity were clear...We infused the best with our DNA, and then let nature take its course."

"Then what you're saying is that spontaneous creation and evolution are, in actuality...one in the same," Padrino offered.

Lucy nodded. "As yet, most of your species has no concept of time. What you interpret from your Bible as spontaneous creation was to us millions of years and to the Entity...but the blink of an eye."

"I'm confused," said Bone.

"Why am I not surprised?" quipped Padrino.

"So you believe in God?" asked Bone.

"The Holy Entity? Of course…don't you?"

"Well, sure, but…"

"Bone, the best way to get out of a hole is to stop digging."

Lucy giggled. "I thought it was interesting that the three million year old fossilized hominid, Australopithecus afarensis, discovered in 1974 in Ethiopia, was named *Lucy* by your scientists."

"Yes, the hominid was nicknamed after the Beatles song *Lucy in the Sky with Diamonds*," added Padrino

"Now that's spooky," Bone said.

"Your science has only recently proven that every Homo Sapiens on the Earth carries the mitochondrial DNA from one single woman…"

"So there was an Eve?" said Padrino.

"In a manner of speaking."

"I'm still gettin' a headache."

Lucy placed her hands on both sides of his head. There was a brief blue glow. "How's that?…Better?"

Bone blinked several times. "Uh, yes, ma'am. Thank you…That's just slicker than a greased baby's butt."

She grinned and continued, "Anyway, since my ELT beacon's wave travels in sub-space, it doesn't exceed the speed of light. It takes the wave a little less than hundred years to reach my world of Tyrin…"

"You named your dog after your world?"

She nodded. "I am expecting a rescue craft anytime…so, you can see, I can't leave this location. The Reptoids or Global Energy could ruin everything and prevent me from getting home."

"ET phone home…Yeah, my gut tells me they're not done…Either one." said Bone.

"That's what I fear. I have to be in this location and wearing what you would call my space suit."

"You kept it?" asked Padrino.

"Of course…Just a moment, I'll show it to you."

Lucy walked over to a cedar chest in a nearby shed, opened it and took out a one-piece gray hooded body suit with built-in large almond-shaped black eye lenses. She held it up for them to see…

GLOBAL ENERGY WAREHOUSE

Williams and his crew finished loading up in their vehicles. The overhead door was raised and they drove out. The three vehicle caravan led by Williams' SUV turned on to I-35 and headed north for Cross Timbers County…

LUCY'S YARD

Bone jumped up from the bench. "Holy cow! That looks exactly like the drawings I've seen…And they were right on with that TV show SG 1."

"And very similar to the Aldebarian's suits, but they weren't wearing the helmet," added Padrino.

"The helmet or hood can get tiresome after a while, as you can imagine…Earth's atmosphere is similar to ours and provides some protection…Without it, I can still get a sunburn."

"Still a neat getup," said Bone.

"Of course we have been seen on occasion. The suit is almost indestructible…except for your more primitive high velocity solid projectiles…It has complete telecommunication capability and the large built-in lenses protect our eyes from the unfiltered UV, gamma and cosmic rays in space…They also allow us to see in low light. It serves much the same function as the flight suits your fighter pilots and astronauts wear."

"No wonder you are described as *Grays*...Why didn't your people pick you up since they're apparently still coming here?"

"Undoubtedly they thought we were destroyed as a result of the battle damage to our communicators...The emergency locator beacon only sends a tight, narrow beam to our home world. And due to the earth's rotation, it can only broadcast once a day. Every time it comes into alignment with my world, the transmission is automatically triggered...I wasn't aware they were actually looking for me."

"Vesta and Rania said that your people were looking for you...they knew you had crashed," said Padrino.

"That could very well be...but there would be no way to find me unless they accidentally crossed my beacon during its pulse like the Reptoids did...I think you refer to it as a needle in a haystack."

Bone looked down at her wrist and saw a bracelet identical to the one he found in Aurora. He reached into his shirt pocket and took the other one out and held it up. "This look familiar?"

She took the bracelet from him. "Oh, my...This belonged to Garrin...my mate." Her eyes filled with tears. "Where did you find it?"

"About a hundred yards from the crash site in Aurora. It had apparently been thrown to the base of a limestone outcrop during your crash, where it lay hidden 'til I found it with my handy-dandy metal detector."

"May I keep it?"

"Yes, ma'am, of course...It belongs to you anyway."

Padrino pointed at the bracelet. "What are those symbols?"

"They're our identification codes, similar to your social security card...Except for one thing."

"That would be?"

"Each bracelet has the power to make the wearer invisible to ordinary light waves, by using a fifth order wave vibration for up to an hour...There is a sequence code."

"You'll have to explain what a fifth order wave is sometime...Guess we'll add it to the list with inertialess drive and cosmic energy accumulator."

"Be happy to, but it will take a little while. Your inventor, Nikola Tesla, was very close to discovering it. He had actually discovered forth order waves and correctly assumed there was a fifth."

"Could you show us how it works?"

355

Lucy touched four of the symbols on her bracelet. She shimmered and then disappeared.

"Amazing…A light refraction force field."

"Holy moly!"

There was another shimmer and she reappeared.

"You used that when you came up on the Captain and me when we were hunting."

"Yes, I wanted to see who you were. The field extends outward about three feet…so it included Tyrin as well."

Tyrin looked up from what was left of his beef knuckle, thumped his tail on the ground and whined.

"We don't use the holographic projection like the Aldebarians and Reptoids…we just prefer to be invisible when necessary."

"Uh, Lucy, could I borrow that bracelet back for a bit?…I have something I want to try."

"Certainly, here is the proper sequence of the symbols…" She showed him the correct order. "This is the cancel symbol…You must be wearing it for it to work, but its latch is broken and it has to be in a continuous circuit."

"Oh, I'm pretty handy at fixin' things."

She grinned. "I'm sure you are."

"Ya'll excuse me a moment. I've got to go check in...Be right back." Bone stood up and walked to his truck.

CROSS PD
DETECTIVE'S OFFICE

Loraine sat at her desk proofing a supplemental report when her S4 phone rang. She swiped her thumb across the screen and brought the receiver to her ear. "Inspector Rodriguez...What's up, Bone?" She paused and smiled. "Uh huh...Yeah...Got it...Cool. Sounds like fun. Figured that's where you were...Glad you called, I was getting kinda bored." She pushed the off button on the side after the call disconnected.

"Stella! You and Newman get in here...and go get Peach, Wanda and Moomer.

She picked up her desk phone and hit the intercom button. "Captain...Bone's out at Lucy's...just said to tell you it's show time."

"On my way." St. John hung up, grabbed his paddle holster with his .40 cal S&W M&P and headed to the armory.

LUCY'S YARD

"I feel like I'm looking through my ancestor's eyes."

"You both carry much of our genetics."

Bone walked back to the table. "Padrino, it's almost sundown...We'd better let Lucy get on about her chores and I need to get back to the office."

"Why don't you come back later this evening and pick me up...I'd like to stay and visit with this remarkable lady a little longer..." He turned to her. "If that's all right?"

"I'd love the company."

"I can do that...Ya'll keep your eyes open...Laterbye."

He walked back to his pickup, cranked up and pointed it in the direction of town.

INTERSTATE 35

The three Global Energy vehicles from the warehouse, were still in the convoy headed toward Cross. They would be turning west on Hwy 922 when they reached the town of Valley View. The jeep with Reid and Pelosi was in the lead.

"What's our ETA?" Reid asked from the shotgun seat.

"'Bout an hour...It'll be dark thirty by then."

"Perfect. This shouldn't take long...You buyin'?"

"Thought it was your turn," said Pelosi as he lit a cigarette.

"Crack your window a bit. You smokers never have any consideration...Ever hear of second-hand smoke?...Stuff'll kill you."

"Aw, screw you," he said as he powered his window down halfway.

LUCY'S HOUSE

Lucy and Padrino sat at her round oak claw-foot dining table enjoying a meal he had prepared.

"Your cold fusion generator is remarkable...Our scientists' conventional wisdom says it's impossible."

Lucy laughed. "They also said your world was the center of the universe...that a man would die if he exceeded the speed of sound...and the most humorous of all that global warming was going to destroy the planet. Eventually they'll realize that climate is cyclical...always has been and most likely always will be."

"Conventional wisdom is usually just that...conventional... with blinders. If they didn't discover it...it doesn't exist or their findings depend upon who's funding their grant."

She nodded and daubed her mouth with her napkin. "Your chicken chili is wonderful, Padrino."

"Thank you, my Queen..."

"I think we can dispense with the Queen title...Don't you? Just call me Annuna or better yet...Lucy is what I've grown accustomed to."

He laughed. "I apologize...Lucy, but all my life, I have studied your visits to my people and of your attempts to rid our society of the barbaric practice of human sacrifice."

"That was the one thing we couldn't seem to get the Nasca to abandon...And I think it proved to be their, as well as the Mayan civilization's, downfall..."

Tyrin got up from under the table growling.

Padrino looked down. "Bone must be coming back."

"I don't think so…He has never growled at him and he already knows the sound of his vehicle…I think my other visitors are back."

"You're right…Let's kill the lights."

The convoy of the Global Energy mercenaries moved slowly down the ranch road—their running lights out. The moon would not rise for several more hours and with Lucy's ranch far from any town, there was little to no light pollution. The stars resembled thousands of tiny campfires spread across the sky.   They pulled off the road and parked a few hundred yards from her house—behind the hill from which they had been spying on her. Williams, Farlow, Reid, Pelosi and the four roughnecks got out of their vehicles and readied their weapons.

Reid held his two napalm IEDs. "I'm setting the timers at three minutes." He held a red-lensed Mag Lite in his teeth.

"All right, everybody knows what to do…" said Williams. "Let's spread out and take care of business."

They moved into a line abreast formation and crept toward the house and barn. When they were about thirty yards from their vehicles, the front end of the jeep Pelosi and Reid had driven exploded in a cloud of steam—the hood flying straight up into the air and flipping end-over-end. The blast was followed two seconds later by an echoing loud boom of a distant .50 BMG rifle.

Lucy and Padrino both jumped up from the table when they heard the rifle's report.

"Down, Lucy! Get down!" He grabbed her and pulled her to the floor and under the table next to Tyrin.

"I think everything is all right, Padrino."

Tyrin covered his broad muzzle with both paws.

Williams and the others turned around and stared at the destroyed jeep, steam was still spewing from large hole in the radiator.

"What the hell?" exclaimed Williams.

Farlow looked at William's chest. "You've got a problem."

He looked down at three red dots forming a triangle and then he looked over at Farlow and saw two red dots on his cohort's chest. "We both do."

He glanced down. "Oh, shit!"

Moomer lay prone on the ground at the top of a hill, a little over a half mile away behind a Barrett M82A1 .50 cal sniper rifle with a Morovision night scope. A wisp of smoke curled from the muzzlebrake.

Officer Wanda Stanton was lying beside him as spotter, with a monocular night vision spotting scope and laser range finder. She looked through the eyepiece. "Dead center of the radiator."

"Well, yeah, Wanda...It's only a thousand yards."

All the other mercenaries stared at red dots on their chests. Reid glanced at the timers on the napalm canisters.

"Oh, God! Oh, God!" He threw them as far as he could and started running back to the other two vehicles. Just before he reached the SUV's, a line of automatic fire stitched the earth in front of him. He dove to the ground, rolled over once and began firing his Uzi blindly into the darkness.

The roughnecks also began shooting into the blackness. Two of the hired thugs took hits from the returning fire and went down.

There was a loud blast from a nearby .50 cal handgun. The massive muzzle flash that lit up the entire area seemed to come out of thin air. A third roughneck came off the ground—flew backward five feet, smashed down hard and never moved again.

There was another tremendous boom and the ground just inches in front of Reid' face exploded, covering his face and eyes with dirt.

From the darkness came Bone's commanding voice, "Throw your weapons down! NOW!"

All the others complied.

Loraine called out, "On your knees, hands behind your head! Do it!"

They quickly did as she ordered as the red dots remained on their chests. Loraine, Stella, Newman, St. John and Peach rose up out of the grass like wraiths.

Car lights suddenly came on behind the officers and Sheriff Brennan stepped forward from his county vehicle.

Everyone but the Sheriff was dressed in black BDU's, black tiger-striped face camo and were equipped with the latest military issue night vision equipment. They were holding MP-5's or M-16's with laser sights still pointed at the mercenaries. Former DEA agent, recently elected sheriff, Will Brennan was dressed in his brown and tan county uniform and his trademark silver-belly Stetson. He lighted his cigar.

"Just who the hell are you, anyway?" asked Williams from his knees.

"We're the welcome wagon," said Stella.

Bone materialized just in front of Williams, with his .50 cal. pistol—equipped with a Crimson Trace laser—pointed at William's forehead. "Looks like you're a real slow learner...Slick."

"Jesus H. Christ! You again...Where the hell did you come from?" He looked around, then back at Bone.

"Oh, I had the Asgard beam me down..."

"What?"

Reid was on his knees, trying to get the dirt out of his eyes.

"What did you set the timers on, asshole?" Bone asked Reid.

"Three minutes."

Bone looked at his watch. "Damn...Everybody down!"

They dove to the ground just as the napalm canisters exploded one after the other in two gigantic fireballs thirty yards away where Reid had thrown them—the flames lit up the countryside.

Padrino, Lucy and Tyrin walked out on the porch and watched the fires.

"I knew Bone would be here."

"As did I…He doesn't know it yet, but he's a sender as well as a receiver."

"I know."

The officers got back to their feet. When Bone glanced over at the fires, Williams scrambled up and sprinted for his SUV in desperation.

"Bone!" Stella yelled.

He spun around and saw the man running. He pitched his 500 to Loraine. "Hold this, be right back."

Sheriff Brennan leveled his M-16 at the other bad guys still on their knees. "Simon says, everybody freeze."

Bone sprinted and caught Williams just as he arrived at the Suburban and tackled him to the ground. Williams twisted free, jumped up in a martial arts stance.

Bone laughed. "You really are a slow learner, slick…Resisting arrest can be dangerous to your health."

"I'm gonna show you how this is done, big man."

"I love it when people say that...Go ahead dummy...Any time..." Bone threw a straight John Wayne jab into his nose that knocked him back against the truck. "Let me know when you're ready to start."

Williams bounced off the fender, and tried several punches and strikes which Bone rapidly blocked. Then he stepped back one step and attempted a spin kick. Bone caught his foot in midair, gave it a quick twist, throwing the hapless thug to his back.

Williams sprang up quickly. Bone skillfully swept his feet out from under him and he slammed into the ground again, harder than before. Bone calmly placed his foot on the man's neck and grinned.

"Now, last time I checked, I weighed somewhere around 280 pounds...I don't think you really want me putting a lot of that on this foot...Do you?

Williams wheezed out a, "No."

"Then say calf rope and I'll let you up while you can still breathe."

"What?"

"I said, say calf rope."

"Ca...calf...rope."

Bone reached down and grabbed Williams by the front of his BDU blouse, lifted him to his feet and pushed him back toward the others.

Moomer and Wanda drove up on a four-wheel ATV. She rode behind him and carried the big Barrett.

"Nice shootin', Moomer."

"Nothin' to it, Bone...Had a good spotter."

"That's what it takes."

"You're just saying that 'cause it's true, Moom," said Wanda, almost embarrassed.

"Did we miss some more fun?" asked Moomer.

Loraine replied, "Not really." She pointed at Williams. "This nabob here just had a case of temporary insanity...He's over it now."

Will stepped forward and pointed to the six star badge pinned on his shirt. "All right, all the rest of you inbreeds...on your feet. I'm Sheriff Brennan of Cross Timbers county and you're all under arrest for terrorist activities, unlawful discharge of pyrotechnic devices, attempted murder, conspiracy to commit murder, possession of illegal firearms, resisting arrest...and anything damn thing else we can think of when we get back to town."

Bone glared at the mercs. "You egg suckers are lucky Sheriff Brennan is in charge here...I'da killed you where you stand and let God sort it out."

"Captain, think we got enough handcuffs?"

"If we don't, I bet we can find some bailing twine...or rusty barb wire...Loraine, you guys start cuffing and reading these miscreants their rights...Peach, you gather up their weapons."

"Bless your heart, Captain, can I keep 'em?"

"They go in the evidence locker, Peach," St. John replied.

"I know...Can't blame a girl for askin'."

"Oh, and Loraine, better radio an EMT for those two over there. And the ME for the other one. When Bone shoots somebody with that 500...they stay shot."

"All right...But, I think we ought to leave 'em for the coyotes, though."

"What's a miscreant?" Farlow asked

"It means you weren't born...you were poured from a colostomy bag."

Padrino, Lucy and Tyrin walked up. The pit bull moved over to Farlow, lifted his leg and urinated on him.

Farlow jumped back. "Son-of-a-bitch!...I thought I killed that damn dog.

"You tried...but, he has remarkable tenacity...as well as a good memory," Lucy commented.

Tyrin woofed.

"I still want to know where the big man came from. One minute he wasn't there, the next he was," said Williams.

"You ever heard the song, "Lucy in the Sky with Diamonds?" asked Bone.

"Well, yeah."

"There you go."

"Huh?"

Bone walked over to Lucy and held out his left hand. The bracelet was latched around two of his fingers. "Here, Lucy...Thanks. Worked like a charm, I used some links from a gold necklace I had and soldered the latch back together."

Lucy slid the bracelet off his fingers. "I was wondering how you were going to do it."

"Where there's a will, there's a way." He winked.

***

CHAPTER FIFTEEN

CROSS POLICE DEPARTMENT

Bone replaced a cup of coffee on St. John's desk with an identical cup. He took the old one with him as he exited the office and headed down to hall to his own. He passed St. John as he came out of the head. "Hey, Cap'n, everything come out all right?"

"None of your damn business...What are you grinnin' at, Bone?"

"Oh, nothin'. It's just a great day."

"You're up to somethin', aren't you?"

Bone got a hurt look on his face and placed his hand over his heart. "Moi?"

"Forget it."

St. John entered his office and shut the door.

Bone went into his own office, sat at his desk and started working on the booking reports for the Global Energy mercenaries. Loraine was at her desk across the room doing the apprehension supplemental reports for the Sheriff's department.

"Don't know why we're doin' all this damn paperwork... The Feds will be here tomorrow to take those maggots off our hands," he said.

"We have to give them a good civil rights violation case as well as trespassing, attempted arson, assault on officers of the law, possession of destructive devices, illegal weapons and the terrorist aspect," commented Loraine.

"Yeah, save the county some money."

"What about Davis?"

"Ranger Carmichael said they were serving an arrest warrant on him this morning."

"More paperwork...Speak of the devil." She indicated the hallway.

The sheriff passed by the open door with a handcuffed Jeff Davis. Brennan stepped back and stuck his head in the doorway.

"Rangers delivered Mister Big this morning. Want me to take him on down to booking?"

"Yeah, let him cool his heels a while in the tank," said Loraine.

"Works for me," Brennan said as he continued down the hall with Davis.

"God bless the Texas Rangers," said Bone as he went back to his paperwork.

Down the hall, St. John was doing his own paperwork. He subconsciously picked up his cup and brought it to his lips and started to take a sip—a stream of coffee dribbled from a tiny hole in the side of the cup onto his new paisley tie and light blue shirt.

From down the hallway and through a closed door came the Captain's scream, "DAMN YOU, BONE!"

"What did you do now?" Loraine asked nonchalantly.

Bone feigned innocence again.

She grinned and shook her head. "You think Lucy and Tyrin will be all right now?"

"Oh, I think so."

Stella walked in with a small package a little larger than a shoe box wrapped in brown paper tied with a white string. "This box was in the break room this morning, Bone. There's no delivery notice, but it has your name on it...It's heavy...to be such a small package."

She set it on Bone's desk. He picked it up, looked all over it and finally saw a small capital *L* on one corner.

"It's from Lucy." He continued to stare at the box.

"Well, open it," Loraine prodded.

He pulled his Uncle Henry knife from his pocket, opened it, cut the string, sliced the packing tape and removed an envelope from inside. He opened it, took out two documents, unfolded and read them to himself. "Well, slap Aunt Gussie in the face..."

"What?" asked Stella.

"It's the deed to Lucy's ranch and the title to her Cord...Made out to me!"

"You're kidding," said Loraine as she got to her feet and walked over to Bone's desk.

"Not likely...Wait, there's also a small bag..." He took out a dark blue velvet bag, opened the draw strings and dumped the entire contents on his top of his desk pad. "Suffering Mother of Jesus!…Diamonds!…A whole handful."

Stella rushed over. "Let me see…" She gasped. "Oh…my God!"

He looked back in the box. "The car keys to her 1930 Cord, a bracelet…in my size…some long gold bars and a note…" He unfolded the hand-printed note and began reading, *"MY DEAR BONE, THIS PACKAGE IS JUST A SMALL TOKEN OF MY APPRECIATION FOR YOUR HELP. I KNOW YOU'LL SHARE THE CONTENTS WITH PADRINO, YOUR CAPTAIN AND THE REST OF YOUR FRIENDS WHO HELPED. I ALSO THOUGHT YOU MIGHT HAVE NEED AGAIN FOR THE BRACELET SOMETIME, I HAD SOME EXTRA LINKS ADDED BY MY PEOPLE.*

REMEMBER, I TOLD YOU TO NEVER SAY NEVER. I HOPE YOU ENJOY THE AUTOMOBILE, I KNOW YOU'LL TAKE CARE OF IT.

I HAVE TO LEAVE NOW, BUT, I WOULD ASK OF YOU ONE LAST FAVOR. I CAN'T TAKE TYRIN. I KNOW YOU'LL GIVE HIM A GOOD HOME. YOU HAVE A WONDERFUL HEART. MAYBE I CAN COME BACK FOR A VISIT SOME DAY. WE DO STILL KEEP AN EYE ON YOUR PLANET, WAITING

FOR THE TIME WHEN YOU HAVE MATURED ENOUGH TO JOIN OUR FEDERATION. YOU STILL HAVE SOME EVOLVING TO DO. MY BEST TO ALL, LUCY."

Bone took the bracelet, and gold bars out of the box and laid them on his desk. The keys he added to his key ring.

"Is she talking about our Bone?" asked an incredulous Loraine.

Stella looked over his shoulder and then up at Loraine. "I'd say so."

"Well, if this doesn't beat all...I need to go out there. Tyrin is probably upset...Anybody going with me?"

Bone got up and started to the door.

Loraine grabbed her bag. "Undomesticated equines..."

Stella finished for her, "...couldn't keep us away...Lead on, o' ye of wonderful heart."

"Don't get smart, little bit..." He stopped and turned to Loraine. "Undomesticated equines?"

"Yeah...And if you try to use that bracelet to get in the ladies bathroom...I'll shoot you right between the eyes."

"Would I do that?"

"Do I need to answer that?"

LUCY'S YARD

The sun had set and it was another moonless night by the time Bone and the others got out to Lucy's. Tyrin just sat in the yard, looking up at the sky and softly whining.

Peach knelt beside the big dog and put her arm around his muscular shoulders. "It's all right, boy."

Bone, Loraine, Padrino, Stella, Newman, and St. John also looked up into the sky in the direction of Orion.

"She was really from another planet?" Stella asked.

Padrino put his arm around her. "So it would seem, Stella...So it would seem."

"Where is Daniel Jackson when you need him?" commented Bone. He slowly brought his hand to his brow and saluted. "Via con Dios, Lucy." He knelt down and put his hand on the faithful dog's head. "Let's go home, Tyrin..." He looked around. "On second thought...I guess we are home."

A large silver triangle space craft moved across the star-speckled sky out beyond the orbit of Earth's moon—also in the direction of the constellation Orion. A distortion appeared in front of it—the craft entered. There was a quick bright flash and the giant disappeared…

***

CHAPTER SIXTEEN

INSIDE JUPITER ORBIT
CALLISTO

A small greenish globular craft appeared out of a distortion near Jupiter's moon, Callisto.

Two creatures with four arm-like appendages, each with four tentacle-like fingers stood on two elephantine legs at a console in the center of the craft—they had no necks. Their snake-like heads with alligator jaws sat directly on top of their square scaly green torsos. Four eyes were on short prehensile stalks that were capable of directing each of the four tentacle arms independently. Their speech was a series of clicks and consonants.

"Set the electromagnetic detectors and shields at maximum. The hated Tryranians are surely on patrol in this sector," said Rdydl, the larger of the two.

"Should I activate the cloaking device?" asked his copilot, Klyn.

"No, it consumes too much power. We'll activate only when necessary. Possibly we can slip through their net surrounding the third planet."

Their craft shuddered violently…

A triangle-shaped silver craft emerged from behind Callisto and fired a purple force beam, striking the globular craft. The shield of the sphere flared to violet. The globe instantly returned fire with a green pulse laser.

The shield of the triangle craft flared a bright orange as an identical vessel emerged from behind the small moon.

The tentacles of the creatures flashed over the symbols on their large flat screen.

"Engage the cloaking device…now!" ordered Rdydl

The globular craft suddenly disappeared as its shield flared into a frenzy of violet shades from the dual fire of pure beams of force from the two triangle ships.

Two small Tyranian gray creatures inside one of the flat triangle vessels looked at each other and communicated telepathically.

"Did our combined fire vaporize the Reptoid vessel?"

"There is no data to indicate if their vessel was destroyed or went to hyperspace. There is no sensor data at all. It's possible they finally have a cloaking device as we do."

"Log the encounter and notify Central to increase surveillance, we are returning to patrol."

The two craft turned under impulse power and headed back toward Calisto.

FIRST STATE BANK
CROSS, TEXAS

Bone and Loraine took cover behind his silver-gray pickup—weapons drawn as four masked armed robbers exited the bank with money bags.

Bone rose to a firing position from behind the front fender with his S&W 500 revolver. "Freeze, assholes!"

She moved into position from the back of the vehicle with her Kimber .45 cal 1911A. "Drop 'em!...Don't be stupid."

One of the bandits lunged to grab a woman who was exiting her car.

The .50 cal in Bone's hand recoiled from the loud *boom*.

The man was slammed back against the side of the brick building from the force of the shot. He collapsed down into a motionless heap. The woman screamed as a light yellow puddle collected at her feet.

Bone yelled, "Get down!"

She quickly dropped to the sidewalk as another of the bandits turned to fire his shotgun at the big detective. Loraine squeezed off a quick double tap. The crook took both rounds in the chest, two millimeters apart and went down.

"Anybody else?" Bone demanded.

The other two bandits dropped their weapons.

"On your face! Hands behind your head!" Loraine ordered.

They dropped to their stomachs and clasped their hands behind their heads.

A news van from KTEN pulled into the parking area of the bank. Newscaster, Lisanne Adamson quickly exited along with her cameraman.

GLOBULAR CRAFT

The moon flashed by as the Earth got larger and larger in the viewscreen. The cloaked craft pushed the thin atmosphere in front of it, creating a crescent shaped distortion with eddies and swirls behind. The atmosphere began to glow slightly from the velocity of the invisible craft.

The vessel continued its long arc through the mesosphere, the stratosphere and finally the troposphere, punching a temporary hole in the cloud cover.

The velocity of the globular ship slowed almost to a hover over a rural farm in the north Texas county of Cross Timbers, and then settled to the ground behind a barn—creating a disturbance of dust and flattening the grass.

"Disengage the cloaking apparatus," said Rdydl.

"Apparatus disengaged," confirmed Klyn.

"This is the last reported general vicinity where scout unit K-225 was when they disappeared."

"It's possible the same Tyranian patrol we encountered destroyed them before they could cloak."

"Possible, but not likely...It is fortunate there is a source of P-239 in the area also. We must replenish our fuel stores."

A twelve year old boy was near the barn, teaching his dog to catch a frisbee. The dog barked at the pale green metallic ball just becoming visible behind the youth. He turned around.

"Whoa! Where the heck did that come from?"

A portal opened up in the side of the craft. A vapor issued from inside as the door hissed open. Rdydl appeared at the opening, stepped out to the ground on his elephantine legs. He held a pipe looking device attached to one of his four arms.

The boy stared, stunned for a moment, and then started backing away.   "Run, Sparky!"

As they turned to run, Rdydl pointed the tube device. The boy and dog glowed green briefly in mid-stride and instantly vaporized. Rdydl shuffled forward as Klyn followed and they moved toward the nearby farmhouse.

FIRST STATE BANK
CROSS, TEXAS

Patrol officers Stella Johnson and Joel Newman were putting the two surviving bank robbers in the back of a squad car.

"Let's go sunshine," she said as she pushed the man's head down to clear the door.

Lisanne was interviewing Bone and Loraine as two assistant MEs loaded the bodies in an EMT ambulance.

RURAL FARM

The farmer lunged for his shotgun above the fireplace mantle. Klyn vaporized him in mid-air. The man's wife entered just in time to see her husband disappear in a green cloud. She screamed and started backing into the kitchen. Rdydl and Klyn followed. She fainted and collapsed to the floor.

A small TV was playing on the counter beneath a cabinet. On screen, Bone and Loraine were being interviewed by Lisanne.

Rdydl gazed at the screen for a moment. "I think we can use those two humanoids for our holographic images to blend in with these soft and puny Tellurians. I'll take the larger. You may have the smaller with the odd protuberances on the front."

They each manipulated an attached device on one of their long snakelike appendages—Rdydl and Klyn holographically became exact copies of Bone and Loraine.

"Attach the neural transmitter to this creature that we may learn their language," directed Rdydl/Bone.

Klyn/Loraine attached a small device to the front and back of the woman's head. They paused for several moments. The farmer's wife eyes opened wide, she spasmed violently and then died.

"The woman has ceased to be…We have all her knowledge…This is an unbelievably abysmal language," observed Rdydl/Bone.

"I agree. So primitive, so many words to say the same thing," agreed Klyn/Loraine

"Retrieve the coordinates for that P-239 storage facility nearby. We don't have enough power to get out of this solar system, much less activate a warp to get back to our home world. The new cloaking device is much more energy intensive than we anticipated, plus our little encounter with the Tyranians drained much of our reserve."

"We only need a few ounces. If these primitives knew how to utilize P-239 at 100% conversion as we do, they would be dangerous. After we re-power, we can continue our search for our friends."

"It is unusual for Cldyl not to report in…There is a wheeled vehicle outside. We'll take that."

Outside, the two disguised Raptoids got in a tan '96 Chevy pickup with a blue replacement door on the driver's side. Rdydl started the engine—they pulled out of the yard and headed to the road.

CROSS POLICE STATION
ST. JOHN'S OFFICE

Bone had a roll of clear double stick carpet tape and his pocket knife. He cut several strips and placed them in parallel on the extra cushion pad in the captain's chair. Finished, he put the rest of the roll in his pocket with his knife and walked out the door whistling the marching song of the 7th Cavalry, *Garryowen*.

He met Loraine coming out of the ladies' room.

"Hey, girl, everything come out all right?"

"Kiss my ass, Bone…You just get back here from lunch?"

"Oh, been here a few minutes…Had your coffee?"

"Going to get some now."

"Black. I'm gonna get started on the supplementals for that fracas this morning."

"Who waits on you when I'm not around?"

Bone just gave her his look, blew her a little kiss and headed to his office.

St. John walked out of the Chief's office and down the hallway toward his.

"Afternoon, Cap'n."

"Right…Nice work on that bank 211 this morning, Bone. You started on the novel you're gonna submit?"

"On the way, boss."

"Sometime today," St. John said over his shoulder as he turned into his office.

He started shuffling the stack of papers on his desk, reached for his coffee cup, slightly lifting it up and looking under it to make sure it was not glued to the blotter. He picked it up, got to his feet and headed to the door—his chair pad stuck to his butt.

St. John ambled down the hallway to the break room with his cup. He passed several uniformed officers who greeted him with nods. As they passed, they turned and looked at the him walking down the hall—wide grins appeared on their faces.

He met Loraine coming out of the break room with a cup in each hand.

"Afternoon, sir…" She glanced down then back up and tried to stifle a grin.

"What?"

"I'll never understand men's fashion."

St. John looked down and behind, saw the chair pad stuck to his rear. "Damn you, Bone!…" Then quietly he mumbled, "Paybacks are hell."

GOVERNOR'S LOUNGE

Bone, Loraine, Stella Peach, Newman and St. John sat around a circular table just off the small dance floor.

"Gotta go see a man about a dog. Be right back," said Bone as he got up and made his way to the rest room.

St. John waited until he was out of sight and pulled out a bottle of Tabasco from his coat. He took Bone's beer bottle and dumped a good slug of the fiery sauce in it. The others just looked and grinned.

"Pay backs are hell."

"Bless his heart, it's about time somebody paid him back for one of his pranks," said Peach.

"I think you should have put more in," added Stella.

St. John glanced at her, grabbed the bottle and added another slug for good measure.

"Here he comes," warned Newman.

Bone walked back to the table pulled his chair out and sat down. "Miss me?"

"Oh, were you gone?" popped back Loraine.

He picked up his beer and chugalugged the entire bottle.

"Damn, that's good...Vertis, need another round."

The owner, Vertis Jolley, an attractive middle-aged woman with premature gray hair was wiping down the bar. "Why don't I just run a hose over there?"

"Damn, why didn't I think of that?" He belched loudly.

The others looked at him then at each other and shook their heads.

"Hey, Bone, where were you and Loraine going this afternoon? I passed you out on 678 and you didn't even wave," said Newman.

"Yeah, ya'll gettin' stuck up in your old age?...Or just goin' blind?" asked Stella with a big grin.

"Excuse me? Loraine and I were in the office all afternoon doing supplementals on that 211."

"We came straight here from the office," added Loraine.

"Now look, I know it was ya'll. You were in a tan Chevy pickup with a blue driver's door...I even honked. You looked straight at us."

"Well, we must have a couple of dopplegangers out there, 'cause we never left the office...and neither one of us has a tan pickup."

"OMG! One Bone is enough," Stella chimed back.

"I'll second that," added St. John.

BONE'S RANCH HOUSE

Bone walked in, Padrino glanced up over his reading glasses from his recliner then back down at the copy of *Haunted Falls* he was still reading. Tyrin was lying at his feet, also paying no attention to him.

"Tyrin ignores me and you don't speak?"

"That's like the pot calling the kettle black," Padrino replied still not looking up.

"Come again?...What are you talkin' about?"

He finally looked up. "You and Loraine almost ran me over at Hunter's station...and where the hell did you get a tan pickup?"

"This is startin' to get weird."

"How's that?"

"You're the second person that says they saw Loraine and me in a tan pickup today...What time was it?"

"'Bout six."

"No way. Loraine and I were in the Governor's Lounge knocking back a few after work with the captain and half the shift."

"I think I know you when I see you...I'm not that old."

"We won't go into that...What are the chances of having someone that looks like exactly like me with someone that looks exactly like Loraine?" His cell rang with the tune of Bob Seger's *Old Time Rock and Roll.* "Bone."

"Bone, have you lost your mind?"

"That's probably open to debate...What's up, Cap'n?"

"I just got a message from dispatch on you."

"'Bout what?"

"You got gas at Hunter's and drove off without paying...in a tan pickup with a blue door."

"Around 6 pm?"

"Right...Hey, wait a minute. We were all at the Governor's Lounge at that time."

"I know...Padrino was at Hunter's and someone that looked like me almost ran him down...Something's goin' on here. Startin' to sound like Twilight Zone."

"I'll put out a BOLO on that truck."

NRC CROSS TIMBERS FACILITY ROAD

The tan pickup cruised slowly past the fence of the Nuclear Regulatory Commission Facility. The Bone and Loraine doubles scanned the area with an alien type of Geiger counter. Klyn/Loraine studied the small LED screen.

"I'm getting a high radiation signature from the interior of the large building."

"High enough to be P-239?" asked Rdydl/Bone.

"Yes."

BONE'S RANCH HOUSE

Bone punched in Loraine's number.

She answered on the third ring. "What?"

"You asleep, pard?

"Let me check…Nope, I was, but some jerk-off just called.

"That would be?"

"You're the detective, you figure it out."

"Love you, too."

"Now that I'm awake, what do you want?"

"Padrino said we almost ran him over at Hunter's around six and the Captain said we drove off without paying."

"Dip stick, we were at the Governor's Lounge."

"Exactly."

"What the hell's goin' on?"

"I don't know, but we're fixin' to find out…pick you up in thirty…Laterbye.

Bone slipped his Galaxy S4 in his pocket, walked over to a credenza and opened a drawer. He took out the bracelet from Lucy and put it on. One of the stones in the bracelet instantly began to glow. "What the hell? Never done that before…Damn, wish she had sent an instruction manual."

"Wait…as I recall, Lucy said the bracelet performs many functions, including alien proximity warning. Remember…she said they got along with most alien races except for the Reptoids," said Padrino.

"You think this could…"

"I think it's a high probability."

"Why do I have a really bad feeling about this?"

Tyrin looked up at him and whined.

***

CHAPTER SEVENTEEN

NRC CROSS TIMBERS FACILITY ROAD

A Cross Timbers County Sheriff patrol unit cruised past the NRC Facility. He passed the tan pickup with the blue door parked along side the road. There were the silhouettes of two people sitting inside.

The deputy picked up his mike. "Dispatch, Unit 28."

"Unit 28 go ahead, Richard."

"Got a visual on that BOLO for a tan truck with the blue door, Holly."

"10-4, what's your 20?"

"Just outside the NRC facility, FM 904."

"10-4, 28, stand by."

CROSS TIMBERS COUNTY
SHERIFF OFFICE, DISPATCH

Dispatcher Holly Stuart, a twenty something black girl, dialed a number on her phone unit and waited for two rings. A voice answered.

"Captain St. John, sheriff dispatch."

"Yeah, whatcha got, Holly?"

"We have a visual on that tan pickup BOLO, any instructions?"

"What's the location?"

"FM 904, parked near the NRC Facility."

"Have the deputy ID the occupants and call me back."

"You got it, Captain."

She disconnected the call and pressed another button on the comm panel. "Unit 28, dispatch."

"Unit 28, go ahead," Deputy Green responded.

"Cross PD requests ID on the occupants of the tan pickup."

"Roger that...28 out."

NRC CROSS TIMBERS FACILITY ROAD

The sheriff's cruiser executed a u-turn on the roadway and pulled up behind the truck a little over twenty feet and popped his red and blue flashing lights.

He could easily see the two occupants through the rear glass of the truck from the beam of his headlights and his bar light. Deputy Green exited his patrol vehicle and started walking toward the pickup. He recognized Bone's face clearly in the reflection in the large outside rearview mirror mounted on the side of the truck.

The two aliens—as Bone and Loraine—sat calmly in the front seat—Rdydl/Bone watched him walk toward the truck in the mirror.

"Eliminate him."

Klyn/Loraine slid the rear glass open and pointed her right arm at the unsuspecting deputy.

Green heard the partition slide open. He looked over and saw what he believed to be Loraine pointing her arm with a unusual tube in her hand at him. His Marine Corps training and combat experience in

Afghanistan served him well as he instinctively dived to the right ditch just a split second before she discharged her weapon.

As often happens in combat and other instances when there is an instantaneous flood of adrenaline, everything slowed down for the deputy as he dove through the air. He could see the end of the pipe weapon glow green. For a brief instant, the arm disappeared and the scaly tentacle arm of the Reptoid was visible. *Holy Mother of God! What in hell is that?*

Behind him, the patrol car glowed green briefly and then vanished in a vapor. *This ain't happening!* Green rolled into the ditch, rapidly belly-crawled away and disappeared into the darkness as the pickup started up and drove off—spraying gravel behind.

Green made it underneath some brush and watched the truck drive away—he keyed the mike attached to his shirt. "Dispatch, dispatch! 28!"

"Dispatch, what happened, Richard?"

"Shots fired…Well uh, I think I was fired upon, I… uh, hell, I don't know…Uh, officer needs assistance."

"Is your unit damaged?"

"It's gone!"

"They stole it?"

"No, dammit! It's just gone!

"Gone where?

"How the hell do I know? It's just gone…disappeared, vanished, poof!…It was Bone and Loraine. Repeat…officer needs assistance, Code 3! Code 3!"

"Bone and Loraine? Verify, 28."

"I say again, Detectives Darrell Bone and Loraine Rodriguez…and they made my unit disappear! Loraine pointed something at it and it…it vanished."

"Uh, 10-4, 28…I think."

CROSS TIMBERS COUNTY
SHERIFF OFFICE, DISPATCH

"All units, all units, officer needs assistance, uh, Code 999. FM 904 near NRC Facility. Say again, Code 999. FM 904 near NRC Facility."

The phone on the night stand rang. David St. John rolled over.

"Who is it?" his wife Beverly asked.

"Don't know yet." He picked up the receiver. "St. John."

"Captain, this is Holly with the sheriff's department, uh…got that ID on the occupants of the tan pickup…uh…"

"Well, are you waiting for an invitation, Holly?

"No, sir…Uh, Deputy Green IDed them as Detectives Bone and Rodriguez."

"Something tells me there's more."

"Yes, sir. They made his unit uh…disappear, sir, and drove off."

He sat straight up. "They did what? What the hell do you mean, disappear?"

"That's just what Deputy Green said, sir. His unit vanished, into thin air…just gone."

"I see. And he was sure it was Bone and Loraine?"

"Yes, sir. Very sure. No question."

"When did this happen?

"About three minutes ago, sir."

HUNTER'S SERVICE STATION

Bone and Loraine sat in the office going over the surveillance tapes from the security camera. The small screen showed a poor quality, but recognizable, image of Bone filling the tank with Loraine in the passenger seat. Then it showed him getting back in, driving off and almost hitting Padrino in his vehicle as it was pulling in.

"That's us! We're both wearing the same clothes that we wore all day. I didn't change 'til you got me out of bed," she said.

"Yeah, that's us, but it ain't us. I mean it can't be us 'cause we were at the Governor's Lounge...weren't we? Look at the damn time code."

"Of course we were...But, that's still us...Can you make out the license plate?"

"Nah, too banged up from hooking onto a trailer."

His cell phone rang with his signature ring. "Bone."

"Where the hell are you?" St. John demanded.

"Loraine and I are at Hunter's looking at surveillance tape."

"How long have you been there?"

"'Bout twenty minutes. I picked up Loraine and came straight here...Why?"

"Deputy Green says you and Loraine just made his unit disappear three minutes ago out at the NRC facility."

"Disappear? Damn I knew we were good, but not good enough to be in two places at the same time...That's long way out of town."

"Be that as it may, Brennan is looking for you. You better make yourself scarce."

Just then the door to the office opened and two sheriff deputies, Chuck Watts and Serena Carter came in.

"Too late. Laterbye." He punched off his phone.

"Bone, the sheriff wants to see you and your partner," said Watts.

"Tell him we'll drop by in the morning."

"Now," Serena said somewhat icily.

"Or now's good...Come on partner, looks like we're real popular tonight."

CROSS TIMBERS COUNTY
SHERIFF OFFICE
INTERROGATION ROOM

Bone and Loraine sat in wooden chairs at a gray metal table. Sheriff Brennan and Deputy Green were seated on the other side.

"Now, dammit Bone, I don't know what you're trying to pull, but Deputy Green says ya'll made his unit disappear or dissolve or whatever...I've had a belly full of your practical jokes…This ain't funny…Now where the hell's my cruiser?"

"I'm tellin' you, Sheriff, Loraine and I were at Hunter's lookin' at surveillance tape…"

"I know what I saw and I saw both of you in that truck… Clothes were different though," said Green.

"How the hell did you do that, Bone? You some kind of God damn magician?"

"Sheriff, it's a good 10 miles out to the plant. How could we be there and at Hunter's at the same time?" asked Loraine.

Brennan started looking like he could chew nails. He got to his feet and motioned to Green. "Outside Deputy, we need to talk."

The two county law officers exited the room.

"Pard, I'm not inclined to sit here in this circle jerk all night…We got work to do."

"I'm open to suggestions."

Bone pulled up his sleeve to reveal the bracelet Lucy had sent him. They got to their feet.

"Put your arms around my waist and when they come in, we'll slip out."

"You just want me to hug you."

"That too…but, come on, we don't have much time."

They walked over and stood next to the door. Loraine got behind him and wrapped her arms around his waist. Bone keyed the combination into the bracelet. They shimmered, and then vanished.

Brennan and Green reentered the room leaving the door open.

"What the hell?" exclaimed the sheriff.

Green looked behind the door. Brennan glanced under the table then at him.

"Don't look at me…They were here when we left."

BONE'S PICKUP

The real Bone and Loraine drove away from the Sheriff's station in his truck.

"Well, that went well…Sheriff Brennan is probably having a conniption, though," she said.

"He'll get over it. We just couldn't sit there while our dopplegangers or whatever are out causing mischief…My first inclination is to head out to the nuclear facility…"

"Every damn cop in the county will be out there and they all know our vehicles."

"That's a fact. Let's go get Padrino's."

CROSS TIMBERS COUNTY
SHERIFF OFFICE
INTERROGATION ROOM

Sheriff Brennan had been steady chewing on Green's butt for the last five minutes.

"Now, dammit, I don't know how you managed to let them get out of here…"

"But, Sheriff, we were both in the hallway and we came in together…Maybe he's a magician or an illusionist like that Copperfield guy…You know he once made the Statue of Liberty disa…"

"I don't want to hear it! You get your butt back out there and find 'em and don't come back 'til you do. Clear?"

"Yes, sir. Clear…Can I check out another unit?"

"Just go, dammit

DIRT ROAD

Rdydl/Bone and Klyn/Loraine pulled the tan truck into a copse of trees off a dirt road near the NRC complex and shut off the engine.

"We should move on the facility quickly before too many of their law enforcement personnel become involved," said Rdydl/Bone.

"I would not worry, they have no beam weapons that can breach our new force fields. Their technology is still primitive," replied Klyn/Loraine

"We will obtain entrance at the main gate. There was only one humanoid guard. From there, we will then proceed directly to the storage area."

BONE'S RANCH HOUSE

Padrino sat on the couch looking through a box on the coffee table as Bone and Loraine entered the front door. Tyrin lay on the couch beside him him—he woofed a greeting as they came in.

"Padrino, need to borrow your pickup."

He looked up at the pair. "I don't think so. I have seen how you drive…Why don't you drive that Cord Lucy left you?"

"Like you said, I don't think so. Promised myself I wouldn't use in for work."

"Ya think…Look here."

Padrino held up a device in the direction of Loraine that looked something like a garage door opener. "I think Lucy may have left a weapon behind."

Tyrin barked a warning.

"Don't point that thing!" Loraine exclaimed.

Padrino quickly swung the device away from her, accidentally hitting the discharge button. A purple energy beam shot out—a lamp near the wall burst into flame and disappeared, leaving just a small pile of ash. Tyrin covered his stubby nose with both paws.

"Whoa! Be careful with that thing. Better let me have it."

"Sorry, I guess that button on top is the activator."

"I'd say that's a good guess." He took the device gingerly from Padrino, examined it, and then dropped it in his shirt pocket. "Might come in handy...Now about your truck."

"Like I said, I don't think so...I'll drive."

"This could get hairy."

In case you don't know, Loraine, I was Force Recon Marine in 1968 in 'Nam...I'll watch your backs...Looks like someone needs to."

"Fill you in on the way."

"Where we goin'?"

NRC ROAD

Deputy Green's new patrol unit was parked, with its flashers going, on the side of the road where his other unit disappeared. He walked up and down the shoulder with his flashlight scanning the ground for anything out of the ordinary. A set of headlights appeared and approached. Green stepped out and waved down the oncoming vehicle.

Loraine sat in the middle of the bench seat with Bone riding shotgun and Tyrin in the back seat. Padrino pulled over to the side of the road when he saw the officer waving.

"Shit...Quick, Pard, sit on my lap."

"Excuse me?"

"That's Green...We gotta disappear again."

"Ah, damn."

She quickly shifted over into his lap while Tyrin jumped the seat and sat in the space Loraine had just occupied. Bone keyed the bracelet—they shimmered and vanished again.

Deputy Green walked up to the driver's window and shined his light on the glass. Padrino squinted, blocked the light from his eyes with one hand and rolled down the window with the other.

"Evening officer. Is there a problem?"

Richard flashed his light over the inside of the truck and into the bed of the truck.

"Evening, sir. Have you seen a tan Chevy pickup with a blue door?"

"No, sir. Just a whole bunch of police cars...I just left the domino hall, headin' home. What's goin' on?"

"Just police business, sir. If you see that truck...do you have a cell phone?"

"Don't everybody?"

"Yes, sir, just about...Well, if you see it, please call 911...and do not approach it."

"Got some desperadoes in it, does it?"

"Can't say for sure, sir, just don't approach it, okay?...You have a safe trip home now."

Padrino pulled away from the shoulder and back on the pavement. A hundred yards down the road he heard a loud *smack*. Bone and Loraine materialized—he was rubbing the side of his face. Tyrin jumped back over the seat.

She crawled off his lap and back into the middle. "Damn you, Bone! You watch those octopus hands."

"Can't, they were invisible."

"Well, practice your Braille on me again and I'll break every bone in your body."

"That might leave a mark," chipped in Padrino.

Tyrin woofed in agreement. Bone looked over his shoulder at the light yellow and white pit bull sitting on the back seat.

"Don't need anything from you."

Tyrin just cocked his head.

NRC CROSS TIMBERS FACILITY GATE

The tan truck pulled up to the guard shack at the main gate. The single Hispanic guard approached the driver's window. Rdydl/Bone rolled down the glass.

"May I help you, sir?" the guard asked.

Klyn/Loraine pointed her arm across in front of Rdydl/Bone. Her true form briefly became visible as her energy weapon discharged. The guard glowed green and then dissolved into a light green vapor that drifted away on the evening breeze.   "I do not think so," Rdydl/Bone said as he put the truck in gear and drove through the gate and up to the largest building.

NRC CROSS TIMBERS FACILITY ROAD

Bone and Loraine both saw the vehicle as Padrino slowly drove past.

"There, there…the pickup! Pull in," Bone and Loraine said simultaneously.

Padrino whipped into the entrance. "Where's the guard?"

"There's nobody here," observed Loraine.

"Don't like the looks of this," added Bone. He looked down at the bracelet—one of the stones was glowing brighter and was now flashing. "Oh, boy…Park over there in the dark, out of sight."

Padrino pulled over by a nearby smaller building and parked in its shadow. Bone and Loraine got out. The big man leaned back in the window.

"You stay here and keep your eyes open, we'll go check the building."

"Right." He watched them walk off and turned to Tyrin in the back. "I ain't stayin' here like a sittin' duck, you?"

Tyrin reached up and placed a big paw on the top of the front seat. Padrino leaned over, opened the glove box, took out his 1911A .45, racked it and got out.

"You stay."

Tyrin cocked his head and then jumped out the window.

"Damn, you're hardheaded as me."

The muscular dog looked up at him.

NRC CROSS TIMBERS FACILITY ROAD

Deputy Green cruised past the facility, looked in the parking area and spied the tan pickup. He quickly pulled in the gate and keyed his radio. "Dispatch, Unit 28, request 10-40 for a possible 459 in progress."

"Unit 28, dispatch, what's your 20?"

"NRC facility, FM 904. Tan pickup spotted."

"Oh, no...10-4, 28. Will send back up. Dispatch out."

Green parked near the pickup. He unlocked his tactical shotgun and exited his unit, racking the slide. He knelt behind the fender as he spotted Rdydl/Bone and Klyn/Loraine leaving the building with Rdydl/Bone carrying a small metallic looking case.

He aimed the shotgun over the hood of the car. "Freeze, Bone!"

Klyn/Loraine raised her arm and pointed at him.

"Oh, shit, seen this before!"

Green sprinted away from his unit as she discharged the weapon. Her Reptoid form was again visible for a millisecond. The patrol unit glowed green briefly and vanished.

"Damn you, Bone!"

Just then the real Bone and Loraine came around the side of the building and witnessed the patrol unit being vaporized.

"Good God almighty!" exclaimed Bone.

The two aliens turned and saw the real Bone and Loraine. Klyn/Loraine raised her arm and fired—again becoming briefly visible—just as the two detectives dove in separate directions.

Bone rolled over on the ground, quickly reached into his shirt pocket and took out the Tyranian weapon and fired multiple purple beams of force at Rdydl/Bone and Klyn/Loraine. The shields of the two Reptiods flared a pale violet in sequence—the aliens were unaffected.

Once again Bone fired the small energy projector and again their shields just flared. Rdydl/Bone and Klyn/Loraine quickly entered their truck and dug out heading straight for Green. He stood his ground and aimed his shotgun at the oncoming truck.

"Halt!"

They didn't—he leaped out of the way just in time as the truck roared past. Green jumped up and fired two quick shots at the retreating vehicle, blowing out the back glass. The truck exited the gate, fishtailed onto the road and sped away into the darkness.

Bone and Loraine walked up behind him.

"Nice try, Green."

He turned and saw Bone, looked back at the receding truck and quickly pulled his shot gun back to his shoulder.

"Freeze, Bone. Damn you, I don't know how you just did that, but you're both under arrest."

"You moron! That wasn't us, I mean it was, but it was somebody else bein' us…"

"Don't even try to explain," Loraine nudged his shoulder with her hand.

"I don't care, drop your weapons!"

"No, son, I suggest you drop yours," came a voice from behind him.

Green looked over his shoulder at Padrino pointing his .45 at his face and wisely laid his shotgun on the ground.

"We'll explain later…Right now our doubles are getting away. Loraine, get the truck."

Padrino tossed the keys in the air, she snatched them, turned and sprinted to the truck.

"Come on, Tyrin."

The big dog was quickly on her heels.

"Now pick up that scattergun, we may need it."

Green bent over and retrieved his weapon. "What the hell is goin' on, Bone?"

"Later," he said as Loraine slid to a stop next to the three men. They wasted no time in getting in as she tore toward the gate even before Green had closed the back door.

***

CHAPTER EIGHTEEN

CROSS TIMBERS COUNTY
FM 904

Deputy Green, in the back seat, keyed his radio. "Dispatch, Unit 28."

"Unit 28, dispatch, go ahead."

"We are in hot pursuit of the tan pickup, headed west on FM 904. Notify backup."

"10-4, 28…We?"

"Explain later, dispatch. Just notify backup."

"Notifying. 10-4."

The tan truck sped down FM 904 at more than eighty miles per hour. A sheriff's patrol unit was headed in the opposite direction, its lights flashing.

Deputies Watts and Carter were en route to the NRC as backup for Green—Serena was driving. They passed the perpetrator's vehicle going at high speed in the opposite direction.

"That was the tan pickup!" she said as the two vehicles passed each other.

The radio crackled to life. "Unit 36, dispatch."

Chuck Watts grabbed the hand set. "Dispatch, Unit 36, go ahead."

"Cancel the backup at NRC. 28 is in hot pursuit of suspect vehicle, tan Chevy pickup heading west on FM 904."

"10-4, dispatch. We just passed it. Will pursue. 36 out."

Deputy Carter, slammed on the brakes and executed a sliding 180. As she took her foot off the brake, Padrino's truck swerved around them at a high rate of speed.

"Jesus! Who the hell was that?" Serena shouted as she floor-boarded her unit and hit the lights and siren.

Watts keyed the mike. "Dispatch, Unit 36."

"Unit 36, dispatch, go ahead."

"We are in pursuit of tan pickup and were almost blown off the road by a silver Titan crew cab also pursuing."

"That must be 28. I'll check 36."

Padrino, Bone, Loraine and Green could see the taillights of the pickup with their doubles.

"We're gaining on 'em," said Loraine.

Green's radio crackled. "Unit 28, dispatch."

"Unit 28, go ahead."

"28, are you in a silver Titan?"

"That's affirmative, dispatch."

"Where's your unit, 28?"

"You really don't want to know, Holly."

"You just passed Unit 36."

"We know. Tell 36 we're the good guys. 28 out."

"10-4. Dispatch out."

"I guess that's the cavalry," offered Padrino.

"One unit ain't gonna be enough…Richard, tell Holly to patch through to Cap'n St. John," said Bone.

"Dispatch, Unit 28."

"Unit 28, dispatch, go ahead."

"Patch through to Captain St. John, Cross PD."

"10-4. Patching."

He held for a short moment.

"St. John."

Bone reached back and took the mike from Richard. "Cap'n, get Stella and Newman to intercept us on FM 904. We're headed west in hot pursuit of the tan pickup in Padrino's silver Titan with sheriff unit 36 behind us."

"Already done, Bone. I've been monitoring the sheriff's channel. You should see them anytime."

As St. John spoke, the four saw the flashing red and blue strobes along with headlights headed their way fast down CR 222 on the right.

"Got 'em," said Bone.

Stella and Newman's unit slid sideways as it entered 904 just behind Padrino's truck, cutting off the sheriff's cruiser. Carter in Unit 36 slammed on her brakes, hit the shoulder and narrowly missed Stella's patrol car. She fishtailed twice back onto the pavement and stomped on the gas—all three vehicles continued the pursuit.

Stella held the wheel in a death grip. "Damn. I think I peed my pants."

"The hell you say, it was on my side," countered Newman.

"I think I peed my pants," said Serena in the sheriff's car as the radio came to life.

"Unit 36, dispatch."

"Unit 36, go ahead, Holly," answered Watts.

"That is 28 in the silver Titan. Cross PD is joining the pursuit."

"Yeah, we know...Thanks for the heads-up, Holly. Got a regular convoy now. 36 out."

"Johnny on the spot info," commented Carter.

The tan pickup turned left off FM 904 onto a gravel road—CR 212. Padrino's truck followed the turn, still a hundred yards behind. His truck was followed another hundred yards back by Stella's Cross PD unit with the sheriff's unit right on her bumper.

The convoy barreled down the caliche road in a cloud of white dust.

"I can't see a damn thing," said Padrino as he leaned forward as if being closer to the windshield would help.

"Just follow the red glow of his tail lights," Bone offered.

The alien's pickup made a hard right onto the dirt driveway of the rural farm where their spacecraft was.

"Holy shit!" Padrino slammed on the brakes and slid into the turn, taking out the mailbox in the process.

"Dammit!" Stella slid past the drive, stopped and started to back up.

"Hold it!" shouted Newman. "Unit 36 is on our ass."

Serena slammed on her brakes and stopped just three feet from the Cross PD unit. She threw the gear shift into reverse and quickly backed past the dirt drive where a little dust still lingered in the air.

Stella spun a 360, pulled into the drive and was followed by Serena's unit down the long entryway.

The alien's truck slid to a stop near the pale metallic green globular craft behind the barn. Rdydl/Bone and Klyn/Loraine exited quickly with Klyn/Loraine carrying the case from the NRC facility. She ran to the craft as the hatch opened.

"Quickly, install the P-239 while I stop these natives," ordered Rdydl/Bone

Padrino's truck slid to a stop at the side of the barn. Bone, Loraine, Padrino and Green jumped out simultaneously.

"Scatter and get down!" yelled Bone.

The others did as he ordered, drawing their weapons in the process of going prone.

Bone pulled out the Tyranian weapon and fired a pure purple energy beam at the big alien—his force field flared a bright violet.

Rdydl/Bone raised his arm, aimed at Bone and triggered his laser projector—becoming momentarily visible. Bone dove out of the way of the pulse and rolled, throwing aside the Tyranian weapon.

"The hell with this." He drew his S&W 500 revolver, got to his feet and stood sideways like Wild Bill Hickok with his right arm extended.

Rdydl/Bone just smiled and raised his arm again. Bone fired the .50 cal.

The solid copper hollowpoint slug penetrated the force field as if it weren't there and a hole near the size of of hot dog appeared in the alien's chest. A grayish fluid began to leak out. Rdydl/Bone looked down in surprise for a moment, then glanced back at Bone and fell backward.

The hatch on the globular craft closed and it started to hum as it began to rise. Bone fired his last four rounds into the skin of the door in a tight pattern. Padrino, Loraine and Green also jumped up and emptied their weapons at the glowing sphere.

The Reptoid craft continued to rise more rapidly leaving a vapor trail coming out of the numerous holes in its outer skin.

Stella and Newman's Cross PD unit braked to a stop. The two officers exited with weapons drawn as the sheriff's unit stopped right behind them, Carter and Watts also jumped out with weapons in hand.

Tyrin, who had been hiding under truck, ran over, picked up the Tyranian weapon and took it to Padrino. He looked around and quickly put it in his jacket pocket.

They all stood with mouths agape and watched as the globular craft rose silently into the darkness. Suddenly, a triangular craft dove in from high in the atmosphere, chasing the Reptoid craft—they both quickly disappeared from sight. In a short moment, there was a bright flash high in the heavens followed ten seconds later by what sounded like a rolling clap of thunder.

"I think Lucy's friends just cleaned up the situation," said Bone as he holstered his pistol.

Stella, Newman, Carter and Watts ran up to join Bone, Loraine, Padrino, Green and Tyrin.

"Bone, what in hell just happened?" asked Stella.

"It's a long story."

He walked over to Rdydl/Bone and looked down at him. The big alien was just barely alive. "Well, that's me, all right."

Then, as they all watched, the creature tried to reach a control pad on his left arm. Bone stepped on his right hand. Rdydl/Bone looked up at him with pure malevolence for a moment, and then changed to its alien Reptoid form as it died.

"Now, that is one butt-ugly son of a bitch."

"I don't know, Bone, might be an improvement," said Loraine as she moved closer for a better look.

"Bite me."

Two black Suburbans pulled into the farm. Four men in black suits exited each one. One man walked over to the group, held up a badge and ID folder.

"NSA, Special Agent Gibson. We're in charge here." He turned to Bone. "You Detective Darrell Ulysses Bone?"

He nodded. The agent took him by the arm and led him away from the group. The other men in black took the rest of the group off to the side—away from Rdydl's body. One of them opened a briefcase, took out some papers and gave one each to Loraine and the others.

Special Agent Gibson, with Bone, took out a folded paper from his coat.

A black stealthy helicopter with whisper-quiet rotors suddenly appeared from over the barn and settled to the ground near the alien body.

Four men in white biohazard suits jumped out with an enclosed capsule stretcher and approached Rdydl's body. They opened the unit, loaded the dead Reptoid inside and closed the lid. Without a word to anyone else, they carried the capsule to the still rotating chopper, loaded it on board and got back in.

The helo increased rotation, lifted from the ground, banked to the right and headed off into the darkness as quietly as it had come.

Agent Gibson handed Bone the paper from his jacket. " Sign this."

"What is it?"

"It's a United States National Security Act nondisclosure document…Sign it."

"I don't suppose I have a choice?"

"You do not. This never happened Mister Bone…Do I make myself clear?"

"I gave my oath to protect and defend the Constitution when I joined the Marine Corps. An oath is forever. I know the drill… How did you guys get here so fast?"

"We monitor all nuclear facilities closely by video and via satellite. We saw everything as it went down at the NRC complex and then we tracked you here with a RQ-170 Sentinel drone…Now, I repeat, this never happened…Sign it." He handed him a pen.

"What never happened?" Bone said as he scrawled his name on the paper.

"I see we're going to get along just fine, Mister Bone."

"It's just Bone."

"Ok, Bone…Oh, tell Sheriff Brennan he'll be getting two new cruisers, state of the art…courtesy of Uncle Sam."

"Thanks, it'll get him off my butt for sure…What about the residents of this farm?"

"It is regretful. We'll have the public record reflect that they moved and send a crew to clean up around here tomorrow."

"How'd you know who I was?"

Special Agent Gibson just looked at him.

"Yeah."

The NSA agent turned and headed back to the lead vehicle as Padrino and all the others signed their documents. The men in black collected the papers and returned to their vehicles, loaded up and left the property.

Loraine and the others walked over to Bone.

"Well, you were right. It wasn't you, it was…but, I mean it wasn't."

"What wasn't, Deputy Green?" Bone said with a big grin.

"It wasn't…Oh, right. Nothing…But what do I tell the Sheriff?…I lost another cruiser."

"Tell him it was government business. He'll be getting two new cruisers…State of the art."

"Wow, that'll work."

Bone glanced around. "I suggest ya'll fill out your reports as a false alarm…" He turned to Padrino, Loraine and Tyrin. "Well, let's load up kids. Deputy Green why don't you ride back with Carter?"

"No problem."

They loaded up in their respective vehicles and pulled out of the farm and back on to the caliche road.

Padrino drove, Bone was back at shotgun with Loraine in the middle. Tyrin laid down in the back and quickly fell asleep.

"Still can't figure out why the Tyranian weapon had no effect."

"I think it's obvious, Bone. The technology was over a hundred years old. Don't you think the Reptoids have made both offensive and defensive advancements in that period of time?"

"I think they forgot one thing though," said Loraine.

"That would be."

"How to stop a .50 cal 300 grain slug traveling at over 2,000 feet per second."

"Good point, there, Pard. They designed their shields against what they know…directed energy beams or laser technology. Not physical matter…Padrino, let me see that Tyranian weapon."

He pulled it from his shirt pocket and handed it over. Bone held it in the palm of his hand and studied it for a moment—it vanished.

"What the hell…"

They looked through the windshield and saw a silver Tyranian triangle craft moving at their same speed. Tyrin jumped to his feet in the back seat. The overhead craft 'waggled' and darted off out of sight into the night sky.

Padrino looked over at Bone. "Lucy?"

Bone nodded and grinned. "Lucy."

Tyrin woofed.

The truck abruptly died, the lights went out and it coasted to a stop in the middle of the road. A blindingly bright blue-white light infused the truck, both inside and out. Loraine screamed…

BONE'S RANCH

In a few seconds, the light faded. The truck engine started again and the headlights came on. Padrino slammed on the brakes just before running into the white picket fence surrounding Bone's newly acquired ranch house.

"My God, what just happened?" asked Loraine.

"I'd say we're back home," replied Bone as he opened the door and stepped out.

Padrino, Loraine and Tyrin also got out and they stood at the gate looking around just to make sure they were back at the ranch. Just inside the yard, the air shimmered and a small gray alien appeared. The figure reached up and removed the smooth round covering with the large black almond-shaped eyes from its head—it was Lucy. She shook her light brown pixie-cut hair loose and smiled.

"Well don't just stand there, come in."

The stunned trio entered the yard as Tyrin trotted to her, wiggling all over and laid down next to her feet.

"How come he's not kissin' all over you, Lucy?" asked Bone.

"Because he knows I'm not really here...I'm a hologram."

"But, how did we get here?"

"Teleportation, Bone," offered Padrino.

"A four thousand pound truck?"

"My dear Bone, if we can move blocks of stone weighing a thousand tons, your little vehicle is not much of a challenge."

Loraine shook her head. "Huh?"

"They helped build the pyramids, Tiahuanaco, Stonehenge and a host of other sites in antiquity where massive cut stones or monoliths were transported many miles and erected," said Padrino. "They apparently not only mastered the physics of anti-gravitation, but also teleportation as well."

"Are you in orbit?" asked Bone looking up into the sky.

"Yes, in one of our small two-seat scout craft. Our mother ship is in what your scientists call a Lagrangian Point just outside Earth's orbit. They refer to it as L2."

"Come again?" Bone questioned.

"It's a point of gravitational equilibrium, named after the Italian-French mathematician Joseph Louis Lagrange in 1772. There are five Lagrangian Points in Earth's orbital plane around the sun. It doesn't take any power to maintain the position because of countering gravitational effects," said Padrino.

"Right…There's not going to be a quiz, is there?" Loraine asked with that deer-in-the-headlights look.

"It's really quite elementary, Loraine. We've been out there for millennia…But, back to the matters at hand. Due to the increased activity of the Reptoids, I picked up some items you might need when I was home. Hold out both hands, Bone."

"You've already been home and back?"

"Yes, as I mentioned, it doesn't take long. Now your hands."

"Yes, ma'am." He held them out, palms up.

A device similar to the one that vanished, appeared in his right palm and a duplicate of a new Galaxy S5 cell phone materialized in his left.

"Far out," he exclaimed.

"The weapon is an updated particle force beam projector that will…at least for now, penetrate the new shields of the vile creatures. The phone is identical the newest version of your existing one except for one thing."

"That would be?"

"Activate the screen."

He pushed the button on the side and swiped his thumb across the face. The Galaxy app icons appeared on the screen.

"Do you see the tiny little one that looks like our suit?"

"I do."

"That app will summon this hologram if you should need to communicate with me. I can teleport you anywhere on the planet…and it will also do a number of other things."

"Son of a gun! Shades of Star Trek," exclaimed Bone. "Beam me up, Scotty…or in this case, Lucy."

"No, I can't beam you up. One, you wouldn't fit in our scout/fighter craft and two, even if you could, you would have to have one of these suits in your size."

"Well, I do have a birthday comin' up…"

Lucy laughed. "We'll see."

"Our scientists have said there is not enough computing power in the world to create a transporter," said Padrino.

"We've had that discussion about your scientists, Padrino…"

"Yes we have, sky queen. They just don't know what they don't know."

"I didn't know that," offered Loraine.

****

PREVIEW
OF
THE NEXT EXCITING NOVEL FROM

TIMBER CREEK PRESS

ACROSS THE RED

BY

KEN FARMER
&
BUCK STIENKE

Book four in the Bass Reeves saga

CHAPTER ONE

COOKE COUNTY, TEXAS
DELAWARE BEND

Texas Ranger Bodie Hickman instinctively ducked when he saw a puff of rifle smoke from the other side of the Red River. Approximately one second later he heard the crack of a bullet just as it clipped the top of his gray center-creased Stetson and took it from his head—followed immediately by the boom of a big gun. The big rawboned redhead dove from the back of his line-back dun mustang, Lakota Moon, rolled to a crouch, still holding on to the reins and tapped the horse's left front foot in the signal to lay down.

"Git down, Billy!" he shouted at the young posseman behind him as he reached up and jerked his brand new 1886 Winchester lever action rifle from its boot.

The warning came too late as the second booming report of the distant big gun was followed by the sickening *twack* of the round striking flesh. Bodie turned at the sound as Moon dropped to his knees and rolled over on his side. He was just in time to see a cloud of red explode from Billy Malena's chest, the young man flip backwards out of his saddle and fall to the ground. His panicked horse lunged up the side of the draw and ran into the woods on the south.

The two lawmen had been riding single file—tracking some rustlers moving a small herd of horses—down a shallow three foot deep wet-weather wash that headed west toward an area known as the *breaks* along the Red River, still some three hundred yards away.

The heavily wooded area close to the wide, but usually slow moving border river between Texas and the Indian Nations had become a sanctuary for the lawless—allowing the malefactors to head into the Chicksaw Nation if the Texas Rangers got too hot behind them.

The sweeping six square miles of the bubble-like horseshoe on the west side of the much larger Delaware Bend of the Red was ten miles directly east of Marietta, IT and twenty miles northeast—as the crow flies—from Gainesville, Texas. It had been a past haven to the likes of Charles Quantrill—the guerilla chieftain of the south—as well as the James brothers and now was a crossing point for stolen cattle and horses bound for the Nations—especially in early summer when the water level was going down

"Billy!" Bodie shouted in vain at the motionless body of his friend and brand new posseman four yards behind him in the gully. Another *boom* sounded and a slug slapped the sandy bank just above his head a half second later. "Son of a bitch!" He raised his head just enough to see over the edge of the ditch and could make out a small cloud of gunsmoke coming from atop a forty foot bluff just across the Red. "Damnation! Purtnear a quarter mile...Gotta be .45-70...Got a shooter up there, Moon. Stay down...That bastard don't know I got surprise for him."

He belly-crawled forward—his rifle cradled across his arms—in the gully as quick as he could about fifteen feet to a low scrub bush over the northern lip of the bank. Bodie adjusted his Lyman tang sight up to where he saw the four hundred yard range notch was marked and took a deep breath. He levered in a long .45-90 round and brought the rifle snugly to his shoulder. He rose up slightly and found the desired sight picture on the slowly dispersing cloud of smoke, concentrated on the front sight, exhaled half his air and fired.

The big cartridge—originally created for taking buffalo at long distance—bucked hard, but he paid it scant heed as he quickly cranked another into the chamber and shot again. Both rounds were discharged in less than a second with the distinctive roar of the big bore echoing up and down the Red River valley. "Bet you weren't expectin' that, were you, asshole?" *Not like I had a chance of hittin' anything, but maybe I scared 'em off.*

The cloud of his own gunsmoke gradually drifted away, but not before he had smelled the pungent aroma of burnt sulfur from the black powder load. Bodie drew a pair of the cigar sized rounds out of his custom-made gun belt and shoved them past the Winchester's loading gate as he contemplated his next move.

He waited for return fire for a good five minutes—nothing. *White man...Injun would have the patience to wait me out.* Just to be safe, he crawled back to his horse. "Git up, Moon."

The big mustang got to his front feet, followed quickly by his back—he shook, as horses will do after getting up from the ground. The young ranger led him over to the woods on the side near Billy's mount, ground-tied him so he could graze a bit and solemnly walked back to his friend's body.

His hat lay near Malena. He picked it up, slapped the dirt off on his thigh, stuck his index finger through the hole in the top of the crown. "Yep, forty-five." He jammed the Stetson firmly back on his head and knelt down beside Billy and caressed the side of his face.

"God, I'm sorry, boy...Yer first day, too...What in the world am I gonna tell yer mama?" He slipped his arms under the still warm body, easily lifted the wiry teenager and carried him over to the horses.

DEXTER, TEXAS

Bodie slowly walked Moon—leading Billy's blood bay with the young man draped across the saddle—down the dirt main street of the dying little north Texas town.

At one time, Dexter had been larger than Gainesville, the county seat, until the highly anticipated Santa Fe Railroad went south through Woodbine—instead of Dexter—to Gainesville.

He passed by the Sugar Hill combination store and saloon with two cowboys leaning against the porch posts smoking roll-your-owns. One—a reed-thin man in his twenties—touched the brim of his dark Montana pinch Stetson, gave the young ranger a surreptitious grin and blew a cloud of smoke in his direction.

The two working cowboys sported batwing chaps—as opposed to shotgun chaps preferred in Montana and Wyoming because they were cooler and gave greater freedom of the lower leg when mounting. Each wore store-bought white boiled work shirts without vests. The thin one had a Colt Peacemaker strapped to his hips and his shorter, heavier friend a Smith & Wesson Schofield in reverse grip.

Bodie noticed the two, but didn't acknowledge or even look their way. He knew who they were and would bet money they were involved in the rustling ring that was plaguing north Texas and the Indian Nations across the Red. He just couldn't prove it—yet.

Every step Lakota Moon took increased his dread, not of the two ne'er-do-wells he just rode past, but of having to tell Billy Malina's mother what happened. *Damn, I'd rather git whipped with a wet rope...but I ain't got no choice.*

He drew rein in front of a small, but well-kept, white painted clapboard house—with a galvanized standing-seam roof and flowers along the front porch—on the outskirts of Dexter. Bodie stepped down and quickly moved to Billy's body. *Hope I can git him down 'fore she comes out the door...Don't want her seeing her son draped over his saddle.*

He slid the young man down and cradled him in his arms like a baby, turned and stepped toward the porch only to see the widow Millie Malina standing on the stoop, both hands to her mouth. She was a very attractive, 5' 2" brunette in her late-thirties—widowed at the age of twenty-eight when her bank teller husband had been killed in a robbery.

"I'm...I'm sure powerful sorry, Miz Malina. We was bushwhacked near the Red..."

She dropped her hands and said in a soft, but steady voice as her eyes filled, "Bring him in the house...Need to get word to Father Miller...He'll need…need his rites…read proper." She choked back a sob and held her head up as she opened the screen door for Bodie.

"Yessum, I'll see to it right away."

"Lay him there." She directed him to place her only son on his bed against the wall and then grabbed Bodie's arm after he had gently laid Billy on the patchwork quilt cover. Millie lifted her chin in resolve even as the tears continued to course down her cheeks. "You find who did this, Bodie Hickman…You hear me?…You find them."

He nodded.

"I want them punished…he was just a baby…my only baby. But he was a man…Wanted more than anything in this world to be a Texas Ranger…You catch 'em…and I want to be there when they put the noose around their necks."

A lump built in Bodie's throat and he rasped out, "You can count on it, ma'am." He swallowed and headed to the door. "I'll go fetch the priest."

Even the closed door couldn't keep him from hearing the anguished wail from the bereaved mother inside as she couldn't hold back her grief any longer. He wiped his own tears with the back of his hand, mounted, reined Moon in the direction of the small

Catholic chapel and Father Thomas Miller and bumped the gelding into a hand gallop. It was less than a mile away.

GAINESVILLE, TEXAS
COOKE COUNTY SHERIFF'S OFFICE

"Damn shame on Billy…Boy had the makin's of a fine lawman," said Sheriff Wacker—a trim middle-age man with a full head of light sandy hair and mustache—as he filled his cup from the coffee pot on the wood burning stove in the corner.

"Pure out and out dry gulchin', Tal…uh, Taggart…Didn't have a chance. Shot from near 400 yards away…"

"Takes a hellova gun to do that.…45-70 you think?"

"I mind that would be it. But it was a repeater…weren't no fallin' block or trapdoor, I can tell you that."

"I'll give Sheriff Colcord up to Oklahoma City and that new Sheriff at Ardmore, Pullman, a call and have them check their area for sales of .45-70 ammunition. We can do the same here."

"I reckon there's quite a number out there since the '86 Winchester came out."

"True, but it at least would narrow the field."

A messenger from Western Union came through the front door. "Got a telegram here for Ranger Hickman."

"That would be me, son." He took the yellow flimsey and flipped the young man a dime from his tan canvas vest pocket.

"Thank you, sir. Ya'll have a nice day, hear?" he said over his shoulder as he closed the door.

Bodie stared at the envelope for a moment.

"Well, you gonna open it?"

"Oh, yeah, sure…Just wasn't expecting a telegram. That's all."

"You know what they say about a guilty conscience?"

"No, what?"

Wacker paused for a second. "Damned if I can remember…but if I think of it I'll let you know."

"Cain't wait." Bodie ripped open the thin paper and unfolded it. "Well, butter my butt and call me a biscuit."

"What?"

He chuckled. "Listen to this…'Finished arrangements for the church and the preacher. Stop.

Preacher has never done a double wedding before. Stop. Mama and Father are en route by train from Alabama. Stop. Sent telegram to your mother. Stop. She will contact you when she will arrive in Gainesville. Stop. Sent telegrams to Marshals Reeves, McGann, Lindsey and Hart. Stop. Wedding is June 18. Stop. You don't show up…Texas isn't big enough to hide in. Stop. Love. Stop'."

"Wonder what she means by that?" Wacker said with a smile as he pulled out his Bull Durham pouch and papers from his shirt pocket and started to build himself a cigarette.

"Guess…Hell, she's a better shot than I am. Reckon I better show up."

"Ya think?" He lit the end of the twisted paper, drew the fire into the fine cut tobacco and blew a cloud of blue smoke over his head. "What's that about a double weddin'?"

"Colcord's deputy, Willie Agee…Told you about him gittin' shot an' all…and Annabel's best friend, Theresa Chadwell…"

"Ah, the other girl in the kidnappin'."

"Right…Well, anyways, they're tyin' the knot too."

"Don't that beat all…Sounds like ya'll are gonna have a hellova chivaree."

FORT SMITH, ARKANSAS

The young teenage messenger hopped up and stabbed his boot in the stirrup once the cinch was tight. The telegram he had placed in his saddle bag was addressed to US Deputy Marshal Bass Reeves. The boy knew exactly where the famous black lawman lived. He had delivered telegrams out there a half dozen times before and had always been rewarded by one of Bass' signature tokens—a shiny Morgan silver dollar that was worth more than his daily pay of seventy-five cents.

He turned the Standardbred mare up the street from the Western Union office and quickly brought her up to a road trot.

REEVES FARM
VAN BUREN, ARKANSAS

Mame Reeves, Bass' tall blond adopted daughter, was visiting after teaching school in the nearby town. She heard the knock on the door as she and her dad sat drinking iced tea and enjoying one of their infrequent visits. Riding the Indian Territory for Judge Isaac Parker—known as the *Hanging Judge*—did not give the big man much time for a home life.

"I'll get it, Daddy. You deserve to sit back for a change."

"Much appreciated, baby girl," he said as he settled his 6' 3" frame back in the overstuffed chair. His catahoula dog, Buttercup lay back down at his feet and sighed.

"I'm not a baby girl anymore," she said over her shoulder.

"You are to me."

She smiled, opened the front door and saw the eager messenger waiting outside on the porch.

"Telegram for Marshal Bass Reeves."

She opened the screen door. "Come right in, young man. I do hope it's not a call for him to come back to work already. He just got home two days ago."

The boy shrugged and snatched his cap from his head. "Couldn't say, ma'am. Ain't allowed to read 'em." He held out the envelope as Bass got to his feet. Reeves took the message and handed it to Mame, as the former slave had never been taught to read—that was a privilege his owner had denied him.

She opened it quickly and read it aloud. Bass beamed as he glanced over at a Dr. Thomas' - Eclectic Oil calendar on the wall.

"That falls smack dab in the middle of my time off, I reckon. Looks like me and Momma have us a little trip to Oklahoma City a comin' up." He fished into his pocket for some money and handed it to the messenger. "Send this reply, if you would be so inclined...Mister and Missus Reeves will be most proud to attend yer wedding."

The young man jotted down the missive on his note pad, grinned, put the dime, a nickel and the silver dollar in his pants pocket. *Boy, oh boy, oh boy, made a dollar fifteen tip today.* "Thank you, Marshal! I'll be sure the message gits sent soon as I git back to town."

He nodded politely to Mame, donned, and then tipped his short-billed baseball cap. He spun around and headed for the door. Once he was gone, she smiled at her dad. "Are those the two young girls you were telling me about? The ones you rescued out in the Glass Mountains?"

He nodded. "Yes, honey...Got there just in the nick of time. A few more seconds and they would'a been gonners, fer sure."

"And you get to see Jack again...And this time, nobody will be takin' pot shots at you."

He laughed. "We can only hope, baby girl...We can only hope."

MCGANN CABIN
ARBUCKLE MOUNTAINS
CHICKASAW NATION, IT

US Deputy Marshal Jack McGann sat in a slat-backed rocker on the front porch of his and Angie's spacious log cabin next to Honey Creek. He was holding a bottle for his adopted daughter while she fed. His big white wolf/dog lying beside the chair got to his feet—his tail wagging. "Somebody comin' you know, Son?'

He looked over at his master with his unique golden eyes, danced on both front feet and wagged his tail harder.

Jack glanced back up to see Marshals Selden Lindsey and Loss Hart round the corner from the wagon road and jog-trot up to the hitching rails set outside the whitewashed slat fence.

"Hey, Jack," the broad shouldered, mustachioed Lindsey said as he dismounted, loosened the girth on his big black stallion, Dan, and looped the reins around the shaved hickory rail.

"Hey, Selden, Loss. Ya'll come on in...Are you lost or in trouble?"

"Neither," Lindsey said as they climbed up the four steps to the wide front porch. "I'd shake hands, but looks like you got yours full...how's Baby Sarah doin'?"

"Aw, growin' like a weed...Gonna be knee high to a short frog 'fore you know it."

Jack's wife, Angie, opened the screen door and stepped out onto the porch. "Well faith and wouldn't ye know the worst pair of hooligans in the Nation would be showing up at lunch time," said the attractive fiery redhead.

Loss looked at Selden. "You mean to tell me it's noon already?...I gotta git my watch fixed."

"The divil fly away with ye, Loss Hart. Don't try to spread the blarney with me. I've known ye too long...Well, just so ye know, I fried up a big hen to go with some creamed new potatoes, so best ye wash up...Would ye be wanting me to take Baby Sarah, husband?"

"'Spect so, she's finished her bottle. She burps better fer you than fer me."

She took the squirming six month old from his arms. "Ye think she's a bag of grain."

"Aw, do not."

"Do to." Angie draped the child on her breast with her head on a clean cloth she had placed on her shoulder and rubbed three circles on the middle of her back, and then gently patted her just below her shoulder blades. She was immediately rewarded with a long burp. "See, husband. That's how ye do it."

"Balderdash, you jest know how to hold yer mouth right." He turned to the grinning Selden and Loss. "And what brings you boys out to our neck of the woods...sides lunch time?"

Selden pulled a Western Union envelope from his coat pocket and handed it to Jack. "Come this mornin'."

"Hope it ain't from the judge." He ripped it open and read the telegram. "Well, well, well...Knowed this was a comin'."

"Loss and I got one just like it," Selden said as he grinned.

"Woman of the house!"

Angie came back to the screen door. "What, husband? Do ye need me to teach ye something else?" she said as she stepped out on the porch.

He handed her the message.

She quickly scanned it. "Well bless Paddy!"

DEXTER, TEXAS

Bodie was one of six men asked by Millie Malina to serve as pall bearers at her son's funeral. He was the second oldest, as Billy's favorite uncle, Earl Russell—Millie's older brother from Gainesville—was at age 39, the most senior member serving in that solemn capacity. All the rest were teenage friends or cousins, each dressed in black as was the custom.

The grave had been dug at a Catholic cemetery just south of town—just on the east side of dirt road between Dexter and Callisburg. A few mature live oak trees dotted the premises, offering shade for those attendees not inside the 15' x 15' green tent that had been erected near the grave site itself. It was a spot selected next to Billy's father's resting place—one he himself had visited many times since his father's passing, back when the young man had been just a lad.

The men lifted the simple wooden casket from the glass-sided hearse, as a pair of magnificent shiny black Standardbred horses—festooned with dyed black ostrich plumes on their browband headstalls—stood quietly in their traces. A skinny beanpole of an undertaker held the rear door open and whispered cautions to the men as they slid the box out and took their assigned places at the brass handles—three on each side.

Father Thomas Miller, the smallish local priest, finished the service and invited the small throng gathered to pay their respects to Millie. Most of them did so, although a couple of them simply turned and made their way to their horses and departed.

Sheriff Tacker stood in line behind a few of Billy's distant cousins and finally got to address the grieving mother personally. They had never met before and he was immediately taken by the beauty of the thirty-eight year old widow. Despite the strain of burying her only son, her flawless alabaster skin, classic bone structure and enchanting dark eyes caught his attention, even through the black mourning veil she wore.

"Ma'am, I cannot tell you how sorry I feel for your loss. I knew Billy through Ranger Hickman and I felt he had the makin's of a fine lawman." He took her hands in his and gave them a gentle squeeze as she nodded, but said nothing. The sight of tears streaming down her cheeks caused tears to rim his own eyes as well. "If there is anythin' I can do for you…anythin' a'tall, Miz Malina…please contact me over at the sheriff's office."

She squeezed his hands in return, touched by his sincerity and managed to whisper out a weak, "Thank you, Sheriff Wacker. So kind of you to offer," as their eyes locked on one another for a few more seconds.

He released her hands and tipped his hat as he moved to speak with the other relatives.

Bodie stayed until the service was completely over and the relatives were escorting Millie home. Earl approached him and stuck out his hand.

"Thanks for coming, Ranger. Billy meant a lot to us…Would you like to drop by the house for a bite? I'm sure there's plenty to go 'round. You know how it is…Well meanin' folk always seem to bring enough food for a month, thinkin' the family won't feel like cookin'."

The Ranger shook his head as he gripped the uncle's hand firmly. "Thank you kindly, but there's somethin' important I got to do." He swallowed at the lump that had been in his throat since the service started. "Nice meetin' you, Earl. Just wish it coulda been under happier circumstances."

"Likewise," Earl replied as he released the handshake. He watched as Bodie tightened the cinch on the dun and stepped into the saddle.

The lawman nodded once and reined Lakota Moon west and jog-trotted up the dusty road.

He's headed back up where they ambushed him and Billy. Man's got guts, I grant you that, Earl thought as he watched him ride away.

He unshucked the big Winchester—just in case—stepped down and let Moon's reins fall. The mustang stood still, except for an occasional swish of his tail to try to keep the flies at bay and cropped some of the early summer grass growing along the tree line.

Keeping a sharp eye on the bluffs on the far side of the Red, Bodie made his way down to the wash and found his footprints where he had bailed off after the first shot.

He studied his tracks as he played the memory of the awful event over and over. *Here's where I was crouched down. Billy fell yonder on the second...and the third hit right about...there.*

His eyes found a small depression in the sandy wall of the wash. He took one more look back at the bluff from which the deadly shots had come. *I wonder if somehow those jayhawkers knew we were comin'?* Bodie shook off his question and reached for his sheath knife he wore on the left side of his gun belt and began to slowly dig at the sand under the obvious point where the bullet had impacted. The loose sand eventually fell clear of the disturbed surface, leaving a clear tunnel about a half inch in diameter. *Now we're getting somewhere.*

He searched around for a small stick to probe with, but the wash was pretty barren. *Dummy, you got a pencil in your coat.* He pulled it out and stuck it in the hole, but didn't make the contact he was expecting. He left the pencil inside and resumed digging beneath the bullet-bored tunnel, carefully taking the outer layers of moist dirt away. After another minute of digging, he tried probing again and felt something solid this time.

Coming up from underneath, he was rewarded with his persistence by a long heavy bullet dropping into his hand along with some tightly packed sand and his pencil. *That's what I came here for.* He cleaned off the slug and examined it carefully, and then took another look up at the bluff. The bullet itself was not exactly what he had expected to find. It lacked deep lubricating grooves and certainly was not as big as the .45-70 round that had knocked off his hat or the one that killed his posseman. *This here slug was paper-patched and ain't no bigger than .40 caliber.* The evidence in his hand told a story, and one he didn't much care for as he came to the most logical conclusion. *Two.*

COOKE COUNTY, TEXAS
CALLISBURG

The waxing gibbous moon that had just risen above the tree line offered the only light inside the old abandoned Butterfield stage depot just a block from Billy Rousseau's Dry Goods and Grocery store. The faces of the three men inside were hidden in the dark shadows broken only by the pale moonlight streaming through the broken window panes and by the meager glowing ends of their handmade cigarettes.

The Butterfield Overland Mail was a stage line that carried passengers and mail from two eastern termini, Memphis, Tennessee and St. Louis, Missouri to San Francisco, California. The trail merged in Ft. Smith, and then curved south through Texas, New Mexico and finally terminating in San Francisco, California. The line only operated from 1857 to 1861. The US Government revoked the contract of the company in anticipation of the coming conflict, but the operation continued on a limited basis for the Confederacy through 1862. A few abandoned way stations still stood along the route—the building in Callisburg was one.

"That ranger is going to be gone for a while I hear," said one.

"Gittin' married, is he? Haw!" said another. "She might be gittin' widdered purty soon when he gits back."

"Maybe you'll do better the next time."

"Hey, wadn't our fault he ducked."

"Not worried about that…just now. But it is an opportune time to move that herd of horses we been collectin'. My buyer in Love County has been ridin' me to take possession and to move those cattle south."

"When's he leavin'?" asked the first man.

"My understanding is next week...Monday, I've been told."

"We'll move on Tuesday night. Be a full moon," said the second man.

"You don't get paid 'til both herds are delivered."

"Yeah, yeah, this ain't our first rodeo."

***

TIMBER CREEK PRESS